Croft na Beinn

RÙMHOR

Ben
Machrie

PORTVOYNACHAN

Hamish's/Mathew's
Cottage

Loch
Sliach

...gmhor

Bob's
Biggin

S O U N D   O F

RHANNA AT WAR

RHANNA
AT WAR

Christine Marion Fraser

Blond & Briggs

Also by Christine Marion Fraser:
Rhanna

First published 1980 by Blond and Briggs Ltd., 44/45 Museum Street, London WC1

Printed in Great Britain by The Anchor Press Ltd and bound by Wm Brendon & Son Ltd both of Tiptree, Essex

SBN 85634 104 5

To Tam and Rita,
in memory of Soirighsis

AUTHOR'S NOTE

While I have tried to make the raids over Clydebank on 13th March 1941 as authentic as possible, there may be some discrepancies. According to statistics from German sources there was no Bomber Squadron I.K.G. 3 over Clydebank on 13th March 1941.

I wish to express grateful thanks to Alistair Ashfield, John McKee and Walter Muir for invaluable information on various subjects throughout the book.

C.M.F.

CONTENTS

CHAPTER ONE

The Chosen One

Rhanna, 13th March 1941

Biddy McMillan stirred from a deep, satisfying sleep. She was unwilling to relinquish her dream world, but something apart from the drowsing quiet of the Rhanna night seeped through the house, penetrating her state of oblivion.

Her wiry grey hair straggled over the pillow, spikes of it falling over her forehead in English sheepdog fashion. She opened her eyes slowly, blinked, and peered unseeingly into the face of a battered alarm clock on her bedside table.

"Ach, these damt cows roarin' on the hill again," she muttered disgustedly. "The buggers might have the decency to let folk sleep."

She sucked her lips inwards and slapped her tongue against the roof of her mouth to dispel her stale taste. Then she turned and snuggled into Bracken, a fat, comfortable black cat whose eighteen years on earth showed only in a white muzzle and a slight paunch. The cat began to purr loudly, her claws curling into the blankets with pleasure.

"Will you be quiet, you fat Cailleach, and take your paw out my ear!"

Bracken changed position, stretching a hind paw against Biddy's nose but she was already dropping off again, her lips pulled into her toothless mouth till her nose almost touched it.

But the sound that had first roused her became intensified and was now recognisable as a loud knocking on the door below.

The old midwife struggled to sit up. "Can a body never sleep on this island?" she mumbled in annoyance, groping on the table for her spectacles. She glared at the clock but could see nothing in the darkness. She found a box of matches and after much fumbling managed to light the candle, stuck at a crazy angle in a saucer. She peered at the clock. The hands had never been the same since she'd thrown it at the wall because it had stopped going. Amazingly it had started again and had ticked furiously since, the hands, though crooked, still managing to scrape the hours away.

"Half past eleven! I've just been in bed an hour!" Biddy exploded into the empty room. "What damty bugger has the cheek to knock me up at this queer hour? None of my bairns are due yet for a whily."

The old midwife invariably referred to the unborn as 'her bairns' because, no matter how much she complained, she loved her profession.

She put her blue-veined legs over the bed and recoiled from the cold of the March night. Searching with her feet for her slippers she found one and slipped it on to the wrong foot. The other eluded her and a fresh burst of knocking from below sent her groaning to her knees to peer under the bed. The dim light from the candle was of little help but she could make out the dark bulge of her large chamber pot. She grabbed at it, pulling it out to stare at her slipper gaily riding the swell of slopping urine.

"Dirty bugger!" Biddy addressed the slipper as if its advent into the chamber pot had nothing to do with her.

Scrambling painfully upright she reached for her dressing-gown, pulling the blue woollen folds gladly round her shivering skin. Then she limped to the window, trying to keep her un-slippered foot off the cold linoleum.

She opened the window and peered out, cringing into her dressing-gown as the sharp air from the mountain rushed in to rob her body of heat. The great hump of Sgurr na Gill loomed black against the moon-silvered sky, burns rushing down through corries were freezing flurries of sound; to her left, the Sound of Rhanna sparkled in a faint hush of peaceful rollers. The white blur of the small fishing village of Portcull huddled securely round the harbour, quaintly picturesque. The moon slid gently into a cloud, throwing the Glen into deep shadow and Biddy stared with hostility into nothingness.

"Who's there?" she rapped. "Whoever you are will you stop bangin' my door or the bugger will fall down!"

"It's me, Biddy," said a disembodied voice, tinged with apprehension at the expected annoyance caused by the intrusion, but a strong note of urgency uppermost.

"Ach, who's me? Am I expected to know every one o' you by just a voice?"

"Angus McKinnon, Biddy! My wee lad has fallen out o' bed and split his face open. Awful it is. Blood runnin' out his nose and never stoppin'. Ethel and me are feart he'll bleed to death!"

"And was he sleepin' on top o' a mountain or have you hung his bed from the ceiling?"

"Ach no, Biddy. It is one o' they beds on layers so it is. I made it myself to save space and wee Colin being the oldest was on the top shelf and had quite a journey down to the floor."

Biddy shivered and snorted. "And what way did you not call in at Lachlan's? He's nearer than me and him being the doctor it is more of a job for him.'

"I did call in at Slochmhor but the doctor was called away to Todd the Shod who's been taken bad with his appendix. Bad, bad it is. Phebie says the doctor will likely have to operate and asked me to ask you to go over to the Smiddy to help out after you've seen to Colin."

The disembodied voice was becoming conversational, full of a suppressed interest at the plight of Todd, the island blacksmith.

"Wait there," instructed Biddy dourly. 'I'll come down and unlatch the door. You can bide in the kitchen till I get dressed."

Angus fell thankfully through the door the minute it was opened. His thick-set figure lumbered into the warm kitchen where he stirred the remains of the fire into an orange glow, then helped himself to a buttered bannock from Biddy's supper plate.

"I have the trap, Biddy," he called into the dark lobby.

"Just as well," came the sharp reply. "My auld legs are no' what they were!"

She appeared a few minutes later, cape and hat askew, her spindly legs clad in black woollen stockings.

"Well, what are you waitin' for?" she demanded of Angus who had been impatiently waiting for her.

But Angus wasn't dismayed. He had been blessed with good

humour and his black eyes snapped with the same kind of mischief that was in his sisters, Nancy and Annie. His indelicate use of language, while not so alarming as the rest of the family, nevertheless raised the eyebrows of strangers unused to the McKinnons.

Biddy climbed stiffly into the trap while he stood behind to give her a helping push. "See you don't fart in my face now," he said cheekily.

"I'll pee on it if you're not more mindful o' your manners," she answered with alacrity.

He bellowed mirthfully and climbing beside her took the reins but his pony, having found a few sadly distorted cabbages among the roadside weeds, was in no hurry to move and nibbled avidly at the tit-bit.

"Get goin' you lazy brute!" yelled Angus.

The pony snorted in response, dared to browse for a minute more, but another shower of abuse sent him plodding tranquilly up the dark ribbon of road through Glen Fallan.

"My teeths!" cried Biddy suddenly. "Stop the cart! I've left my teeths in the glass!"

"Ach, Ethel won't mind," said Angus placidly.

"And who said anything about Ethel? It's me that minds!"

"Well, we can't be turning back now, Biddy. Colin is bleeding real bad and Ethel has no stomach for these things. A wee spot blood anywhere and she near faints so she does."

Biddy muttered under her breath and tucked a threadbare tartan rug tightly round her spindly legs.

Angus urged the pony into an unwilling trot and they were soon passing Slochmhor, huddled in darkness against the lower slopes of Ben Machrie. They trundled on, past the sprawling buildings of Laigmhor, and the white blur of Portcull became clearer, individual crofts and cottages quite distinguishable in the pale, cold light of the moon.

Little Colin McKinnon was huddled in a huge rocking chair by the flickering peat fire, his bloody face full of patient resignation as his mother fussed about ineffectually, putting wet cloths on his brow and holding his head back till he felt his neck must surely break.

Ethel had administered to her small son, relying on her rather indelicate sense of touch. She blundered about, her eyes squeezed

12

shut so that she wouldn't see the flowing blood and on two occasions she had clamped the cold wet cloth over his mouth. When Biddy arrived he was more in danger of suffocation than anything else and stood up gladly when the old nurse came through the door. The cloth fell to the floor accompanied by an assortment of keys which slid down his vest and out the legs of his baggy underpants.

Ethel blushed and hastened to explain. "I was hearing keys were the thing for a nose-bleed so I just grabbed hold of every one I could find and shoved them down his wee back. Och, I'm feeling right sick so I am! Have you anything you could be giving me, Biddy?"

"A piece o' my mind I'm thinking," snorted Biddy. "It's a silly woman you are indeed. It's wee Colin I'm here to see. You could be making yourself useful by putting the kettle on for a cuppy!"

Ten minutes later Colin's face was clean, though his mouth was grotesquely swollen and his nose patterned with bruises. Biddy patted his curly head tenderly. "There now, my wee man. I told you Biddy would make it better though you won't be smilin' at the lassies for a wee whily. There's three teeths gone from the front but they were baby teeths anyway. A big laddie like you has no need of them."

Colin stretched his swollen lips gratefully, a sure sign that he was gaining his manly control. He stretched out a sweaty palm in which reposed the bloody teeth. "I'll put these under my pillow and maybe a fairy will give me a silver threepenny." He studied Biddy's face mischievously. "Did you leave your teeth under your pillow, Biddy? I'm thinkin' the fairies won't be affordin' them all."

"You cheeky wee upstart!" laughed Biddy. "Back to normal I see. Now, it's up to bed with you and no sweets to be chewin' for a whily."

Angus swept his son up in his arms and Biddy gulped down her tea. "I must be gettin' over to the Smiddy. Lachy will be waitin' for me." She turned to Ethel. "Will Angus take me over in the trap to save time?"

"Ach yes, of course," said Ethel who had reverted to her usual placid self. "Poor auld Todd! It will be awful gettin' his appendix out . . . worse than teeths I'm thinkin'."

"Ay, well, he won't know a thing for he'll be under the gas. He'll be his own hero now, we'll never be hearin' the end o' his appendix."

Angus came downstairs, into the halo of light cast by the oil lamp. There was an air of suppressed excitement about him and Biddy eyed him suspiciously.

"What's with you? You're like a cat waitin' for the cream."

Angus hastened to compose his ruddy features into serious lines. "Och Biddy, it's just pleased I am you helped wee Colin. C'mon, take my arm out to the trap and I'll tuck in your legs for you."

Ethel hovered at the door, her round freckled face beaming. "It was the keys, Biddy. Do you think it was the keys? I'm no' much good at these things but sometimes I just seem to hit on the right thing . . . a wee way I have."

Biddy looked at the eager young mother and bit back a sharp retort. "Ay Ethel, the keys would help," she said softly. "But next time, mo ghaoil, try using your head as well."

At that moment the low, unmistakable drone of an aeroplane floated peacefully down from the night sky. The trio at the cottage door craned their necks to look up into the velvet blue-black night where millions of stars glittered brightly. The moon was peeping sullenly from behind a curtain of silver-lined cloud, her pale halo making the heavens vast and coldly infinite. The ragged peaks of Ben Machrie and Sgurr nan Ruadh reared up to embrace the great emptiness of space with intimate approval, shutting out the tiny speck of man from the secrets shared by the heavens and the highest places of planet Earth.

But the three onlookers had no eye just then for things of beauty. They were all concentrating on the sound that invaded the sky. If the world had been at peace the sound would perhaps have provoked a slight interest, but the world was not at peace and things that were involved in war now brought unease to those that heard the throb of flying machines.

"It will just be one o' they Coastal Command planes," Angus murmured faintly. "Can any o' you see it?"

"Never even a glimpse," said Biddy. "I think it's went away."

"It . . . was sounding funny," whispered Ethel uncertainly.

"Ach well, it's away now and it's Lachlan will not be sounding funny if I don't get over there quick," said Biddy, moving over to the trap.

"I'll be gone a wee whily!" Angus called to Ethel. "I'm seeing Father at the Headquarters."

Ethel accepted the explanation without question but Biddy snorted and muttered. "Some o' these days we will all be findin' out there's more goes on over at Tam's than meets the eye."

"It is not women's business," said Angus with dignity and for the rest of the short journey lapsed into tight-lipped silence.

Lachlan McLachlan, the doctor who had tended the islanders for more than nineteen years, gave a cry of relief at sight of Biddy. His dark, handsome face was tense and he raised an impatient hand to brush a lock of hair from his brow.

"Thank goodness, Biddy!" he acknowledged gratefully. "We've caught it in time! I've opened him up but we'll have to go easy, it's on the point of rupturing.'

Biddy looked at Todd lying prone on the well-scrubbed kitchen table. His rounded belly stuck up in a pale dome from the surrounding area of weatherbeaten flesh. His round, pleasant face, relaxed into a beatific smile under the anaesthetic, peeped out from wind-bleached folds of gleaming white linen.

"Would you look at him." Mollie McDonald patted his shining bald pate affectionately. "Innocent as a bairn. I scrubbed him up for the doctor." She looked at Biddy proudly. "My best linen and plenty carbolic. Clean as a new pin he is now and needin' the wash, the dirty auld bodach. Wait till I tell him about his feets. Like coal they were and it is shamed I am just . . . but, och" – she beamed down at her husband – "he's not been well this whily and never even goin' to the Kirk on the Sabbath so he's not been having his usual bath this week or two."

Biddy put her nose near Todd's mouth and sniffed suspiciously. "Never mind his feets, it's his belly needs washin' out. He's been drinkin', the auld scunner. No wonder his appendix started grumbling."

Mollie reddened and Lachlan nodded. "You're right, Biddy . . . and very near anaesthetised himself with the stuff. It only took a tiny whiff of ether to put him out."

Angus had been shuffling uneasily, carefully keeping his eyes well averted from the neat little incision on the right side of Todd's abdomen.

"I think I'd better be goin'," he said hastily. "I have Father to see, then I'd best get back to Ethel. She'll be worried about wee Colin and I'm tired out after all the excitement. My back is feelin' funny too. I think I wraxed it carryin' Colin up to bed."

"Ay, away you go!" said Biddy sharply for she had no time for Angus and his tales of backache. With the war worsening, a number of young Rhanna men had gone off to fight. Angus McKinnon had suddenly and unaccountably developed a bad back and to prove the fact had crawled around bent double for almost a week. "The bugger is just lazy," was the general verdict but Lachlan was unable to make such a ready diagnosis. Backs were a very contrary part of the human body, and there was no real way to tell if Angus's case was genuine or not. Ethel, her sense of loyalty to her husband born through a languid indifference to his devious ways, looked sadly sympathetic when his condition was sarcastically mentioned and bore the heavier tasks around their little croft with scant complaint.

Ethel's mind wasn't inquiring enough to wonder why Angus was able to perform the most athletic contortions in his efforts to satisfy his healthy sexual appetite. One night she plucked up enough curiosity to say, "Angus, does it no' hurt your back to go jumpin' up and down like that?"

He had stopped his lustful activities to explain earnestly, "Och, mo ghaoil, it's my rooster doing all the work, nothing at all to do with my back," and while he tackled her body with renewed enthusiasm Ethel had tried to work out the authenticity of the explanation.

Angus had solved the matter of a rather uneasy conscience by becoming a keen member of the island's Home Guard, formed by the older men who were anxious to contribute to the war effort. At first the idea had been received with sour acclaim by the womenfolk.

"It's just an excuse to strut about wearin' they arm holders and playin' with guns," sniffed Behag Beag, the doleful, fault-finding postmistress of Portcull.

"Ay, and the buggers' heads will be so big they'll be lookin' like thon queer barrage balloons on legs," supported Kate

McKinnon. "There's no need for it on Rhanna! We'll never see any of the Nazi folks here."

But the attitude of almost everyone changed from complacence to anger after bomb attacks on the Orkneys and Shetlands. Rhanna people were slow to rouse. Temperament generally was as smouldering as a lump of sodden peat. Once fired with enthusiasm, however, they threw themselves into a venture with all the determination of will inherited from generations of dour, sturdy-minded Gaels.

"If the buggers can throw bombs on the Shetlands they can do it here!" cried old Joe McKinnon who was a retired navy man and renowned for his tales of the many adventures that had befallen him in the long years of his travels. He was well endowed with a fanciful imagination and his listeners were never sparing in their attention. "It's up to us to protect our land!" he continued. "What would we be doing if there was a raid over Rhanna with parachutes dropping like mushrooms and us not trained to do a thing about it!"

"Och c'mon now, man!" spat old Bob McDonald who was the shepherd of Laigmhor. "These Germans won't be wasting their time or their bombs on us! It was the naval base at Scapa Flow they were after and the bridges at Rosyth and the Forth. What way would they be droppin' bombs on a few wee bit farms and crofts?"

"It's the land," retorted Tam McKinnon cryptically. "I'm hearing thon bugger, Hitler, is trying to get his feet in the door of all the countries in the world! I would not be liking to sit back and watch him getting a hold of the islands!"

His words were met with a roar of agreement and it was decided there would be a Home Guard on Rhanna. Soon after the Local Defence Volunteers had been raised in May 1940, a group of Rhanna men went away to special schools of instruction, returning strong in the faith that they were fully equipped to face any emergency that might possibly come to the island. But while their minds were filled with splendid ideas for preservation of people and places their outward appearance gave no clue to the changes within and much fretting and wailing had ensued before spasmodic supplies of equipment came their way. Now it was March 1941. Each member of the Home Guard was able to sport an arm band.

A promised issue of suitable weapons still hadn't arrived but the Rhanna men were unperturbed.

"We have our pitchforks," said Bob, "and our shotguns."

"Plenty of those," grinned Robbie Beag, "if all the poaching on Burnbreddie is anything to go on."

Fergus McKenzie, tenant farmer of Laigmhor, was one of those who had joined the Home Guard and he had also been appointed Chief Warden. At first the islanders had been informed that, as the likelihood of Rhanna and the associated islands of the Outer Hebrides coming under air attack was small, there would be no need for Air Raid Wardens.

Rhanna exploded at this. Indignantly they enquired if that was the case why then did they have to draw curtains and blinds to comply with blackout regulations? Could they now light their lamps and let them shine from windows while the German Luftwaffe flew back and forth on their bombing raids? The local authorities had passed the matter on to the Regional Commissioner who saw no reason why Wardens should not be active on an island no matter how small.

Rhanna glowed with achievement and Fergus, while feeling that matters had been taken to a ridiculous extreme, nevertheless accepted his appointment with dour gratitude.

Behag Beag's wizened jowls fell apart in astonishment when she heard that the ancient wireless transmitter, neglected and forgotten in a little outhouse adjoining the Post Office, was to be resurrected. It had been operational during the 1914–18 war for the purpose of maintaining a watch on Atlantic shipping but that had been some years before Behag's time as postmistress of Portcull. She glared malevolently at the strange machine with its bewildering array of knobs and wires and told everyone sullenly, "Ach, it is just a lot of palaver I'm not understanding," but inwardly she was thrilled that her little Post Office was given the grand label of a Report Centre. After a course of instruction she soon lost her first feelings of resentment and now regarded herself as a very distinguished person. For years the receiving and dispatching of gossip had been one of her chief occupations but now she had no time for such frivolities. She stared with fresh eyes at the War Office notices pinned on the walls. The large headings jumped out at her with a strange insistence. IF THE INVADER

COMES – What To Do – And How To Do It. *She* would know what to do. Privately she christened herself 'The Chosen One' though she hastened to her pew in the Hillock Kirkyard on the Sabbath to bow her head and commune with God in earnest and give thanks for the sublime duties bestowed on her, ending rather fearfully, "It is yourself Lord who is the Chosen One indeed but I can't get it out of my mind that I have been chosen to do a special job too . . . though nothing as grand as some, you know. But we are all here for a purpose, so we are, and while there have been times I have wondered what mine was, I am knowing now. The waiting has not been in vain. Thanking you Lord and begging your humble pardon for putting sheets to dry in Isabel McDonald's hayshed last Sabbath, I am your faithful servant, Behag Beag, Amen."

So taken up was she that her brother, round-faced, good-natured Robbie, who had suffered years of constant nagging, now found himself living a life of comparative peace. His job as gamekeeper of Burnbreddie had been the solace of his life. Within the confines of the Laird's estate he had strolled through leisurely, contented hours, close to the earth that he loved. He turned a blind eye to the odd poacher, shared out his own spoils among his friends and was beloved by many. But inevitably the end of his working day took him from Heaven to Hell with faltering steps. The coming of the wireless had changed all that. Behag was tight-lipped and preoccupied. In the evenings an eerily beautiful peace descended over the parlour. Only the ticking of the clock and the warm crackling of the fire invaded the silence. Robbie began to feel so confident that he made frequent trips to the 'wee hoosie' to swig deeply from his hip flask, a pleasure that he only dared indulge during his daytime wanderings. Behag not only looked like a depressed bloodhound, she also had a nose like one and could sniff out whisky fumes however well masked by 'Grannie sookers'.

One night she disappeared out to the wee hoosie and was gone so long Robbie went out to look for her, the better side of his nature hoping she hadn't met with a mishap, the worst side vaguely praying that she had taken a brain storm and was stumbling about the Muir of Rhanna, perhaps even wallowing helplessly in a peat bog.

Eventually he traced her to the little outhouse adjoining the Post Office where by the feeble light of a paraffin lamp he saw her sitting by the wireless, staring fixedly at the knobs and dials. The earphones were clamped to her head, embracing her threadbare scarf under which lurked her long ears, and she neither heard Robbie's intrusion into her Report Centre or his silent exit from it. It was then that Robbie realised his sister was living for the day when she could use the set to send out some really important message instead of the insignificant little reports that had been her lot to date.

Robbie had hugged himself gleefully. He prayed that the day would be long in coming because, till then, Behag's anticipation of such an event looked like keeping her thoroughly occupied, leaving him free to enjoy a life of unparalleled peace.

Over and above the Home Guard, Rhanna also boasted an excellent one-man Coastguard Service in the shape of Righ nan Dul who manned the lighthouse at Port Rum Point. Righ had kept his lonely vigil for years as had his father before him. No one was better qualified for Coastguard duties than Righ because he had a vast knowledge of local conditions. The lighthouse afforded him a perfect lay of both land and sea. Already he had made several sightings that warranted investigation and Behag, redfaced with importance, had accompanied him to the object that everyone else carelessly labelled 'the contraption' but which was lovingly referred to as 'my radio contact' by Behag.

But her big moment had yet to come and when it did the whole of Rhanna would pat her on the back and thank the Lord for seeking her out to be 'The Chosen One'. The one chosen to save the island and its people.

CHAPTER TWO

Bomber Adrift

The shower of incendiaries that came spitting out from the planes of the Luftwaffe, Third Air Fleet, were profuse enough for some to find their way into inflammable areas of industrial sites. The black spaces of the surrounding open fields seemed to push the orange flames into a giant torch which greedily devoured the little town into its voracious throat.

Thin curls of oil-laden smoke eddied through the streets. Niall, working with a rescue party clearing the debris of a crushed tenement that had received a direct hit from a 500 kilo bomb, coughed on a mixture of soot and dust that flooded his lungs.

Another wave of bombers was arriving from the East, looking like evil black birds of prey against the cold, pale sky. Within seconds they were dropping altitude and more bombs were falling, together with parachute mines, allowing no time for people in the target area to sort out one thought, one fear, from the other. The times the sky was clear like that, to actually see the enemy planes, were of split seconds, when the fires held the smoke in a livid intake of oxygen, when a tiny lull cleared the world of the pink glow of landed incendiaries and the rapid, vulgar flashes of the H.E. bombs. Enormous craters split the tarmac asunder, blowing water mains and gas mains to smithereens. Because three Auxiliary Fire Service Stations had been put out of action earlier in the evening, the problem of dealing with the Clydebank inferno was overwhelming. Many of the hydrants were dry and the fire-fighters were driven to use the muddy waters filling the craters.

Niall had lost his gas mask. He breathed in choking dust and hot smoke till his lungs were raw. Someone pushed a dirty hanky at him. "Here, tie this over your face or we'll end up rescuing you!"

They came upon a pile of battered corpses quite unexpectedly. They were so twisted and bloody it was difficult to believe they were people. From out of the heap of dead flesh a terrified voice cried for help and they extricated a young woman, pulling at her arms as gently as they could, trying to ease her free from the ensnaring bodies that held on to her legs like the sucking mud in a bog. "She's the only one in this lot," said one of the men. "Dear Jesus! There's dozens of them gone!"

A squad of rescue workers raced up, filthy spectres with reddened eyes and pale lips showing through the grime. "The next street!" panted one. "We need some hands!"

Niall ran and somehow he knew, even before he turned the street corner, that the place he called 'home' in Glasgow was no more. The entire right side of the building was sheared off at the front. It was as if someone had taken a giant axe and split bricks and mortar down through the centre in the way one splits open a log. Underneath the great mound of smouldering debris were buried all the people that Niall had helped to 'safety' just a few hours before. The portions of the front walls that had been blown away, ludicrously exposed all the little domesticities of family life. In one kitchen an elderly couple were seated at the table as if about to start eating supper. They sat on their chairs looking at the table but their eyes were sightless because they had been killed by bomb-blast, unhurt and whole, but all the air sucked from their lungs. It was like the kind of tableau seen in a waxworks museum only in this case the motionless figures were flesh and blood.

Two houses along to the right, old Mr Maxwell's table stood sturdy and intact amidst its humble surroundings. In the kitchen above, Miss Rennie's rocking chair sat by the jagged ruins of the range. On the mantelshelf china plates remained unbroken, on the smashed hearth a plaster dog lay on its side, its painted eyes staring out from the ruins. The Brodies' bedroom lay fully exposed to the elements. All the furniture was intact but the bed mat had flipped upwards to drape over the wardrobe and a lamp shade hung from the brass knob on the bed end. Eerie sights, made spine-chillingly macabre by the curious whims of blast.

Blackie O'Riorden stood at the edge of his kitchen on the top flat, waiting to be rescued. A torrent of abuse, directed at the bombers in the vaults of the heavens, drowned out the instructions of the rescue squad.

Some of the dead had been blown into the air and had landed so far from where they'd first been struck it seemed they might have been dropped from the sky. They littered the road like broken dolls, arms and legs twisted beneath them. But had they been dead when they were blown into the air? That was the question that drummed into Niall's brain as he stared around him in disbelief.

He looked at a crumpled ball of orange fur lying on the cracked pavement and realised it was Ginger Moggy stretched in a pool of his own blood, his lips drawn back over his fangs in a grimace that showed he had suffered a painful death. Above him, alive by some freakish escape, Joey perched on a crazily leaning lamp-post, feebly muttering 'Goodnight Mammy! Mammy's pretty boy.'

Miss Rennie's broken body was being lifted from the rubble. The jagged spars of Joey's cage were embedded in her chest, light pink bubbles of lung blood oozed out of the little holes.

Half sobbing, Niall ran to the heap of masonry and began to tear at it with the strength and blindly unthinking rage of a bull. Voices roared at him to be careful and several pairs of hands tried to pull him away but he shook them off and went on with his demented searching. There was no whimper of life from the piled rubble, nothing to tell him that a soul still breathed or the flicker of a heartbeat kept someone alive till help came. He found Ma Brodie quite suddenly. Her eyes were open, gazing up at him out of the debris.

"Help me get her out!" he shouted desperately but the other men were already pushing aside lumps of jagged stone, carefully freeing what was left of Nellie Brodie's diminutive frame. The teapot was still clutched in her hand, fragments of a teacup were embedded into the flesh of her arm like crazed paving on soft ground. Her rib cage had been smashed, splinters of bone stuck through the gay, flowery apron Niall had given her at Christmas. It was soaked in blood which had congealed quickly in the powdered dust and crushed brick which had caved in on top of her.

"Ma Brodie – mo ghaoil," whispered Niall brokenly and gently closed her eyes. He knelt beside her, too shocked to move. Deep within the crazily strewn heap of glass and masonry there came an almost imperceptible little sob. Holding his breath he cocked his good ear and it came again – the stifled ghost of a human voice. "Someone's alive in here!" he called to the long line of men who were expertly shifting rubble in the fashion of a human conveyor belt. They scrambled towards him and carefully began the arduous task of rescue.

An hour later they came upon a small boy, so petrified he was unable to move or speak, his life saved by a massive beam that had jammed above him to form a wedge-shaped tunnel. Niall was slim and agile yet neither he, nor any of the other men there, were able to wriggle in through the narrow gap.

"Haud on, I'll get in there." Johnny Favour appeared at Niall's elbow.

"Johnny! I thought you were having a night with Shirley Temple!' grinned Niall, feeling a great sense of unaccountable relief at seeing Johnny's familiar, friendly face. He had changed his creased tweeds for a rather shiny navy blue three-piece with a watch chain hanging from the pocket of his waistcoat. But he still wore his battered cap as proudly as a king might wear a crown.

"I left the wife at the La Scala," he explained cheerfully. "She'll be safe there and I'll be better use here." He squirmed out of his jacket and handed it to Niall. "Guard it wi' your life, son, it's my best. I'll get in beside the bairn and try to hand him out."

He disappeared in through the small opening. A moment later his voice floated out. "I'll need help, the lad canny move. I'll start making the hole bigger from this side. We'll shore it up with some bits of wood."

Fifteen minutes later Niall was able to crawl in beside Johnny. The child lay in a bed of suffocating dust. He was a ghostly little figure with his face and hair coated in white plaster but Johnny was saying things that made him laugh and one side of his face bulged with toffee from Johnny Favour's trouser pocket. His legs were pinned under a lump of concrete but he showed no pain and Johnny whispered to Niall, "At a guess I'd say the poor wee bugger's legs are crushed. I'd be a lot happier if he was greetin'. Then we'd know he was feeling something. C'mon, let's get to work."

The job of freeing the child was painfully slow but eventually his torn and bleeding limbs were exposed. Both men looked and knew the child might never walk again.

"Sod it!" Johnny drew a grimy hand across his face. "Sod the bloody lot of them!"

A First Aid party had arrived. One peered through the opening. "Can you get him out to us? We've got an ambulance waiting."

"Pass us a blanket," said Johnny tonelessly. "He's shivering a bit."

They wrapped the child carefully in the blanket and at Johnny's insistence tucked the shiny navy blue jacket round the small shoulders.

"You're a wee man now, son," Johnny grinned down at the boy's pale face. "And just to prove it . . ." He whipped off his battered cap and placed it on the child's head. "There you are. It's maybe no' much to look at but it'll keep your brains warm."

The little boy peeped out from the peak that came over his eyebrows. "Ta, Johnny. I'll wear it when I'm playin' football – well, when I'm doing my goalie. Goalie's always wear a cap."

"You do that, lad," nodded Johnny. "Get going now. You get out first, Niall. Take his shoulders."

In a short time Niall was placing the boy into the arms of the First Aid party who bore him quickly away. Niall felt dizzy with relief. At least one small life had survived the holocaust, but what of the others? The boy's parents? Old Mr Maxwell with his little thermos flask and his assurances that he would be safe under the kitchen table. He would still be alive if he had stayed there! And Ma Brodie! The dear, big-hearted warmth of such a wee body – dead – and for what? He remembered the teapot still clutched in her hand, a symbol of a life that had cared unstintingly for everyone she met.

What of Iain Brodie? Coming back exhausted from the fires. Back to what? His wife, his home, his memories, all gone forever in a senseless waste of everything that made life tick sweetly for the average, home-loving man.

The ground trembled suddenly and the tunnel from which Johnny was just emerging caved in. He made no sound as he was first smothered in dust then crushed under the tons of rubble that came down on top of him. When it finally settled there was no whisper of life and the men knew that Johnny had performed his last favour.

Niall's mind was going numb with shock. He stared at the

dull gleam of Johnny's watch chain caught among the bricks and everything swam together in a watery mist. The rescue squad were telling him to get out of the danger area but he barely heard. He was thinking of the senseless waste of good lives. Just a short time ago some faceless nonentity had pressed a button and a bomb had dropped. The mind that guided the hand would forget quickly each press of the button, giving no concrete thought to the agony and grief invoked by just the flick of a finger.

If Niall's own thoughts had been more rational, if he hadn't been so emotionally exhausted, he would doubtless have exercised more care in his movements. But his tiring feet were clumsy and he slipped on loose masonry. The beam that had saved the child dislodged from its precarious hold and came toppling down towards him. He tried to struggle upright but couldn't. The splintered edge of the massive beam came speeding down. In a mesmerised trance he saw the whole thing in slow motion and he lay helplessly, waiting for blackness to engulf him. Hefty arms grabbed at him, dragging him away from a deadly hail of bricks and glass, but they weren't quick enough to stop the beam from pinning his right arm into a bed of plaster, close to the spot where only minutes before a small boy had lain, too frozen with terror to do more than whimper like a lost puppy.

Carl Zeitler, the pilot of one of twelve Heinkel bombers of Bomber Squadron I.K.G. 3, rocked gleefully in his seat. He squinted down through the Plexiglas panels of the gun cupola to the pink glow where incendiaries and the rapid flashes of the H.E. bombs split enormous craters in the ground and turned the little burgh of Clydebank into a raging inferno.

The rest of the group were heading back to base; but Zeitler, in a gluttony of excitement, was taking the risk of diving once more over the burning town, his skilled manoeuvres curving the lumbering bomber in a triumphant sweep through the murky clouds of smoke.

The feeling of power was strong within him, the strong throb of the Junker's Jumo 211 twin engines seemed to beat right into his heart, giving him a confident sense of security. He was an excellent pilot and, though he was barely twenty-five, there lay behind him an exemplary career as a dive-bomber pilot. He had brought his plane safely over Scapa Flow, Narvik, and Dunkirk, with little more than some superficial damage to show for it. True, on one occasion, he had flown back to base with his navigator peppered with flak, his cries of agony filling the plane before he died. Another time he had lost his rear gunner. No one knew he was dead till the ground crew slid open the rear door and were bathed in blood gushing from the holes in the gunner's face. Dunkirk! The remembrance of that always made Zeitler smile. All those stupid bastards strung out on the beaches like flies on a wall! Just asking to be picked off! He must have wiped out dozens of them. The French had been beaten and the Allied British had taken to their heels with their tails well tucked between their legs.

Even as he turned to make the final sweep over Clydebank he felt echoes of the thrill Dunkirk had given him. His very bones shivered with delight and he threw back his wedge-shaped head in a smile of arrogance. But anger mingled with his pleasure. Anger at the British for still managing to remain on their toes despite the concentrated blitz.

Europe had gone under like a drowning dog! All except the bulldog British. Despite the hammering they had taken those proud, clever bastards were still keeping their heads above water. For someone like Zeitler, tuned into Hitler's wavelengths like a well-programmed robot, the pill was a bitter one to swallow. Deep in his heart he admired the cool-headed British their fighting spirit and their admirable allegiance to the British Premier, Winston Churchill. There was a great leader for you! A good soldier too, experienced in the field of both war and politics. But he was the enemy and Zeitler's hot-headed, fanatical devotion to his own leader, Adolf Hitler, blotted out his rare moments of level-headed thinking.

He stared through the Plexiglas. The moon was beautiful. A cold, bluish disc hanging in the sky. But Zeitler didn't see it as an object to be admired. It was there in the sky to aid the success of these night attacks. This raid was strange, they had come quite some distance to reach this insignificant spot in Scotland. The targets were the docks, shipyards and oil depots. Difficult. The target area was small over this point. The landscape showed a lot of dark patches that were fields. Spasmodic streaks of flak spattered up from the fringes of the town. It was all a bit feeble after the big raids over London and Coventry. These night air attacks on England had caused terrible havoc yet still she remained unconquered. The damned place had nearly been blown off the face of the earth but still Britain popped up smiling, each time with a new trick, a new defence, up her voluminous sleeve.

The pilot's thoughts made his pale blue eyes bulge with chagrin. Dark rings under his eyes made him look older than he was. The illusion was completed by premature balding but with his head enveloped in his leather flying helmet he looked younger, except for the rings under his pale eyes. He removed a large, gloved hand from the control column to adjust his face mask. "Die Späten answers well, eh Anton?"

Anton Büttger, bomb aimer and commander of the plane, lay on his belly on a foam-rubber pad in his vulnerable position in the nose of the gun cupola. The muscles in his jaw tightened and his keen blue eyes snapped like fire-crackers. He guessed the reason for Zeitler making the unnecessary fly-over: it was so that he could gloat. The destruction caused by the raid was pleasing him, exciting his cold, calculating emotions. Whenever bombs smashed into concrete, Zeitler showed, by the sucking of his breath and a strangely sensual rocking of his pelvis, his immense pleasure. During a sortie his most favoured expression was 'Don't shit! Hit!' This he had roared through the intercom so many times in the last twenty-five minutes that the young commander couldn't keep back his seething feelings of dislike for the pilot. He was so completely cast in the mould of so many hot-headed Nazis that he seemed to have no individuality, no character of his own. His personality was about as pleasing as a chunk of cold metal. The voice of the Gruppenführer, ordering immediate withdrawal of the group from the target vicinity, crackled imperatively through the headphones. Anton could see his plane. It was well ahead of them and much higher but Anton knew that the Gruppenführer was keeping an eye open for Zeitler who was renowned for his bouts of foolhardiness. An earlier threat to ground him had cooled him for a time but tonight he was being big-headed again.

"Go now, Zeitler!" ordered Anton. "Make a mess of this one and your days in the air are numbered!"

Zeitler hunched his shoulders, straightened the servo rudder and the Heinkel ripped through the cold night sky.

Anton relaxed slightly. He tried not to think of the scene below but couldn't keep the pictures out of his brain; the spilled blood, the cries of terror . . . the moments of death for the women and children. The hearts of the living world would be filled with anger, frustration, compassion. He shuddered. It was easy to press the bomb-release button. Too easy. There was no challenge, no feeling that you had achieved something the way you did during air combat. He had joined the Luftwaffe because he loved flying. He had never imagined his career would one day turn sour on him. Up here in the gun cupola he always felt a certain measure of unease, often long after a raid was over. The bomb aimer and the gunners perhaps always had more on their conscience than the pilot. But it might be that not everyone felt like he did. He would rather have been at the controls but Zeitler was the better pilot and was arrogantly aware of the fact, using any opportunity to display his prowess and undermine Anton's authority. In an odd kind of way Anton understood. He was younger than Zeitler, he had only recently taken over command of the plane. Zeitler had made umpteen bombing raids with bomb aimer and commander Willi Schmitt, who had been grounded because of illness. Anton knew you had to fly with someone a long time to get in tune with him.

"We have managed to make a pretty little bonfire!" It was Zeitler again, his lips stretched in a gloating leer which the other couldn't see but could feel. "Look! Down there, the flames leap high. An oil depot perhaps! Drop the rest of the high E's, Anton. Might as well put them to good use instead of wasting them in the sea!"

Anton didn't answer. His fingers touched the bomb-button but he didn't press it immediately. He knew he should. If he didn't lighten the load now he might have to later . . . perhaps in a field, or an open stretch of water . . . or on a little country farm with all the people in bed, unsuspecting, unprepared . . . He felt very tired. The kind of dull, heavy tiredness that filled the veins with lead instead of blood. When this kind of exhaustion swept over him he remembered things he had thought forgotten. Far-off days filled with happiness. Small-boy days when his world was of green fields and golden corn. Ambitions to be like his farmer father. The dreams of childhood. The grown-up Anton loved planes. When his father spoke about cows or horses he thought about planes, not the technical make-up of them but the performance of the engines, how fast, how high. He thought about diving and banking, the sensation of zipping through lacy cloudbanks to the blue roof of the sky, to look down on the clouds drifting lazily over the world.

His vision of a flying career hadn't included war and the personal tragedies it brought. The raids over Berlin in the late summer of 1940. Late summer . . . his father out in the fields, working on after last light . . . his mother in the kitchen baking the bread for morning, the fragrant smell of it filling the room . . . and his two little sisters, asleep upstairs. At least they'd had no time to know the terror his mother had known, buried in the rubble of the kitchen. She had lived for a short while after rescue, his father a few weeks, all because of one bomb, one stray British bomb that missed the town and fell on a little country farm.

A sob caught in his throat and for a moment he didn't care about the hail of flak that crackled in the air about them like sparks in the black chimney of a cosy farmhouse kitchen . . . It was the reflexes of his weary limbs that made him roll off the foam-rubber pad to push himself against Zeitler at the controls.

"Take her up, Zeitler!" he said, in a slightly breathless voice. "The searchlights are on us!"

"Did you drop the bombs?"

"Damn the bombs! Get her up!"

In his seat by the radio controls, Ernst Foch, the wireless operator, was barely aware of the searchlights. If he had been up in the gun turret he would have seen the flak and the searchlights through the Plexiglas fairing. Their time over the target area was up, now they would be heading back to base. He allowed his thoughts to stray briefly, back to his family in Germany. It must be eternity since he had last set eyes on his pretty wife, Helga, and his small, sturdy son, Franz. He wondered why it was sometimes difficult to remember their faces. Little scraps of dear, familiar things came to mind but the memories did nothing to soothe him. He wondered how long the war would last. Like Zeitler he was devoted to his country. From the age of fourteen he had been a member of Hitler's Youth Movement, proud to wear his brown uniform and to carry a dagger like a man. His young mind had been very receptive to the Nazi régime. He had felt part of a glorious system. But the softening influences of a wife and child had dulled his enthusiasm for mass regimentation. He didn't want his son to grow into a puppet with a master-mind controlling his life. It took more than a uniform and a dagger to make a man. There had to come a time when common sense and the need for individuality came to the fore. He wondered about Zeitler up front in the pilot's seat. The man was a brilliant pilot but a mindless fool otherwise. If the Führer ordered that every Nazi should burn piss holes in the snow in the sign of the swastika then Zeitler would be the first to open his fly.

A sigh escaped Ernst's thick, fleshy lips and he bunched his hands. It was very hot. Little beads of sweat were popping out on his face like the droplets of moisture on the glass of an ice-cold lager . . .

The searchlights were criss-crossing into the skies, violating the blue-black reaches. Zeitler screwed his eyes against the glare from the instrument panel. He throttled forward and the Heinkel responded by gaining height steadily. But still the beams were on them, clinging like leeches to a leg. Something inside the pilot's head, a built-in instinct of impending danger, warned him that this time his conceit had tempted providence too far. His knuckles tightened on the throttle and he knew an unaccustomed rush of apprehension. The Ack-Ack defence was much stronger than he had first imagined.

The gun crews on a Polish destroyer, docked in John Brown's for repairs, stood by their Ack-Ack guns and sent an almost constant barrage of shells tracing upwards to the planes of the Luftwaffe. The smoke from fires made visibility difficult though John Brown's shipyard was comparatively free of serious blaze. The searchlights were probing, glinting on one plane lagging behind the rest of the unit, the guns swivelled round, a magazine of shells spat fire at Zeitler's plane.

Jon Jodl, the flight engineer and lower rear gunner, lay on his belly near the ventral sliding door, in front of the machine-gun housing. "Why is Zeitler hanging about?" he thought. "Get out of it!" He watched the flak shells exploding about him. Down here it was cold but he felt a trickle of sweat running between his shoulder blades. One of those shells was going to pierce the perspex door at any moment. That was how you always felt when you could see something coming but the thought struck him that the stressed skin and plating on which he lay was probably just as flimsy as the Perspex. He could get up now and go forward . . . but he knew he ought to wait for Anton's orders. A tremor passed through his body. He couldn't stop it. Somewhere inside his skinny frame a tightly coiled knot of nerves made him feel sick.

Zeitler guided the plane into a big fluffy cloud. It was like being enveloped in cotton wool. The searchlights and the tracers disappeared from view. Jon reached out to the tin can jammed between metal plates and retched miserably into it. He was neither a coward or a hero and he didn't give a damn about the Führer and his greedy dream to conquer the world. All his life Jon had been plagued by feelings of inadequacy even though he had shown a great proficiency in his academic studies. His very appearance was stamped with a studious sagacity, from his thin clever face to his long, tapering musician's fingers. But he had never been 'One of the crowd' and he had always walked alone, though sometimes this introvert nature of his made him deeply unhappy. He had seen the German Luftwaffe as an escape to freedom, a chance to prove to the world he was as much of a man as the next.

His big domineering mother had not approved. "You were not made for such things, my Jon," she told him firmly. "You must continue with your music, it is what you were born for."

But at the first opportunity Jon had taken himself off to an air training school and with his high educational standards was soon well on his way to becoming a flight engineer with the Luftwaffe. All the other boys wanted to be top pilots but not Jon. What he was doing took courage enough. With the coming of war he quickly realised he didn't have the 'guts' to cope with the rigours it brought. His tightly strung nervous system simply couldn't take the strain. His world was, after all, in Hamburg with his gentle little hen-pecked papa and his large, overpowering mama who was like an indestructible mountain. All his life she had pampered him and he knew now that he wasn't strong enough to break away from her shadow. "You were not made for such things, my Jon!" Her words were an empty echo inside his head. But it was too late now, there was no turning back. Jon was at breaking point but tension was such a familiar thing in his life he wasn't aware that his crawling nerves were stretching tighter with every turn of the airscrews.

They flew out of the cloud and back into a criss-cross probe of searchlights. The flak was falling short. The crew breathed sighs of relief and Jon Jodl felt the sweat drying under his helmet. "Thank you, my God in Heaven," he prayed childishly and shut his eyes in gratitude. Another raid, another test of nerves was over for a while.

The flak from an Ack-Ack gun on the fringe of the town caught them quite unexpectedly. A hail of lead peppered the fuselage.

"I couldn't get her up high enough!" roared Zeitler in disbelief. "You should have dropped those bombs, Anton!"

The burst of incredulity momentarily suspended his reactions. The plane staggered along for a few seconds then dropped forty feet like a broken elevator in a lift shaft. Zeitler felt his backside rammed down into his seat, the others hit the floor like stones. Shuddering gently, the Heinkel was suspended for a moment in the sky.

Zeitler yelled through the intercom. "Get up here, Jon!" The control column was jammed. The plane continued to lose height though it was now a smooth but steady drop. Soon they were at just 1500 metres but by then Jon had freed the controls. "Good, Jon, good," said Zeitler. He pushed the controls and the Heinkel rose, but sluggishly. Jon's eyes went quickly to the instrument panel to check the fuel and oil but saw that the needles of all the gauges were swinging in senseless circles.

Zeitler was kicking viciously at the rudder bar. The rear part of the fuselage was being tugged from side to side in a violent motion and they all knew that the air was streaming over a damaged rudder, but still Zeitler kicked at the rudder bar.

"Do your best, Jon," said Anton quietly, and Jon went to work, sweat pouring from his brow but his hands steady in those crucial moments. Everyone was very quiet, even Zeitler. He could sense the resentment of the others for putting them all at risk for a few moments of greedy triumph. The more sensible part of his make-up was rapidly coming to the fore now that he was out of the grip of his irrational blood lust.

"We should be thankful that no one was hurt," said Anton. "We haven't much idea of the damage to the plane but I don't think it's as bad as it might have been."

"Except we are on a one-way journey," snarled Ernst. "We can't do much without a compass." He bunched his fists. "You're a bloody maniac, Zeitler! You're not fit even to ride a bicycle in a cemetery!"

Zeitler didn't answer. He didn't need a gauge to tell him that the revs of the starboard engine were falling. God! Not this too! He felt drained, so exhausted that he felt if he shut his eyes just then he would die. He looked down through the Plexiglas. They were flying over a dark mass of land. Silver threads of river glinted. A large expanse of water dotted with islands was familiar. They had come over this way earlier.

"Any luck, Jon?" he asked, pushing hard on the rudder bar even though Jon was working nearby.

"Does it matter?" asked Ernst grimly. "The starboard aileron is torn to hell!"

The Heinkel, with no human hand to steer it, was on a course of its own. Despite a coughing engine it flew steadily, over the dark land mass of Argyll, across the Firth of Lorne and over the high peaks of Mull in the inner Hebrides. After a smattering of tiny islands the dull gleam of water was unbroken by land interruption.

Zeitler, his mind racing with the implications of what a damaged plane could mean out over the open sea, was unable to endure the truth of Ernst's remarks and he reacted typically. His pale eyes bulged with frustrated rage, his guttural tongue issued a string of useless comments. The needles on the panel seemed to mock him in their restless wanderings inside the gauges. He couldn't take the irony of being shelled by an Ack-Ack gun in some remote little part of Britain after all the fire he had come through on the big night sorties. He fumed, fretted and swore till Anton could take no more.

"Shut up, Zeitler! Remember, it was your arrogance that got us into this one. The untouchable Zeitler! There's a laugh for you, only I don't feel like laughing. If we get out of this farce I'll see to it you won't fly for a very long time!"

"And keep your lunatic ravings for those Party Rallies you

enjoy so much," warned Ernst dryly. "Is it fear that makes you roar like a madman?"

"Me, afraid? I would die for Germany if I had to!"

"Enough," said Anton. "This is no time for discussions on bravery!" He crouched down beside Jon. "How goes it, my friend? Can you do anything with the steering?"

"I think I've loosened her a bit. Try her now, Zeitler."

The pilot worked with the controls and the damaged rudder responded unwillingly.

"Good for you, Jon," said Anton. "You're a genius."

Jon spread his long fingers. "There is nothing I can do with the instruments . . . the compass . . . how will you manage . . . can you tell where we are going?"

"I have charts and maps. I'll manage something."

"I'll have another go," said Jon. He looked again at the instrument panel and saw nothing but a misty blur. He felt himself trembling and, licking his dry lips, tried to grab at his remaining wits.

"Come on, Jon," urged the bluntly spoken Ernst who had never been able to understand the shy young man who loved music.

"Shouldn't you be back there at the radio?" asked Anton.

"Kaput!" said Ernst shortly. "The aerial."

Anton gripped Jon's arm, his quick, understanding nature allowing him to see the nerve-racked spirit seething inside the flight engineer's sparse frame. "Just do what you can. You did a fine job with the rudder. The rest of us can thank you."

Jon took a deep breath and pulled his senses together. He wasn't going to let go now. It was foolish after all the big raids he had come through. Each time his engineering skills had been tested and though his was an overwhelming responsibility his quick understanding of a plane's technicalities had seldom let him down. Ernst was always goading him but he had never given him the satisfaction of showing how much it stung. He breathed deeply and went to work but eventually had to admit he was beaten. He squeezed over to Anton who was trying to work out their position from the charts. The young commander felt at a terrible disadvantage. It was so difficult to know where they were. He could get nothing from the scene below, there were no recognisable landmarks . . . only the sea gleaming brightly.

"It's hopeless," said Jon. "We must be somewhere over the Atlantic ocean but . . .'

"Ha!" Ernst's derisive interruption made even Zeitler jump. "Over the sea, are we? God, Jon, you are clever. If you hadn't spoken I might have thought we were on our way to the moon!"

He smiled mockingly, sensing Jon's fear. He had sensed it before, like a tangible thing and, perhaps because it was mixed with the smell of his own, he was forever tormenting it. "Don't worry, Jon," he continued dryly. "If we talk nicely to Zeitler he will perhaps make it to Hamburg and parachute you straight into the arms of Mama!"

Jon swallowed and closed his eyes. The sick feeling was back in him though this time it was born of anger. Opening his eyes slowly he looked steadily at Ernst. "If we get out of this I promise I will thrash you at the first opportunity so that the world will see what colour your gut is. I can safely bet that it's just as yellow as every other swaggering pig who shouts to the world how brave he is."

The look in his brown eyes was reminiscent of a trapped animal and Ernst felt a pang of remorse. "Sorry, Jon. I went too far, we're all on edge."

Zeitler had the least to say. The starboard wing was listing and he knew the fuel pipes had been damaged. The engine could burst into flames at any moment though there couldn't be much fuel left in either tank. Jon had made the fuel change-over some time ago. Anton had released the remaining bombs into the black depths of the sea but even so the Heinkel was losing altitude. They were flying at less than 1000 metres and could see plainly the moon-flecked waves below.

"Land on port side," reported Anton suddenly.

The others peered down.

"I've seen a bigger postage stamp," said Zeitler.

"All right, we go into the sea then."

"I prefer to swim in kinder waters," returned Zeitler sarcastically.

"Drop down and circle the island," ordered Anton.

The Heinkel dropped and Jon swallowed his rising gorge, the thought of the inevitable parachute jump bringing him out in a cold sweat. Anton shoved a tin at him and said kindly, "Don't keep it back, Jon. Air sickness is nothing to be ashamed of. What about Kommodore Vati Mölders? Look at the position he is in despite air sickness."

"Unlike Mölders I have no ambition to be a pilot – ace or otherwise," said Jon sadly.

"There won't always be a war, Jon."

"I know that, Anton . . . but . . . never mind. We'll survive."

Anton crouched by Zeitler. "Take her round once more. The island is split by a range of high mountains but there is a good stretch of open ground just beyond. We must all try and land there."

"I will stay with her," said Zeitler.

"You will bail out and that is an order!" snapped Anton. "It would be madness to attempt a night landing. Look at those mountains . . ."

The plane gave a violent downward lurch. When she steadied rather shakily the starboard wing was listing dramatically. The exhaust manifold spat a sudden rush of bright red flame.

"Rev her," said Anton. "Burn up that fuel. Ready now! Jon, you first, get it over with."

He accompanied Jon to the hatch. The smell of the red hot manifold made them splutter. Jon swayed dizzily, looking down to the sickening curve of the watery world below.

"Now, Jon!" ordered Anton and Jon jumped. The air-stream grabbed him and hauled him away from the plane. Before he pulled his rip-cord the speed of the drop churned up his belly. He choked on his vomit and had barely time to get his wind before the pull of his released 'chute brought him up with a jerk. Now he was floating like a piece of thistledown to the dark little patch of moor.

Ernst had followed close on his heels and was just above but behind him.

"Now you, Zeitler," said Anton firmly. "I will take her now." He was taking no chances with the dogmatic Nazi whose arrogance led him to believe he was the master of any situation.

Zeitler's eyes flashed but he unbuckled his straps and went without a word, leaving Anton at the controls.

The young commander had noticed little white dots of habitation below and he wanted to get the crippled plane away from them. The only uninhabited area appeared to be the dark stretch of land where the others had jumped. He was over it now and would have to try and come back. He looked at the starboard wing. The fire had fizzled out. It meant the fuel was almost gone. A series of shuddering spurts of speed brought him round the western curve of the island once more. At a dangerously low altitude he flew past black humping mountains and his heart pumped into his throat. He had to get the plane up higher in order to jump safely. Relentless slopes rushed to meet him. Even while his pulses raced he thought, 'There are no houses on top of a mountain. It might be better if she crashed now . . .'

Before the thought came to an end he tugged at the controls. There was no response. His face was awash with sweat. This was it! Miraculously the Heinkel responded to his wild handling and lumbered upwards into the sky . . . enough for him to make the jump. He wondered if he ought to try and climb out of the sliding hatch above the pilot's seat . . . No, there wasn't enough time to manipulate himself through the small opening. He ran aft and jumped out of the rear gunner's door. The freezing night air whipped him cruelly, the jagged edges of a massive peak reared up to greet the frail speck of life. Frantically he guided his 'chute away only to see the cold face of a tiny basin of water sparkling in the moonlight. Helplessly he glided down, every fibre in him utterly spent but his instincts of self-preservation striving upwards out of his weary frame.

The cold black waters of Loch Sliach waited to meet him. It was a tiny lochan, huddled under the eastern face of Ben Machrie, the highest peak on the small island of Rhanna.

The bomber didn't burst into flames on the face of the mountain. Instead its remaining velocity carried it round the curving slopes. It tilted steeply, one wing clawing the ground, cartwheeled its way across a field, slid a few hundred yards, scarring deep through peat and heather until finally it came to rest, its nose embedded in a gorse-covered hillock. On its crazy journey it had spewed out bits of its innards. The starboard wing lay in a field, the stench of red hot metal oozed from the exhaust manifold, mingling with the sharp air washing over the moors. Ragged ailerons, trim tabs, the tail wheel and tail gun littered the ground. The fins had snapped from the fuselage in a ragged fracture, the servo rudder hung by mere scraps of material. The bold, sharp symbol of the swastika gaped mockingly, looking terrifyingly out of place in the wild, peaceful stretches of the Muir of Rhanna.

CHAPTER THREE

The Uisge-Beatha

Angus hurried away from Todd's house, taking the shore path that skirted the harbour. The moon had ridden out from its curtain of cloud to shed a pale brilliant light over the Sound of Rhanna which was calm with little wavelets sparkling to meet the white petticoats of the sandy beach. The horizon seemed a timeless distance away and the great stretches of the Atlantic Ocean lay placid and hauntingly beautiful.

The river Fallan rushed down from the mountain corries in mercurial wanderings and the sound of it thundered in Angus's ears as he crossed the little bridge. For a moment he stopped to lean muscular arms on the rough stone parapet, bowing his head to watch the frothing flurry of river tumbling into the sea.

"Uisge-beatha," he murmured softly and smiled benignly at the 'water of life'.

The smell of it was like nectar to his senses. On its journeying it had gathered into itself the crystal clear air of high mountain places; on its flight across the moorlands the tang of peaty heather roots had mixed into the water to give it a clear, amber tint and altogether it was a soft fragrant concoction. A light came into Angus's eyes and his smile was now one of triumph.

"Lovely Uisge-beatha," he addressed the river with approval. "Tonight you will be proving you are more than just a pretty sight. I'm goin' now to be havin' a taste of you."

He lumbered on, over the bridge, but a sound, other than that of the whispering sea, made him stop again and peer upwards into the sky. It was there again, the drone of a plane, heard but unseen, and he twisted his neck to try and catch a glimpse of the machine. His neck creaked and putting up a meaty fist he rubbed the aching muscle ruefully. Without quite knowing why, he felt uneasy. He hated the sound of aeroplanes. They sounded peaceful but he knew that was only an illusion. The war had changed everything. Before its outbreak life had been a pleasantly happy affair with no pressures to make a man feel he had to justify his very existence. Now, no matter how hard he tried he was haunted by an ever present sense of guilt made worse by the knowledge that two of his brothers had joined the navy. His supposedly bad back gave him no more than an occasional twinge; the heart murmur discovered during his medical examination did not detract from his easy, peaceful life, yet it and the exaggerated backache had exempted him from active service.

"The Uisga Hags will get you if the Germans don't," Canty Tam had warned, grinning his aimless grin and staring out to sea as if willing all the water witches of myth and folklore to come leaping out to grab Angus in their evil clutches and carry him off to sea.

"It's a useless idiot like yourself they're more likely to be after," Angus had answered with confidence. Nevertheless he hastened to pray to St Michael, the guardian of those on land or sea, and he was careful to wear his Celtic cross even if he was only mucking out the byre.

A little wind ruffled the sea and to one cursed with guilt it was easy to imagine that the sigh of Hag voices rode in on the breeze. Angus shivered, pulled his coat collar closer round his ears, and went quickly on his way. He was making for his father's wash-house, a place that had been grandly christened 'the Head-quarters'. Here a number of men met once weekly, widely broad-casting the fact that they were, for all intents and purposes, patriotically keeping fresh all the instruction they had received at the training courses.

"He breeah!"

Angus was startled almost out of his senses. His heart lurched into his throat, robbing the breath from his lungs. Speechlessly he stared at the stooped, long-coated figure that had apparently materialised from thin air.

"It is myself . . . bidding you a fine night," said a voice that floated out in notes of gentle doom.

"Dodie!" Angus found his voice in an explosion that split the dreaming night apart. "What the hell way is it you are leaping out of nowhere like a wandering spook! You near frightened the kach out of me, you stupid bugger!"

"Ach, it's sorry I am just." Dodie's voice broke on a sob. He was the island eccentric, living a lonely spartan existence in his tiny isolated cottage on the slopes of Sgurr nan Ruadh and it wasn't unusual to see him on any part of the island, day or night. He was a simple soft-hearted creature, as much a part of Rhanna as the very soil itself. Child-like in his innocence he was unable to understand the complicated natures of those around him and was very easily hurt but Angus was in no mood to humour him now.

"And it's sorry you should be! Are you forgetting the state of my heart? It's things like these could make it stop beating just!" Immediately he regretted the exploitation but simple Dodie believed that he had nearly caused a dreadful mishap.

"Och, don't say things like that, Angus!" he wailed. "I wouldny like to be the cause o' you dyin'. It's just . . . well, I was feart up there all alone. I have been hearin' these airy-planes over the island. I don't like them! They're worse than these motor cars they are having nowadays. They have wings you see and bad — bad it is just — it's only the birds should have wings. It's not natural . . . not natural at all!"

"It is the motor cars have wings then?" asked Angus, his natural sense of good humour getting the better of him.

"Ach – no, no . . . the airy-planes. 'Tis teasing you are. I wouldny like it if the motor cars started fleein' about too, the din would be terrible just. Ealasaid would not be giving any milk at all then, she has the bad nerves you see. It's really my Ealasaid I'm thinkin' about most. I put her out on the hill today it being so spring-like and the bugger never came home. Have you seen her at all, Angus?"

"Ach, no, but she'll be fine, Dodie," reassured Angus, knowing how much Dodie loved his wandering cow. "I'm away now, I am going to have a special meeting at my father's place."

Dodie hovered, unwilling to relinquish the company. Angus walked on and Dodie followed with the long lolloping gait that carried him swiftly and silently on his lonely travels.

"It will be all talk about the war things then?" he moaned soulfully, quite unable to understand what war was let alone things connected with it.

"Ay," agreed Angus, turning up the grassy lane to his parents' house. The wash-house was situated about ten feet from the main dwelling. Connected to it, like a lumpy little growth, was the wee hoosie. Because very few of the Rhanna dwellings had piped water most of the islanders had known nothing else but the wee hoosies and suffered them, with their attendant nuisances of flies, clegs and midgies, with very little complaint. Most of them were discreetly placed amidst coverings of bushes but those round Tam's had been hacked to the ground by Kate in a fit of rage. An urgent call of nature had hurried her outside one dark night and she had tripped and fallen into a flourishing bed of nettles, stinging those tender parts she had hurriedly exposed on her sojourn from the house.

"It was terrible just," she told everyone when she was able to laugh at the event. "I lay in that damt bed of nettles with my breeks at my ankles calling for Tam and him never hearing, the deaf bugger! I got such a fright I just forgot all about goin' to the wee house and was constipated for a week!"

For days she had implored Tam to cut back the nettle-bound bushes but while he was perfectly capable of earning his living as an odd-job man he rarely did any work round his own little stead. In a fit of pique Kate had taken an axe and hacked at the bushes till the wee hoosie stuck out like a self-conscious sore thumb.

Dodie eyed the dark little oblong enviously. At his own tiny croft he didn't have the dubious luxury of a wee hoosie; it was the chamber pot or the bushes for him and whenever he got the chance he childishly used the 'convenience' of anyone's house he happened to be visiting.

"Do you think Tam would mind if I . . ." – he leaned close to Angus and whispered self-consciously – "had a wee use o' the bathroom?" He had heard the word used at Burnbreddie where a huge generator allowed for all mod. cons.

In the darkness Angus gaped. Dodie had made a poor choice for his surprise. "The bathroom! There's no damt bath in there, Dodie, only the kach house – though 'tis a pity," he finished cheekily because Dodie's rather off-putting unwashed scent was a never-ending source of comment, though he was as oblivious to these as he was to his own peculiar smell.

Dodie was making prim noises of dismay at Angus's indelicate language. "Ach, you have no taste the way you say things, laddie. It's some manners you should be learning. The gentry have them though it's funny the way they are polite in some things but never in others."

Angus stamped impatiently. "Away you go in then, Dodie. You'll be finding some paper on a hook inside the door."

"No, no, never that!" Dodie lowered his voice. " 'Tis only a pee I'm needin'."

In the shrouding darkness of the tiny enclosure he fumbled through layers of shabby clothing, undid his fly, and gave himself up to the luxury of a 'good private pee'.

Outside there was the sound of scuffling and loud whispering.

"You're late," came Tam McKinnon's muffled reproach. "We have started long ago."

"Ach, I'm sorry," said Angus regretfully. "Wee Colin fell out o' bed and I had to go for Biddy. She's over at Todd's now. Was he here when he was taken bad?"

"Ay, and a terrible job we had carrying him outside, for he was drunk as a lord. In the end we just put him in the wheelbarrow and took him home while Ranald went up for the doctor. How is things with him now?"

"The doctor had him opened up when last I saw him." Angus gulped at the memory. "He says he just caught the appendix in time."

"Ach, poor Todd, a shame just," said Tam sympathetically. "But come away in now, son. It is even better than we thought. Like nectar it is, so easy it goes down."

Angus had forgotten Dodie. He stood in the doorway of the wash hoosie like a child on the threshold of wonderland. A suffocating heat rushed out to meet him coupled with the palpable, overpowering fumes of whisky.

"I could get drunk just standin' here," he said happily, staring into the little room where flames from a peat oven gleamed warmly on the pot still set into a corner of the room. A concoction of pipes and tubes sprouted from it in a glorified jumble that would have baffled the casual observer. But the sweating, glassy-eyed assembly in the wash hoosie had had plenty of time to acquaint themselves with the still and its intricate workings.

Almost three years had passed since Tam McKinnon had acquired the antiquated machinery in a most unexpected manner. He had been fixing the thatch of a blackhouse at Nigg which was

44

used by blind Annack Gow in which to keep peat and other fuel, though it wasn't unknown for her to live in the house during the winter months because she claimed it was cosier than the 'modern hoosie'.

A rummage in the byre for a hammer had also revealed the pot still, sitting like a nugget of gold amidst an assortment of farm implements and a pile of cow manure. Excitement choking him, Tam had hastened to Annack with an offer to clear out the accumulated junk in the byre.

"How much will you be wantin'?" she had barked, peering at him through her thickly lensed specs. "An old body like myself has no money to spare with my man gone and only myself to work the croft!"

"Not a farthing, Annack," Tam had choked. "Just the odd bit junk you will never be using. Being a handyman I can make use of some of it."

"Ay, well, don't be stealing my dung while you're about it," she had returned suspiciously. "I need all I can get for my vegetables . . . and a creel or two of seaweed wouldn't go wrong either," she ended cunningly.

Tam's face fell at the thought of gathering seaweed and humping it over the hill to Nigg, but the temptation of the still was too much and the deal was made. In the process of clearing the byre he found all the bits and pieces relating to the still and happily trundled the lot home on his cart.

Tam was already adept at making beer and had enjoyed long years of solitary tippling but the delicate art of making malt whisky needed several pairs of hands. Into his confidence he had taken those of his cronies whom he considered tight-lipped enough not to give his illicit little game away.

With much patient devotion the various stages of the whisky-making process were carried out. Tubs of barley were put to steep in the peaty water of the river Fallan; the soaked grain was then spread out till it was dry enough to be tenderly winnowed; the sprouting kernels were placed on shelves above a peat-fuelled oven. This had once been used by Kate to heat her washing water; but with the growing up of her family she had abandoned the wash hoosie, the kitchen tub now sufficing for the needs of the diminished household. Willingly the men had mashed the dried malt in heated spring water, the sting of the hard work taken away by visions of ever-flowing, golden whisky. The most critical stage of the business was fermentation and distillation and the men had taken it in shifts to make sure the temperature of the still was kept constant.

Bewildered wives, wondering at menfolk sneaking off in the middle of the night, were fobbed off with a variety of excuses and long before Tam's still was ever to prove its worth many a Rhanna wife harboured suspicions about the faithfulness of their espoused.

But that was all in the distant past. The first batch of malt, lying in cool wooden casks carefully prepared by Wullie the carpenter, was ready to be sampled; perhaps a little too soon for proper maturation but the men could wait no longer to reap the rewards of their labour. In defiance against superstition they had chosen the thirteenth night of the third month for the tasting ceremony. For weeks they had waited for 'the night of the Uisge-Beatha'. Now it was here. Tam had gone into the cool, little closet extension of the wash hoosie and, with the delicacy normally reserved for the handling of the newborn, brought forth the first cask of matured malt. Quite unconsciously, every man in the gathering reverently removed an assortment of head coverings in a moment of homage to the Uisge-Beatha.

Now they lay about the floor, each in different stages of inebriation and in their midst, propped shoulder to shoulder, sat Kate McKinnon and Annack Gow, a long history of temperamental differences drowned in the happy haze of delirium induced by the Uisge-Beatha.

Annack's arrival had caused quite a stir, for she came on the arm of Tammy Brown, one of the confraternity. It soon transpired that Annack was neither as senile nor as blind as her demeanour suggested.

"You silly bugger!" she scolded Tam McKinnon. "Did you really think I was not knowing it was my Jack's still you were after? Clean out my byre indeed! You that canny even keep your own grass cut! It's the sheeps that do it for you!" Here she and Kate exchanged hostile glances. "No, it's not daft I am, Tam McKinnon," she continued with asperity. "My Jack was brewing the malt while you were still cutting milk teeths!" A dreamy look came into her short-sighted eyes. "My, the times we had in the black hoosie . . . up there in the wee secret room . . . ay, they knew how to build houses in those days. My grandfather was the one to start the still and the secret of it was passed down to my Jack . . . ay, and much as I've missed him it's a wee taste o' his whisky I'm missing too. Yours will never match his but since you're a beginner to the art I will give you fair judgement."

"But how did you know it was tonight, Annack?" asked Tam humbly.

"Hmph! Anybody with half a nostril could tell, so don't think I'm the only one to be knowing. Every time I was passing your house my nose is telling me the malt gets riper. I have been keeping a sharp guard on Tammy here . . . all that snooping about at all hours. I knew there was something brewing all these years so I just threatened Tammy with the customs mannie and he couldn't get me along here fast enough."

But Tammy and his ready treachery were soon forgotten in the spree that followed. The whisky, its attraction doubly enhanced by its rich amber colouring, soon transported everyone into an idyllic world where no emnity existed.

Into this gathering came Angus and, close on his heels, Dodie who sniffed the air with his large, carbuncled nose. He uttered a startled "He breeah!" to the assembly, his misty conceptions about the Headquarters and the 'war things' that went on there made no clearer by his first confused impressions of the room.

"I couldny help it," apologised Angus to his father. "He followed me."

"Just for a wee use o' the bathroom!" wailed Dodie with a flash of his broken brown teeth.

Tam looked startled but muttered an urgent, "Bring him in and shut the damt door!"

Thus Dodie was introduced to 'the Headquarters' and his concept about war became even more vague as his innards warmed to his first taste of the Uisge-Beatha. His fuddled mind spun happily till 'airy-planes' and his dearly-beloved cow were mere ghosts in his memory. So relaxed was he that he even let Annack remove his greasy cap and fondle his head of baby-fine hair without the hint of a blush.

From his elevated position in the lighthouse situated on the wind-swept cliffs of Port Rum Point, Righ nan Dul had been keeping an anxious eye heavenwards. He had noticed a plane approaching Rhanna but although it was low in the sky he wasn't yet sure what type of plane it was. Something in the shape of it introduced a niggling sense of unease into his mind but, certain that it wasn't a Coastal Command aircraft, he limped out on to the balcony to shade his eyes from the glare of the moon and crane his neck upwards.

The aircraft had disappeared from view though he could hear the sound of it on the hush of the wind over the Muir of Rhanna. He stood there, a lone figure outlined against the pale bulk of the lighthouse. The cold of the night air swept over him but Righ was oblivious to it; he wasn't known as the governor of the elements for nothing. In his time he had been one of the crew of the Rhanna lifeboat and had fought against lashing gales and mountainous seas. The keen cold of that March night was like a soft little summer breeze against his nut-brown, leathery skin.

The plane was circling the island and he knew by the odd, coughing sound of the engines that it was in trouble. It came round towards him again. A small gasp of surprise escaped his lips and he arched backwards against the balcony rail to get a better view of what was now distinctly a German bomber air-craft. It was flying so low now that he ducked down instinctively, breathlessly watching it juddering round the village of Portcull. For a long incredulous moment he watched it embracing the slopes of the mountains, heading for a crash on the quietly menac-ing shoulder of Ben Machrie.

"Jesus – God – St Michael! Help us all!" he muttered aloud to all those unseen guardians of life. Then he was off, limping hurriedly down the spiral stairs to emerge atop the smooth, cropped turf of the Point. To his left lay the needles of the Sgor Creags – grey, jostling pinnacles of treachery, the swish of the sea deceptively peaceful in its picturesque frothing round the slimy, barnacle-encrusted rocks. To the right of him lay the natural little harbour of Portcull, protected from the worst weather by the long finger of Port Rum Point.

Righ scuttled hurriedly along the path to the Kirk sitting starkly aloof at the top of the peninsula. With its creaking elms and black, huddled headstones casting long moon-scattered shadows, it was an eerie place, but Righ had no time to let himself be haunted by monuments to the dead. His thoughts were for the living and he gave the gate a mighty push that set it creaking on its rusty hinges.

The Kirk was never locked. On Rhanna people seldom locked anything, and to the bible-thumping Reverend John Gray an ever-open Kirk door meant an ever-available sanctum to repentant sinners wanting to unburden their minds to the Lord.

Righ lost no time in getting to the bell pull and soon the mournful notes were crashing rudely into the peacefully dreaming Rhanna night. For several minutes Righ kept doggedly at the ropes, until finally, with aching arms, he withdrew from the Kirk and hobbled away to the other old gate set into the wall atop the Hillock.

Little black blobs were scurrying from all quarters, hastily pulling outdoor clothes over night attire. The tall figure of John Gray came rushing from the Manse, followed closely by his small dumpy wife who was inserting her false teeth as she ran. No catastrophe on earth was worth the price of her dignity to which she clung fiercely on an island where many of the older generation only wore false teeth on Sundays or at funerals.

"What is it, Righ?" she called out in her softly pleasant voice which was such a contrast to her husband's deep boom.

"A German bomber has come to the island!" gulped Righ. "I am not really knowing if it has crashed – or – or, landed!"

"I heard it – I heard it!" bellowed the minister. "I said to Mrs Gray that I thought I heard a plane with failing engines! Is that not so, my dear?"

Her reply was lost in the general confusion that followed, but after a few bewildering minutes a certain order began to emerge. The efficiency of the Home Guard was hampered somewhat by those members who had come staggering out of the Headquarters in a merry drunken heap. Left behind was Annack Gow who sat with her arms lovingly entwined round the cask of malt, her head resting on the barrel in a manner that allowed her generous nose to inhale unhindered the strong sweet fumes of the Uisge-Beatha.

Righ stood on the brow of the Hillock, his arms spread wide to command attention and the members of the immediate community straggled out on the slopes below, listening avidly to what he had to impart.

"Is it no' just like the sermon on the mount?" giggled Agnes Anderson to her youthful cronies who laughed loudly and eyed several of the island lads in the hope that they had attracted their attention. But the boys were too taken up with the novelty of the situation and stared up at Righ. Unlike the parables of hope delivered to a people hungry for a glimpse of a better world, the message that Righ imparted was one laden with urgency to a people already living in a satisfying peaceful environment. To defend that kind of existence meant an instant course of action by all concerned.

Even while Righ was delivering his message the bell he had recently rung was finding its echo all over the island. At Portvoynachan, four miles to the east, Mrs Jemima Sugden, the elderly schoolmistress of the tiny school in that area, was vigorously ringing a huge handbell though she had no earthly idea what was happening.

But the ringing of the Kirk bell at Portcull was a pre-arranged signal to everyone that something connected with war had come to Rhanna and the members of the Home Guard knew to assemble at their various posts to await orders.

At Rumhor, outside the little wooden hut used by John Gray for Sunday afternoon services, a handful of men began to gather, speculating keenly about the meaning of the bell. The use of the hut as a place of worship was a recent innovation dreamed up by the minister because many of his flock grumbled about the journey to Portcull and frequently didn't attend Sunday worship. In truth the excuse was merely a ruse to wriggle out of going to Kirk; now there was no plausible reason to miss it and the shirkers dourly cursed the minister and his diligence to save their souls.

Tom and Mamie Johnston of Croynachan, wakened rudely by the dreadful tearing of metal ripping through earth, were hardly able to believe their eyes when they rushed outside to see bits of a German bomber strewn over their field.

"Don't panic, mo ghaoil," Tom soothed his wife. "It's only bits of an old aeroplane."

"A *German* plane," said Mamie faintly, quickly following her husband who had rushed into the kitchen to fetch his shotgun.

"You stay with the bairns," he told Mamie. "Lock all the doors and only open them to the neighbours or myself when I get back."

Mamie's round pleasant face showed fear but she was a sensible soul and went back upstairs where her two teenage children slept peacefully, oblivious to all.

Tom saddled his horse and galloped to Croft na Beinn, then on to the tiny clachan of Croy, quickly and efficiently gathering together every able-bodied man.

The people of Nigg had no need of warning bells to let them know that something very unusual had happened, because old Madam Balfour of Burnbreddie was standing on top of the high tower of the gloomy old house, lustily banging a dinner gong and shouting at the top of her high-pitched, hysterical voice. Her bedroom lay at the top of the big square tower and the German bomber on its third sweep round the island had flown at such a low altitude she had fully imagined it was coming in on top of her.

With her only son, Scott, the young Laird of Burnbreddie, fighting with the British army somewhere in Greece, she felt vulnerable and abandoned despite the fact that she had the companionship of Rena, her very able daughter-in-law. Having screamed to Rena that the house was under air-attack she made a very agile flight to the roof to bang her gong and shriek. Rena's two children, hearing their grandmother conducting herself in a manner that would have frightened the Uisga Hags themselves, began to scream also and Rena had her hands full trying to soothe everyone.

But Righ had despatched several messengers to places that were bereft of menfolk. The wheels of the bicycle brigade were set in motion and, before long, frightened women and children were receiving sangfroid comfort. Everything was in good hands. Squads of bicycles and horses were moving up to the eastern end of the island, gathering on their way the various little bands of men assembled at their posts.

Robbie Beag was one of the last to leave because he had been told to give his sister certain instructions to be sent out on her wireless transmitter. Behag was greatly excited but the only evidence of her seething emotions showed in a speck of red high on each wizened cheek and a slight trembling of her stubby fingers. She was one of those gathered at the bottom of the Hillock and had barely got the gist of what was happening but her long ears picked up enough to let her know that her great moment was about to be born. She hastened to unlock the Post Office and, with shaky legs, entered the outhouse through a door in the little cubby hole she grandly called her back shop. Slowly and deliberately she sat down in front of the wireless to await orders.

Robbie's bike wobbled alarmingly on the way over the bridge. The Fallan rushed under him, a cold babbling of sound that sharpened the air around it. But Robbie was far from cold. The Uisge-Beatha lay warm in his belly. He tried to unscramble his pickled thoughts but it was useless and he blinked his glazed eyes lazily and beamed happily into the darkness.

Behag heard the approach of 'her messenger' and began to fuss with switches. If only Totie Little, the postmistress of Port-voynachan, could see her now! What a feast of gloating then. Totie had made some disparaging remarks about 'the contraption' but Behag had discounted them by telling everyone, 'Totie is just jealous that the wireless is not under her command'.

But when Robbie's red smiling face came through the door Behag glared at him suspiciously. "What way are you smilin' for?" she barked. "This is a serious business, Robbie Beag!" She sniffed the air in a long series of twitches. "You have been drinking, that you have! I'll be finding out more of this later, my lad! Are you in a fit state at all to know what you are saying?"

Robbie hastened to pull himself together. "Och, Behag! Why is it you always think the worst of me? C'mon now . . . is it not yourself should be a proud woman tonight? My, if Totie could see you now, eh? An important lady is what you are, Behag! You mustny worry about things that don't matter."

Robbie could be crafty on occasion. The malt was bringing out the wiles in him. For once he had said the right thing. Behag fairly bristled with importance.

"Ach you are right, Robbie. Make haste now and give me the message."

"You have to report an invasion. Righ said something about the island was invaded by German bombers." His finishing words were accompanied by a tightly controlled little belch.

Behag glared. "Robbie! What do you mean, 'said something'? I don't know what Righ was thinkin' about sending you. Invaded by German bombers! I heard him say he saw *one* German airy-plane!"

Robbie made a desperate attempt to sort out his happily reeling senses. "Now, now, Behag," he admonished with unusual authority. "Righ saw one plane which does not mean to say that was all . . . in fact . . . now that I recall he said something about – er – *three* Heinkels. People heard planes all over the island. You said yourself you were hearing a plane twice. There could be dozens of Hums all over the place!"

"Huns!" corrected Behag primly, though her voice was now less suspicious. Still she hesitated. This was her big moment. On her shoulders lay the responsibility of sending out accurate information. She wished that Righ was at her side, he could always be relied upon; but he would be showing the men where he thought the crash had taken place.

"Her fine Lady up at Burnbreddie said one near came in her window!" said Robbie in awe, the full import of the event just starting to seep into his head. In an eerie whisper he continued, "Righ said another one near took his head off at the lighthouse – and – and Angus heard one . . . so did Ethel and Biddy!"

It was enough for Behag. If the gentry had reported seeing a plane, and all those other reliable citizens too, then quick action was called for.

Her fingers hovered momentarily above the wireless then with an agile flourish she began to tap out the message, Robbie forgotten in the excitement of her great moment.

CHAPTER FOUR

Paradise

Robbie made a hurried exit from the Post Office and came upon Dodie leaning against a wall. The old eccentric was weeping into his big calloused hands, his stooped shoulders shuddering with long, drawn-out sobs. The happy effects of the Uisge-Beatha were wearing off and he was a bedraggled, unhappy spectacle.

"Och, c'mon now, man, what ails you?" asked Robbie kindly.

Dodie looked pathetically forlorn and lost and it was a long moment before he spoke. When he did so it was in a whisper of embarrassment.

"Oh Robbie, it's feart I am! They are all sayin' the German folk have landed on Rhanna and I'm hearin' they shoot people and throw bombs at them. I'm not knowing a thing about the war and nobody is telling me anything . . . and – and Ealasaid's out there and I'm too feart to go and look for her! It's ashamed I am just!"

He sobbed quietly into his hands, the tears running in dirty rivulets through his fingers. For the first time in his life Robbie thought seriously about Dodie and his lonely simple world. It was bad enough to know about the things that went on in the war but to a simple soul like Dodie, his mind groping at half-formed notions and solitary imaginings, it might be utterly terrifying. To see a ghost was far better than *feeling* that one was there and though Robbie only barely grasped at that idea it was enough to make him feel a great lump of self-reproach in his throat.

He threw a firm arm round Dodie's bent shoulders and said soothingly, "Look now, Dodie, I'm here, I'll look after you . . ." His smile broadened. "I'll tell you what . . . you can come with me. I'll leave my bike here and we'll hitch up Todd's cart. The poor bugger won't be using it for a whily and I'm sure he'd be happy to know he was helping the cause."

Dodie raised his tear-stained face. It was grey and utterly

woebegone in the pale glimmer of the moon's betraying light but a small ghost of a smile lit his weary face.

"Can I really come with you, Robbie? My, it would be right nice so it would . . . and . . ." He blinked away the last of the tears. ". . . We might find my Ealasaid on the way."

Robbie patted his arm. "She'll be fine, will Ealasaid. Now . . ." He pulled out his whisky flask from the generous hip pocket of his ancient plus-fours. "Have a wee droppy o' this. Och yes now, it will do you good. I've plenty and there's enough o' the bonny malt to keep my flask wet for many a long day."

Thinking the household asleep after the labours of the night, and mindful of Todd's post-operative condition, Robbie furtively groped about in the big jumbled barn that served as the Smiddy.

Before many minutes had passed he and Dodie were making their belated journey into Glen Fallan. The road through the mountains into Downie's Pass was eerily silent and Robbie patted his well-oiled shotgun affectionately, finding comfort in its familiar presence. He was equally glad of Dodie's company which though hardly eloquent was reassuringly familiar by the faint waves of odour which even the keen night air couldn't combat.

But despite his caution in Todd's untidy shed, Robbie's impaired reflexes left little room for delicate motion and he made more noise than he imagined. Biddy was asleep by the warm peat glow in the kitchen. Lachlan had departed long ago, despite his long night ready to go out with the rest of the men to assist in the search. Mrs McDonald was asleep upstairs and Todd was ensconced in the big comfortable couch in the parlour. Biddy had declined Lachlan's offer of a ride home, not savouring the idea of being alone in Glen Fallan with Germans reported to be crawling all over the place. She slept the just sleep of the weary but one little part of her subconscious remained alert to danger. The subdued clanks and rattles from the barn brought her awake in a grumbling stupor. She groped for her spectacles because it was a belief of hers that she could hear better with them on. The stealthy movements came again and Biddy held her breath.

"The Germans," she muttered. "The damt cheek o' them! Looking for a place to sleep likely! Well, I'll put them to sleep all right."

Fumbling in her bag she extracted a small bottle of ether, then she grabbed the large brass poker and her spindly legs carried her swiftly to the back door and outside. The little oblong of the side door leading into the barn loomed like a black cavern. It lay slightly open, letting the scent of warm hay and horse manure escape into the night.

Her heart was in her mouth and she gulped, wondering if it might have been wiser to have called upon the brawny help of the local menfolk. But the idea died quickly with the realisation that every man worth his salt was on the other side of the island. Several had been left at various lookout posts but these were widely scattered.

"Now Biddy, mo ghaoil," she told herself, "you have not lived seventy-five years on earth for nothing. The buggers are but laddies, Germans or no."

Tucking the poker under her arm, she made a wad of her hanky then saturated it generously with ether. The only sounds now were the soft little snorts made by two horses and the muffled scamperings of mice on nocturnal prowls. Biddy went forward a step and listened. Robbie and Dodie had made their exit from the front of the shed minutes before, but Robbie had been careless with the bolt and the rather rickety double doors creaked with an eerie menace. The effect of suspense was enhanced by the ghostly beam of moonlight that filtered through the gently swinging doors, turning everyday objects into frightening shadows of the super-natural.

"I know you're in there." Biddy tried to make her voice author-itative but instead it came out in a squeak. "If you come out of there nobody will harm you."

One of the horses snickered softly but it was enough to make Biddy take a careless step backwards. Her foot caught in a mangled heap of junk and she sprawled her full length, one black-clad leg twisting under her at an unnatural angle. Before she had time to feel too much of the searing pain the fumes from the ether-soaked pad wafted up her nose. By a stroke of chance it had fallen where her head now lay and she only had time to grunt once or twice before the anaesthetic carried her into a muffled world of insensibility.

The Smiddy and the rest of Portcull in general sat tranquilly in the moonlight, a complete contrast to the scene on the opposite side of the island. The sight of the twisted wreckage of the plane near Croynachan brought gasps of incredulity from all who gazed upon it; the sign of the swastika on the severed tail-piece made everyone feel oddly uneasy. There was no denying it, the Germans were actually on Rhanna, the evidence was there for all to see. The war had suddenly become a grim reality instead of a distant fantasy.

The islanders bore down on the plane like a horde of ants. Excitement made them revert to their native Gaelic yet caution hushed their voices. The only woman there was Kate McKinnon whom Tam had thought safely ensconced in the wash-hoosie beside Annack Gow. But Kate was made of stern stuff. She had wobbled all the way up Glen Fallan on an ancient bicycle. On the way she had armed herself with a fire besom and she now strode into the scene, nostrils aflare and bosom heaving, wielding the besom in the manner of one expecting to encounter a swarm of German airmen at any moment.

"Get back, woman!" shouted Tam angrily but Kate had stopped short at the wreckage, the Germans forgotten in a tide of wonder. She was a magpie of the human world and immediately she spotted several items that would make dubiously worthwhile additions to her already cluttered household.

A few minutes later, Dodie, in a subdued state of excitement, galloped into the scene. With joy he stared at the wrecked plane, his tall ungainly figure a looming spectre at the feast.

Kate, having been warned to stay away from the plane in case it exploded, was following the trail left by it, like an eagle after prey. Dodie, his fear of the Germans forgotten, followed in her wake to stare lovingly and longingly at the tail-piece with its bold swastika plainly visible in the light of the moon peeping round the shoulder of Ben Madoch.

" 'Tis nice colours on it," he whispered childishly. "A nice pattern so it is."

The men had spread out over the moor, their steps taking them warily through snagging clumps of heather and gorse. Out here in the open a keen little wind moaned in from the sea and wailed softly around the grey cloisters of the old Abbey ruins situated near Dunuaigh, the Hill of the Tomb. It was a lost lonely place and in normal circumstances the islanders gave it a wide berth, even in daytime. Now, in the hushed shadows of night it brought chilling fears to the more superstitious, magnified a thousandfold by the thought that Nazi Germans might be lurking among the time-worn stones.

It was tall, dark Fergus McKenzie of Laigmhor who found Jon Jodl. He was sitting on the ground, huddled against a large mossy boulder, staring dreamily out over the wild dark moors. Jon was in no hurry to move. Drifting down to the springy stretches of heather, his parachute trailing him gently along, Jon had quite magically lost all sense of fear. Standing in the hushed moors with the sea glimmering in the distance and the soft little murmur of a nearby burn making sweet music in his ears, he felt perhaps he had died up there in the last nightmare hours and now he had effortlessly but surely landed in paradise.

The clamour of bombs and guns, the smoke, stink and filth of war seemed very far away from this place of heavenly quiet and soft sweet scents. Tears of relief rolled down his cheeks; the tight knot in his belly uncoiled slowly and he knew peace.

"Just for a little while, God," he prayed silently and through the glimmer of tears on his lashes it seemed to him that the face of God was moulded into a little gauze cloud that drifted lazily above.

Jon sighed and felt he had been reprieved, perhaps only for a little while but enough to let him gather together his frayed nerves. The rank smell of vomit from his clothing revolted him and, grabbing a handful of heather, he dipped it in the burn to scrub at the offending mess, his expression a grimace of shame. What would people think? People! For a moment he panicked but pulled himself quickly together. It was no use hiding. His sense of direction told him he was somewhere in Scotland. The Scottish people were renowned for their hospitality and kindness. Wrapping the parachute round himself he sat on the mossy ground with his back to the boulder and waited to be found.

In his half-conscious state it seemed to him only a very short time before he heard the stealthy approach of footsteps, and a few moments later he found himself looking into the twin barrels of a twelve-bore shotgun.

Fergus McKenzie had only one arm but with it he held his gun with confidence. He had lost his left arm in an accident many years before when out searching for his brother, Alick, in the treacherous waters that swirled round the Sgorr Creags. The loss of the arm had caused him not only physical and mental torture but many years of emotional heartbreak longing for Kirsteen Fraser, the girl he had promised to marry but rejected because of his foolish pride. She had sailed away from Rhanna carrying his unborn son and almost six years were to pass before fate had brought them together again and she had come back to the island in the autumn of 1940. Now she was his wife of nearly six months and he felt that all the years of unhappiness were just a bad dream. Everything in his life was now doubly precious, and strong dark Fergus strode tall and proud, paying no heed to the gossip in the first weeks of Kirsteen's return.

"His lordship will no longer be standing on his pedestal," had sniffed Behag Beag to her cronies. "First his brother gets a girl in trouble and has to be sent away in disgrace. After that we are seeing the terrible shame of his daughter with child and the little hussy holding up that McKenzie head of hers like she was royalty. As if that wasn't bad enough our ex-schoolmistress comes back to Rhanna complete with McKenzie's son born out of wedlock. 'Tis a bad name they will be giving this good place and I hope the Lord will forgive them indeed." At which point Erchy the Post had sent everyone scuttling about their business by opening the door and saying in a loud voice, "And it is yourself, Mr McKenzie! Just in time for a nice cosy gossip!"

The worst of the talk behind them, Kirsteen and Fergus were relaxed and happy. Occasionally there was a clash of personalities because the dominant Fergus liked to get his own way. But Kirsteen had acquired a strong willpower of her own during her years of independence and he was quickly learning that his moody tempers held no water with her. Also too there was the problem of getting to know the little stranger who was his son. On the whole Grant Fergus was a good-natured child, but he was possessed of a temperament which could change like quicksilver from one mood to another. Fergus didn't want to introduce the heavy hand too soon but he was a disciplinarian and was unable to repress the urge to control the boy. This had brought a spell of resentment which had been short-lived because the little boy's irrepressible sense of fun wouldn't allow him to stay sullen for long. His respect for Fergus was growing stronger with each passing day and coupled with sturdy admiration for the big man who had so recently materialised into the father for whom he had always longed.

Overriding all was the warm, wonderful sense of Laigmhor, once more a family home. For too many years it had been a place with an atmosphere of waiting for an infusion of life that Fergus's first wife, Helen, seemed to have taken with her on the night she had died giving birth to his daughter, Shona.

But all that was over now. Fergus was fulfilled and happy. The days were busy with the work of the farm, the evenings filled with the warmth of family togetherness. And the nights belonged to two people making up for their years apart. The room in which Fergus had spent so many nights alone with his memories was now an intimate world of tender love.

When Fergus found Jon Jodl propped like a statue in the middle of the moors he was in a strangely mixed-up mood. The harsh knocking of old Bob on the stout kitchen door had been a rude intrusion into a particularly precious interlude with Kirsteen. For two days she had been cool with him because of a tiff over a matter so trivial that both knew they were being foolish but neither would give in. Earlier in the evening she had kept her fair head averted all through supper. He had watched the fine beauty of her slender body and had wanted to crush her to him because she was even more desirable when she was aloof. Covertly she had observed his strong rugged features with his stubborn set of chin and, as always, the sight of him, his sweet nearness, turned her heart to jelly. Looking at the little white hairs in his raven sideburns always brought a strange choking feeling into her throat. Just to see the muscular hardness of his body thrilled her with its maleness but yet she eluded his burning black eyes. It was childish of her, she knew, but somehow the little times of disagreement between them made the making-up doubly exciting.

He had gone to bed early but she hadn't followed and he tossed and turned, unable to sleep without her at his side. It was late when he finally got up and went quietly down to the warm kitchen. She had just stepped out of the zinc tub and her glistening body was tawny in the glow of firelight, her crisp hair a deep golden halo of ruffled wet curls.

For a moment neither of them spoke then she said coolly, "It seems I am afforded no privacy of my own, no matter how late the hour."

He had felt the laughter rising in his throat. "My darling!" His lilting voice was deep with joy. "Am I to spend the rest of my life finding you in dark little corners wearing nothing but your birthday suit?" He was referring to their first meeting in the fragrant woods above Loch Tenee when he had come upon her drying herself after a swim in the Loch.

She was unable to retain her cold dignity any longer and a soft chuckle escaped her throat. "Fergie." She whispered his name enticingly and in moments he was crushing her against him, fierce in his passion, his lips hard on hers.

His heart was beating rapidly. The smell of her was like the sweet, fresh air on the top of a summer mountain, natural, unmasked by perfumes and cosmetics. She was that kind of woman; clean as a mountain burn; uncluttered by feminine trappings yet so utterly desirable in her own right that his senses reeled with her nearness. For a moment he remembered the first night of their marriage with the bed cool and remote-looking spread with sheets of pure white linen. Unaccountably he had felt awkward and shy, like a young boy entering an unknown phase in his life. She had entered the room looking like a mythical goddess dressed in a white silken nightdress, her hair shining like the pale gold of a summer cornfield. They were like young lovers, awkward and unsure, lost for words in those first breathless moments. The new white sheets rustled in the quiet room, adding to their embarrassment; then their feet touched an assortment of brushes and other bristly accoutrements, placed there by Shona in a moment of mischief. The incident broke the ice and they shrieked with stifled merriment, finally falling into each other's arms in a passion of untamed desire.

The memory made him catch his breath with tenderness even while his mouth crushed her lips and his tongue played with hers. Her skin was like silk, parts of it still damp from the bath, the intimate parts that made him forget all else but his need for her.

But she pushed him away, her eyes going to the windows, which though heavily curtained, were a distraction to her senses. "Not here, Fergie," she whispered. "Let's go up to bed."

"No, here, Kirsteen . . . by the fire . . . like the night at the schoolhouse."

"But – we were alone then, my darling. Shona and Babbie are upstairs, they could come down . . . Grant might come into the bedroom looking for me – you know he does that sometimes and. . ."

"No, I'm not having that!" he laughed. "All those excuses. The house is asleep . . . and I can't wait . . ." He kissed her again and her resolution left her, it always did when he was beside her, doing things to her body that made her forget all else. The hard strength of him excited her; the heat from the fire seemed to burn right into her, till every life force within cried out for a release.

The kitchen drowsed on warmly; Snap and Ginger slept peacefully atop the oven, the clock tick-tocked on the mantelshelf, somewhere behind the skirting-boards a mouse scurried among the plaster.

But the things he was doing to her were drowning out all her usual senses. Now all she heard was his harsh, quick breathing, his lilting endearments. She stroked his thick dark hair, her love for him meeting and whirling with her passions. He had pulled the zinc tub away from the fire and the rug was soft and warm. For a moment she saw the shadows leaping about the ceiling then he pulled her down and in towards him; her eyes closed, driving another of her senses inwards. Somewhere, in the world outside, a plane pulsated, robbing the night of silence; then it was gone; the island dreamt on undisturbed. In his rough search for fulfilment he brought her both pain and pleasure, so deep inside that one could hardly be distinguished from the other; their cries met and mingled together; uniting them in those exalted moments.

The tearing roar of a plane coincided with their ebullience but they were so involved with the beauty of their emotions that nothing could penetrate their world. Kirsteen felt the mist of tears in her eyes and she held his head against her breasts.

"My Fergie," she whispered, "tonight we have made a child. At this very minute our baby is being conceived."

He looked up for a moment, cupping her chin in his hand, his black eyes alight with his love for her. "I had thought that Shona was the only one in the household with a fancy to her imagination.

I can see all that folklore you are hearing at the Ceilidhs is getting at you too."

But her smile was full of conviction. "You wait and see . . . I'll give you the second of those five sons I promised . . ." she giggled. "In fact – just to spite you I might have twins – if Alick and Mary can do it, then so can I."

Somewhere in the distance the German bomber crashed, sending shock-waves through the Glen that were carried on the soft breath of the wind, mere ghostly echoes but unusual enough to make Fergus say uneasily, "What the hell was that . . . I wonder . . . did you hear a plane a whily back?"

"Yes, but . . ."

An urgent rapping at the door made them both scramble quickly to their feet, Kirsteen wrapping herself into her woollen dressing-gown while Fergus, angry at the interruption, quickly made himself decent then went to wrench open the door.

But Bob, his knarled fists bunching on the bone handle of his shepherd's crook, wasted no time with pretty words of apology. He had witnessed the spectacle of the bomber heading for almost certain destruction on Ben Machrie. "Are you deaf, man?" he asked sarcastically. "The damt thing must have come right over Laigmhor! It came down so low it rattled the dishes on my dresser!"

Before Fergus could answer the sound of the Kirk bell could be heard pealing over the countryside.

Shona and her friend, Barbara Cameron, came piling into the kitchen, their faces full of enquiry. Shona tied the cord of her green wool dressing-gown, her blue eyes big in a pale face framed in the thick mane of auburn hair that tumbled down her back. She had left Rhanna to join the Nursing Reserve in Aberdeenshire and had come back to the island only that morning, ordered to take some leave because she had thrown herself into the job with such dedication she was physically exhausted. The leave had come unexpectedly, giving her just enough time to dash off a letter to her sweetheart, Niall McLachlan, who was at a college in Glasgow training to be a vet.

"I thought I heard thunder!" she said breathlessly, "but there's hardly a cloud in the sky!"

Babbie stood beside Shona, a smile of bemusement lighting her freckled face. The flame of the candle she held danced on a shock of red hair and brought out the sparks in her dancing green eyes. Shona's invitation to accompany her to Rhanna for a holiday had come at a time in her life when her ideas for her future were rather uncertain and she had accepted gratefully.

"Is it always as quiet as this on Rhanna?" she asked mischievously, her face alight with a radiance that reached out to embrace everyone. But they were all too uneasy at that moment to respond to her light-hearted words.

The men had left the house quickly and now Fergus stood looking down at the young German. "Up you get now, man," he said quietly. "You will not be hurt if you do just as you're told."

Jon Jodl didn't understand a word but knew what was expected of him. Slowly he unwound himself from his parachute and got to his feet. In the pale glimmering of the moon's light Fergus saw the strained, white face of a youth clad in a German flying suit stained with vomit.

"You are just a laddie and ill by the look of you." Compassion made Fergus's voice soft. He hadn't been able to imagine what his feelings would be on coming face to face with a German. He had expected to feel some sort of resentment, or anger. He had good reason to feel both because of the indirect sufferings that war had brought to his own family. But the slim boyish figure of Jon Jodl, stamped with the vulnerability of the young, brought only feelings of pity . . . yet, this was the enemy. God alone knew what lay in the mind behind the face of a boy!

The others were arriving on the scene in a clamour of excited Gaelic. Jon Jodl heard the foreign tongue and a little smile touched his lips because some of the words were oddly akin to his own language.

"Scottisch," he murmured in satisfaction before he was engulfed in an enthusiastic body of the Home Guard flushing him for weapons. He swayed on his feet and Lachlan strode over.

"Get away from him!" he ordered sharply. "Can't you see the laddie is in a state of shock. He needs all the air he can get! Let me examine him!"

Several yards away Tam McKinnon came upon Ernst Foch in a most unexpected manner. The keen air of morning was bringing

Tam quickly to his senses but the Uisge-Beatha had filled his bladder and he handed his shotgun to Jock the ploughman.

"Hold this while I go for a pee," he whispered and stepping behind a clump of gorse quickly undid his buttons. It was a habit of his to make 'pee patterns' and he distributed the flow of urine over the heather with unrestrained abandon.

Like Jon, Ernst had remained near the spot of landing. He knew he was on an island and that it would be utterly senseless to evade capture. Unlike Jon he omitted to wrap himself in his parachute. Instead he huddled into his thick flying suit, pulled the flaps of his helmet over his ears and went to sleep, letting time bring what it would. He hadn't quite bargained for Tam McKinnon and his guttural roar of surprise split the morning asunder.

He sprang to his feet and there, amidst the heather moors, a highly indignant Nazi and a white-faced, terrified Gael faced each other.

"It's sorry I am, indeed, just!" gabbled Tam, forgetting for the moment that he was addressing the enemy. He stood transfixed, unable to even make the effort of doing up his fly.

A flow of German abuse issued from Ernst's thick lips and Tam, finding his voice, yelled. "Will you be givin' me my gun quick, Jock, before this bloody Hun is after killing me with his bare hands!"

But before the startled Jock could move a muscle a stream of islanders descended on the scene. Ernst was yelling in excited German, Tam exploding in torrents of Gaelic, his fears forgotten with the arrival of his supporters. Both languages filled the air in a great swelling of sound. Wild birds rose in panic from the gorse, sheep bleated in dismay and a flock of gulls rose into the sky, adding their screams of protest to the general mêlée.

Old Bob raced into the scene. "Will you be quiet, you stupid buggers!" he roared. "Or I'll knock your damt heads together."

Ernst, unable to comprehend, nevertheless recognised the voice of authority and suddenly stopped shouting.

"I only peed on him," muttered Tam humbly. "How was I to know I would be doing it on top of a German?"

Ernst was bundled into a trap beside Jon Jodl who was still looking dazed and bewildered.

"Jon!" cried Ernst, glad to see one of his own kind. "You came down safely, then?"

But his companion made no reply and Ernst sniffed at him in disgust. "Spewing again, Jon. This time I don't blame you. I feel a bit sick myself." He folded his arms over his chest. "Good God, it's bloody cold. I could be doing with some schnapps to warm me up . . . or some whisky . . . the Scottisch – they stink with it. We might be lucky enough to sample some while we are here." He sighed dismally. "The war is over for us, Jon, just in time for you . . . but me – I wonder when I will see my wife and son again."

But Jon seemed not to hear a word and Ernst looked away, his eyes raking the moors. He wondered where Zeitler and Anton had landed, there seemed to be no sign of them.

Everyone else was wondering the same thing. The various search parties were drifting back to the scene of the crash to report that there was nothing to be seen of the remaining German crew. The islanders stood around in groups talking in subdued tones while they observed the two captives with dismay. They had been so intent on the search that no one had given a thought about a place suitable enough in which to keep German prisoners.

"It would be fine if we could just chain them up in the Abbey ruins till help arrives from the mainland," suggested Ranald hopefully, his ideas influenced by the adventure stories he read so avidly. "I was reading a war book about prisoners being put in shackles in a cellar and fed only on bread and water."

Tom Johnston snorted and said sarcastically, "Ay, and that was maybe taking place away back in the Dark Ages. They are human beings though they are Jerries and they must be treated with respect."

Lachlan stamped impatiently, his compassionate brown eyes fixed on the wearily crumpled figure of Jon Jodl. "I want to see to that lad and I don't care if I have to take him back to my house to do it! I have a spare room . . . Phebie always has it ready," he added quietly and Fergus looked at him admiringly.

"Hold on! I'm coming! I will take them into *my* house!" The Reverend John Gray burst into the scene. He was covered in mud, his hair was rumpled and a little stubble of beard made his face look haggard. Rhanna, used to a neatly turned out minister

66

with never a hair out of place, his life an orderly affair where it seemed impossible for human indignity to show, stared as one man.

He sensed their thoughts. "I was helping with the search," he explained with dignity, "and I fell into a bog. There was only myself and the Lord and though I nearly drowned he gave me the strength to get out." He looked at his flock sternly. "We should *all* have faith in Him. He is our comfort and stay."

The men muttered and one or two bowed their heads but old Bob said something in Gaelic and the minister glared at him. He had never troubled to learn the native tongue and was continually frustrated by the dour Gaels who took every opportunity to make him feel an interloper, though he had been preaching on the island for many years.

"These men will be quite safe in my house," he continued. "God will guide us all to His way. Their stay will be brief but I would not be doing my duty if I didn't try to nourish their thoughts with the love of God . . . take their minds off war . . . I can speak a little German, we will understand each other."

A gleam came into the eyes of the gathering. What could be better for the enemy than a day or two of bible-thumping under the minister's roof? He would be in his glory trying to save the German souls and they would be only too anxious to save their sanity by getting off the island the minute they could.

"Ach, it's a good man you are just," said Angus solicitously.

Bob's weathered face broke into a deceptively charming smile. "Ay, good, to be learning the German but never a word o' the Gaelic."

The full implication of his words hit home. Everyone looked at each other quizzically and Fergus rapped out impatiently, "Why don't you put your knowledge to good use, Mr Gray, and ask these men a few questions? There's a lot we would like to be knowing."

"Hmm, yes, you're quite right of course but I don't think we will find out very much."

Ernst gave surly replies to 'the interrogation', repeating his name, rank and serial number so many times that even the minister's patience began to wane.

"It's as I told you," he said to Fergus finally. "He will tell me nothing of his mission but I gather he is concerned about his Commander and the pilot of the plane."

Fergus nodded. "Two more to be found but I think we should leave them to the Military. If Mistress Beag got her message through, help should be arriving quite soon, if not we will continue the search in daylight."

Wearily the men agreed and everyone began to move away. Kate McKinnon was waiting by Tam's cart. Into it she had put her bicycle, and under cover of a tarpaulin lay her carefully selected loot. Tam came jauntily towards her and her eyes opened wide. "Tam McKinnon! Is it drunk you still are with your trousers gapin' open for everyone to see!"

He stared downwards and let out a guffaw of mirth. "Ach, I was forgettin' all about them with all the excitement. I was havin' a pee behind a bush, never knowing I was watering a German sleepin' in the heather!" His eyes glinted mischievously. "You wouldny like a wee play while everything is handy like?"

Kate grabbed the fire besom and chased him round the cart. The moors were empty now and their yelps of merriment filled the open spaces. Tam allowed Kate to catch him and grab at her bouncing breasts. Giggling like children they sprawled in the heather in a rough and tumble of sexual play.

Dodie, unheeding the warnings of danger given earlier, lay in an uneasy sleep in the gashed fuselage of the German bomber. Tam's animal-like grunts made the old eccentric sit up with a start and he peeped in embarrassment at the sight of Kate's legs flaying the ground and Tam's well-rounded bottom sticking up in the air.

Dodie shook his head. "Not natural," he sighed, having witnessed one or two such incidents during his many wanderings. The only thing right and proper to Dodie was the mating of four-legged animals. His swarthy skin turned red with shame. "Not natural," he repeated mournfully. " 'Tis only the beasts should be doing it, right enough."

Thinking about animals made him remember his beloved Ealasaid. At the same time all his fears of the night before came flooding back. He stumbled hastily to his feet, looking over his humped shoulder to the bleak stretch of moors. Not so far away were the Abbey ruins. The thought of the 'ghaisties' that lurked

68

there, perhaps in company with wandering Germans armed to the teeth with bombs, the only weapons that Dodie associated with the enemy, hurried his big wellington-clad feet away from the scene.

"Ealasaid! Ealasaid!" he wailed softly and disappeared over the hump of a hillock.

Tam jumped away from Kate in fright and rolled on to a clump of tough moorland grass. He let out a dismayed yell and Kate, feeling sublimely content, said soothingly, "Ach, it's only Dodie lookin' for his cow. He will no' have seen a thing."

"To hell wi' Dodie!" cried Tam indignantly. "I have just had my chookles pierced in a dozen places by that damt grass! You will never be knowin' what *that* feels like!"

But Kate was entirely unsympathetic and shouted with delighted laughter. "Don't I just, Tam McKinnon! 'Tis a punishment you are getting indeed. Are you forgetting the stinging nettles on my poor bum and all because you were too lazy to cut them down! Behag might be an old windbag but she is right when she says we all get our punishment in the end. You had the jagging of your balls coming to you!"

Tam buttoned his fly and got to his feet with dignity. "Balls to Behag!" he said with asperity and walked to the cart, Kate's skirls of merriment ringing in his ears.

CHAPTER FIVE

The Ullabheist

Totie Little, the postmistress of the sleepy little fishing village of Portvoynachan, was on her way to open up the business premises. Totie's cottage was perched on top of a cliff, a good half mile from the village. Her battle with the elements was continual – her little croft was windswept and bare with not a single tree to protect it from the howling gales of winter. The tough wiry grasses of the clifftops fought ceaselessly to reclaim her small plot of cultivated land but Totie fought back, determined to keep her vegetable patch and the roofs on her outbuildings. Endlessly she promised herself a more convenient house in the village but the idea was always half-hearted because she loved the solitude of her cottage with its panorama of rugged cliffs and endless sea. She also liked her privacy. The gossips were never quite given the satisfaction of finding out exactly what she was about.

The morning was keenly cold with a sharp wind biting up from a lively sea. Totie ignored the road to the village. It was far quicker to skirt the cliffs and she hurried along, a strong handsome woman looking younger than her forty-five years. Dawn was still just a promise in the black of the sky. It was really far too early to be opening shop but she had been up all night and hadn't felt it worth while to go to bed now.

In the course of the last few hours she and her neighbours had absorbed enough excitement to keep their tongues wagging for weeks. It wasn't every day that German bombers landed on Rhanna and the event had been of enough import to keep kettles singing over peat fires all night.

The moon had long ago departed the heavens. Totie felt alone but not lonely in the quiet, dark hour before dawn. There was not another scrap of human life to be seen because men and women alike had tumbled into bed to snatch some sleep after such a momentous night. It was much too early for even the children to be going to school and Totie was a lone figure in the hushed, sighing peace of the clifftops where the very gulls seemed to be having a lie in.

At first she thought she had imagined the little black specks moving in the sea far below, but looking further out she could just discern the ghostly shape of a large vessel. It was the womb from which the smaller craft were being expelled and Totie drew in her breath sharply, wondering what on earth was happening.

The black shapes were rubber dinghies flooding into the white sands of Aosdana Bay, Bay of the Poet, so named because of a love-lorn young man who had hurled himself over the cliffs back in the mists of time. It was a place favoured by young lovers because of its seclusion but at the moment it looked anything but romantic. Men were pouring out of the dinghies and quickly disappearing among the rocks. In a very short time both men and craft were gone from the scene. Totie blinked rapidly, wondering if she had imagined it all.

Out at sea the mother ship was gliding swiftly away and was soon lost to view in the velvet reaches of the ocean. Totie's first instinct was to run to the little straggling cottages in Portvoynachan and awaken the sleeping occupants but she was a sensible woman and thought better of such a drastic move. She wasn't yet sure what to make of the stealthy inpouring of men on to the Rhanna beaches. Were they friend or foe? If the latter, what earthly purpose would they have for invading the island? Then she remembered Behag and her jealous monopoly of the wireless transmitter. Totie knew that Behag saw herself as a mighty cog in the wheel of the war effort. For long she had been praying for a momentous happening to warrant the responsibility of her position. In the dark Totie smiled to herself. Behag had obviously got things wrong, and had sent a misleading call for help. Totie had come to the conclusion that the men on the beaches were Commandos, called out to assist an island besieged by Germans. In the end all they would find was one crashed German bomber and its crew.

Totie couldn't help chuckling. She hated Behag and her superior ways. This time the old devil had got her wires well and truly crossed. She changed direction and went quickly up the village street to report the incident to the man of most influence in the immediate area, Dugald Donaldson, a widower and retired police constable.

Dugald had aspirations as a writer and was possessed with a highly developed imagination. She would tell him of the men landing on the beaches but she would omit to say she thought them to be Commandos. After all she wasn't entirely sure if her surmise was correct. She would leave the outcome to the tender mercies of time; meanwhile Dugald would have the chance to let his flights of fancy fly on silvered wings.

Totie hugged herself gleefully as she imagined Behag's wizened face contorted into uglier lines when the whole affair was bounced on to her doorstep in the end.

Dugald had not gone back to bed either. His whole being was alert with excitement, his lively mind unable to settle. He sat by the warm kitchen range, drinking tea and jotting down notes as fast as his fingers would allow.

When the soft little tap sounded on his door he raised his head unwillingly from his work. The second knock was louder, accompanied by a hissed, "It's me, Dugie, Totie!"

Dugald uncurled his long lean figure from the armchair, a smile of pleasure lighting his thin, aesthetic features. For some time now he'd been having an affair with Totie. She took a keen interest in his work but was too tidy-minded for his liking. She spent a great deal of her spare time clearing away his numerous collections of notes and he spent a lot of his precious time looking for them.

She came into the kitchen, her bright green eyes taking in the room in one sweep. "Are you alone?" she whispered.

"Yes." He pulled her into his arms but she drew away impatiently.

"Not now, Dugie, I've something interesting to tell you. I was coming over by the cliffs just now and seeing a lot of wee boats sneaking into Aosdana Bay. There is something funny going on and I was thinking . . . you being an intelligent man might know what to do."

Dugald smiled. "Och, c'mon now, Totie, it's kidding you are!"

"Indeed, am I the sort of woman to bring hysterical gossip?

They were soldiers, carrying guns and wearing helmets. I am wondering if there was something of great importance in that German airy-plane . . . or maybe some high-ranking person. These troops were looking gey suspicious – furtive like. They could have been sent to look over that plane."

Dugald looked amused. "They'll be our own boys come to see what they can find out from the plane. They do it all the time."

"*Dozens* of them! Creeping on to the island in the dark? If it was our soldiers they would do it open-like. These men came off a big boat! I tell you, Dugie, they are on some kind of mission!"

Her words were imperative and Dugald stroked his chin thoughtfully. Things like that did happen, planes carrying highly secret documents had crashed before . . . and it was odd the way this one had come in over the Western Isles. The men might be British . . . on the other hand they might not and Dugald couldn't take the risk of remaining silent.

Grabbing his jacket he ran outside. Once more the exhausted islanders were ousted from cosy beds to be told the latest developments. L.D.V. armbands were hastily fixed in position and the waiting collections of weapons were again brought out from cupboards.

No warning bells were rung this time because Dugald didn't want to alert the new invaders to the fact that their arrival was not unnoticed. Instead messengers on bicycles were sent from village to clachan and it was well into morning before all the members of the Home Guard were well and truly roused.

Those making their way to the scene of the crash now numbered less because vital duties around the crofts had to be carried out. Those that could be spared were all feeling distinctly uneasy. It was bad enough having Germans crashing planes on Rhanna without the possibility of an additional enemy invasion. Men who had walked freely on windswept Rhanna all their lives, with perhaps only superstitious fears to hurry their footsteps along, now felt vulnerable, wary of what might lie behind every heathery hillock. Quite unconsciously many of them walked in a crouched position, cautiously peeping round boulders before going on. They were all glad of the frequent gulps of Uisge-Beatha from Tam's generous flask and long before they reached the end of Downie's Pass the world was beginning to take on a decidedly rosier hue.

Little Grant Fergus was marching up and down the drying green of Laigmhor with a meal basin on his head and a stout tree branch hoisted against his shoulder. He was practising 'being a soldier' and Kirsteen, watching him from the window, was angry at the influences of war reaching out to her son.

"Ach, don't worry yourself, Kirsteen," assured Shona. "All wee boys play at soldiers – girls too – I did it myself when Niall and myself were bairns." She folded the dish towel and turned to pick up a basket from the table. "I'm away over to Tina's with a bite of dinner and I'll do some wee odd jobs while I'm there. Matthew says she can hobble about in the house but she won't get outside to see to the beasts."

Kirsteen looked at Shona's white face and felt a great surge of affection. A memory came unbidden of a slender little girl starting her first day at school; a child with long auburn hair tied back with a blue ribbon and skinny legs clad in black woollen stockings. Kirsteen had just taken up the teaching post on the island so they had both been new to the school. Little had Kirsteen thought in those far-off days that one day she would marry Fergus and become the mistress of Laigmhor. She had always got on well with Shona but her time of separation from Fergus had also separated her from his daughter, the only female in the household after the death of dear old Mirabelle who had been so much more than the housekeeper of Laigmhor. Kirsteen felt that the girl might have resented her intrusion into the domain she had shared so intimately with her adored father but the fears were groundless. Shona was delighted her father had found his happiness; she welcomed Kirsteen with open affection, not as the mother she had once longed for but as confidant and friend. She handled Grant Fergus with a firm sisterly affection and he responded with gruff adulation which shone through his tough little-boy façade.

Impulsively Kirsteen reached out to grasp Shona's hand and looked into the incredibly deep blue eyes. "Shona," she breathed, "you're so sad inside – I can feel it even though you try so hard to hide it. I know what it's like – to love someone and be apart from them. What's wrong between you and Niall?"

For a moment a veil of resentment hooded Shona's eyes. She was growing more like Fergus every day, jealously guarding her most private feelings. But then she saw the genuine concern on Kirsteen's face.

"It's not Niall . . . it's me, Kirsteen. I need time to sort out my feelings. For me he's the only boy in the world. I think I've loved him since we were just children. It was like a fairy story . . . the way we grew up together then discovered how much we cared . . . but . . ." She hesitated then went on in a rush. "It never ended like a fairy story – that's the trouble with real life. I blame myself for that. I made Niall make love to me . . . I was afraid I'd never see him again – the baby was so like him. It's like a dream now . . . the cave . . . me bringing that little life into the world . . ." She paused again and stared at Kirsteen with huge eyes. "What am I saying?" She went on in a whisper. "I didn't give him life – I gave him death. The only time he lived was when he was . . . in here." She touched the flatness of her belly with shaking hands. "He might have lived outside of me if – if I hadn't been so silly about everything – yet I couldn't help it, I thought my Niall was dead – now I feel it's all my fault the baby died. I feel so guilty, Kirsteen. I can't look at Niall without feeling everything is my fault!"

Kirsteen put her arm round the girl's slender shoulders and said tenderly, "Shona, we're all guilty of something. Your father and I could spend the rest of our lives feeling guilt but our time is too precious – love is too precious to waste it on useless self-reproach. A lot of our years were wasted because we were both foolish. Don't make our mistake, Shona."

Shona forced a smile. "You're right of course, but it's easy to be wise after the event – I don't mean that to sound cheeky, it's just the truth. Och, it's so lovely to be back on Rhanna yet it won't be the same till Niall comes back. I wish he were here now but I'm going over to Glasgow to see him. I wrote to let him know I was home. I wonder – will things be the same for us in a city?" She paused to look from the window to the misty blue of the mountains. "This is where we both belong – no matter where I go my heart is always on Rhanna."

"If you really love Niall, you would follow him to the moon. He won't be studying forever, you know."

Shona went towards the door where the hens were cocking beady eyes into the kitchen "I'll have to go now," she smiled. "Thanks for listening to all my worries."

"Be careful out there," warned Kirsteen. "Your father was making quite a fuss about those two missing Germans. He doesn't think it safe for us defenceless females to be wandering about unescorted. Shouldn't Babbie go with you?"

"Ach, the lazy wittrock is sleeping late. I took her up a cup of tea but she just turned over and went back to sleep. She says she is here for a rest."

At that moment a yell came from the garden where Grant had missed his soldierly footing and fallen into the thorns of the rose bed. Kirsteen rushed to the rescue while Shona grabbed a broom and chased the hens from the kitchen. A crestfallen Grant came over the cobbled yard. "Can I come with you, Shona?" he called. "Mother's out of temper and there is still a while to go before school."

Mr Murdoch, the balding, fussy master of Portcull school, had gone to assist the Home Guard in their search, giving all the children an unexpected morning off.

"Aren't you wanting to go down to the harbour?" asked Shona. "If old Joe's there he might tell you a story.'

The little boy loved the harbour with its collection of boats and old men always ready to recount an adventure of the sea. Already he knew a lot about fishing, jumping at any chance to dabble about in a boat. Whenever he could, he went out to help with lobster creels and accompanied some of the older boys when they clubbed together to hire one of Ranald's boats for a day of sea fishing. He was longing for his eighth birthday because his parents had promised that he could accompany the men on a day's trawling but since he had just recently celebrated his seventh birthday he still had a long wait ahead. He hesitated at Shona's words, but seeing the basket of food, decided that a cosy Strupak would better pass what remained of the morning.

"Old Joe has a bad head," he told Shona in his precocious manner, his cultured English already showing traces of the lilting island tongue. "I think too he is weary from chasing Germans all night and told me earlier he was going to sleep off the effects of some meeting to do with the war."

"The war was it?" smiled Shona who had already heard about the 'disgraceful drunken behaviour' of the Home Guard. "On you go and ask your mother then," she conceded, "but mind, you mustny bother Tina with your blethers."

He ran in to tell Kirsteen that he was going with his big sister to 'protect her' and a few moments later his grubby little hand was curled trustingly in hers. The misty fields were frosted with white which scrunched crisply underfoot. The child's normally pink cheeks were soon like red apples in the stinging air. He was a picture with his black curls, snapping black eyes and dimpled chin. Tunelessly he began singing a sea shanty taught to him by the fishermen and soon Shona joined in, feeling something of his exuberance and youthful buoyancy.

The field sloped upwards to a tiny cottage huddled under the brown heather slopes of Ben Machrie. Here, Matthew, grieve of Laigmhor, lived with his ample, easy-going young wife and two children.

Little Donald, a big-eyed dreaming child, was quietly pleased to see Grant and took him off to view a golden plover's nest he had chanced upon.

"Don't be going far," warned Shona. "Remember what Father told you this morning."

Grant gave her a cherubic smile. "I'm minding, Shona, don't worry . . . anyway . . ." He pulled a roughly fashioned wooden dirk from his pocket. "I'll kill any Germans with this! I'll not let them touch Donald or myself."

Tina came limping from the byre, clutching a bucketful of manure mixed liberally with hen's feathers which drifted like snowflakes from the brimming container. At sight of Shona she put up a languid hand to tuck away strands of fine fair hair into two kirbys that were meant to be supporting a lop-sided bun. The grips were totally inadequate for the purpose and loops of hair descended in fly-away abandon.

"Ach, bugger it," she swore mildly, her good-natured face showing not a trace of dismay. The boys scampered off and she told Shona consolingly, "Don't you be worrying your head about wee Grant. Donald might be looking like his head was up on the moon but he is all there and knows every inch of the moor. I was hearing anyways that it was only one airy-plane came down.

77

Matthew says he caught two of the Huns an' the soldiers will find the others later."

Shona had to hide a quick smile. Tina's simple, devoted faith in her husband was such that she believed everything he told her. Her vision of an all-conquering hero was limited entirely to her spouse. It was perhaps her acceptance of his exaggerated manly sojourns that made their marriage one of rare, uncomplicated happiness.

"Ay, you'll likely be right, Tina," said Shona. "Though I hear tell that some of the men have gone out to guard the plane. Father was a bit worried about Grant and myself coming out of the house at all this morning."

"Ach, you'll be fine wi' me. If there is one smell o' a Jerry I'll set my dogs on the buggers!"

They had wandered into the house by now and Shona, looking at the jumbled assortment of canine and feline bodies that were heaped contentedly on hearth and sofa, wondered if even a whisker would have twitched if a dozen Germans had come marching into the room.

Little Eve, who had been having her morning nap in the commodious bottom drawer of the dresser, tottered through from the bedroom, rubbing the sleep from her huge bright eyes. The drawer had been her bed from babyhood and she simply popped into it when the mood took her. She was a rosy, intelligent child, delivered by Shona the Christmas Eve before last. The very timing of her birth seemed to have bestowed on her everything that was reminiscent of Christmas. Roly-poly legs supported a plump little body; stars shone in velvet black eyes; a halo of flaxen hair was a startlingly beautiful feature in a child otherwise so dark.

At sight of Shona she giggled with glee then, turning very solemn, lifted her dress and stretched the top of her knickers till it seemed the elastic must surely snap. Peering over her pot belly she pointed between her legs. "Wet!" she announced and collapsed on to the rug in an ecstasy of baby chuckles.

"I've been training her to sit on the po," explained Tina, "but I'm no' able to bend much just now."

She collapsed into the depths of a huge armchair, pinning the tail of a skinny white cat against the springs. With a terrified squeal it struggled with the ensnaring layers of flesh till Tina was forced to ease herself up an inch. She was still holding the brimming pail from the byre and into this landed the startled cat. By the time he had extricated himself he was in a mad state of indignation and bolted round the room twice before making his exit from the house. Dung and feathers littered floor, furniture and animals, the latter blinked sleepily and summoning enough strength to sneeze away the dusty feathers.

"Fevver!" squealed Eve, crawling amongst the mess to stick fluffy bits of down into her hair.

"Ach, my." Tina clucked in slight anxiety. "This damt ankle is keeping me back right enough. Matthew will be in for his dinner an' me that's so quick with everything will never have it ready, just."

Shona's spirits were rising rapidly. Tina, with her effortless air of unruffled peace and uproarious over-statements, was a breath of spring sunshine. "Don't upset yourself, Tina," she instructed laughingly. "I didn't just come over to blether you know. I've brought some nice things for a Strupak, then I'll get Matthew's dinner going." She eyed the dangling pail in Tina's hand. "Where were you going with that when I came along?"

"Just over to the midden. I'm saving it for the vegetable patch but I'm not wanting Matthew to know. I'd like fine to surprise him with a fine crop this year. Last year the tatties were like bools and the turnip so dry no' even the sheeps would eat it. Matthew hasny the time for it, the soul works that hard. I was having a mind to gather seaweed too but this damt ankle has slowed me down with everything."

In a few minutes Shona had swept the floor clean and the kettle was puffing gaily among the peats. When Tina and Eve were settled with tea and scones she went to get the hens' pot from the jumbled array of cooking containers in the little stone-flagged out-house Tina grandly called a kitchen.

The hens were gobbling greedily when Grant and Donald burst out from the windbreak of firs that sheltered the house from the windswept moors. They were arguing, the way children do when greatly excited. It soon transpired they had wandered up to the shores of Loch Sliach to look for rabbit burrows but had been frightened away when they saw a 'monster' floating on the loch.

"It was all spread out with humps on it!" said a round-eyed Grant. "And it was moving about and making noises!"

"Ach no!" Donald's protest was faintly scornful of an incomer's inability to relate a properly embroidered tale. "It was a Ullabheist right enough but it was dead because it was all white and limp. It was not making one sound but a water kelpie on the wee island was greetin' an' moanin'. Maybe it was crying for the Ullabheist though I don't know why cos they are feart o' them as a rule and should be glad it was dead!"

"We ran away," put in Grant rather feebly, his pale face showing he had suffered quite a scare.

Shona was about to dismiss the childish ravings as of little import but her quick mind suddenly recalled Righ's description of how he thought the German bomber was surely bound to crash on the slopes of Ben Machrie. But instead it had careered round the mountains to come down on the open moor. Everyone had assumed the pilot would have bailed out on to open ground but . . . supposing there hadn't been time? Donald's Ullabheist sounded very much like a parachute.

Making a quick decision she bundled the protesting children into the cottage just as Matthew arrived for his dinner. Taking him into the kitchen on some pretext she hastily imparted the news to him. "Get away now!" exclaimed the youthful grieve of Laigmhor, good-natured and easy-going like his wife, but, unlike her, possessed of an energetic taste for adventure.

"Can you get some men together?" whispered Shona.

"Ach, it would take too long. The last I am hearing they are all up at the airy-plane. Anyways . . ." he puffed out his well-developed rib cage. "I'm here! I'll get my gun and I'll be goin' . . . you will maybe stay here and send some help after me."

But Shona was not a McKenzie for nothing. "Havers! I'm coming with you. I'm a nurse, remember, and the pilot of that plane might be badly injured. It's not a silly wee girl you are talking to, Matthew."

"But Tina has that bad leg and will no' be able to send for reinforcements. I'm no' mindin' going to look for this Jerry so long as I know the lads will be up at my back. The island is crawling wi' strange men. It's surprised I am you havny heard!"

But Shona's brilliant blue eyes were smiling. "Ach, that's just a

80

lot of rumour. Father thinks that Behag sent a wrong message and it is soldiers – *our* soldiers who have come to Rhanna. There will be ructions and no mistake."

Matthew's eyes were bulging and he hissed, "I am hearing it was Robbie took the message to Behag!"

Shona nodded sympathetically. "Poor old Robbie. Behag will never forgive him, his life will be worse than ever. But c'mon now, it's time Grant went down the road to school. I'll get him to stop off at Laigmhor and ask Father to come with Bob and the others."

Grant was given instructions and, fairly bristling with importance, scampered off with Donald at his heels. Shona and Matthew set off, leaving Tina to mourn gently about 'poor Matthew's empty belly'.

The path through the trees was a thick carpet of russet pine needles which muffled their hurrying footsteps. There, in the cathedral of tall trees, it was dim and mysterious, a world apart from the surrounding open spaces. Matthew's steps were a little less jaunty now and he took frequent peeps over his shoulder.

"Did the bairns say something about a Ullabheist?" he asked nervously, the threat of the ethereal appearing to worry him far more than the possible presence of Germans.

"Och, don't be daft, Matthew!" scolded Shona. "The boys were exaggerating and fine you know it! Look, we'll go over the burn here and come out of the woods quicker."

They wobbled their way over slippery stepping stones and, skirting a rise, saw Loch Sliach below. It was a dark, umber pool with the steep crags of the mountains on one side and the amber stretches of the moor on the other. A tiny tree-clad island rose in the centre, separated from dry land by a wide area of deep water. Billowing out from the island was a long length of translucent white material, humped into odd shapes where pockets of air lay locked in the folds. And plainly, on the cool breath of the calm, frosted air, there came an unintelligible thread of sound . . . human, yet, there in the shadow of the sleeping Ben, with the ever-present sigh of moor and sea, frighteningly uncanny and unreal.

"It's a spook, or a Uisga Hag wandered inland," gulped Matthew. "I think we'd be wise to wait for the lads, Shona."

"Nonsense! You have a boat tied up here, Matthew, for I know you go fishing on the loch with Robbie. Where is it?"

Unwillingly he pulled aside clumps of bracken to reveal the boat in a hollow of sand. With a distinct lack of enthusiasm he helped Shona drag it into the water. She sat in it, gently bobbing in a scurry of wavelets, looking at him with quizzical eyes. A few moments elapsed while he stood on the shore, embarrassed but unmoving. She grabbed the oars and began to pull away.

"Wait! I was just coming!" he said peevishly. "I will not be having a lassie doing a man's work."

They reached the islet in minutes. Matthew made a great fuss about tying the boat but Shona climbed quickly ashore. In a very short time she found the delirious figure of Anton Büttger. He lay on a bed of frantically gathered heather and bracken. His eyes were closed but his head was moving from side to side in the madness of his inward nightmares. His uniform was a cold, sodden mess. Of the trousers only tatters remained and blood seeped from a jagged gash in his leg. But it wasn't that which made Shona's hand fly to her mouth. She was staring at his stomach where a cruel finger of rock had ripped it open allowing part of his intestines to escape in a red congealing mass. The skin of his legs was blue with exposure but worse, the fingers of both hands were waxen white with frostbite – the ragged fragments of his flying gloves had afforded little protection from the elements. The pathetic vulnerability of him lying there, his partially covered genitals giving him the innocence of a small boy, made the tears of pity well into Shona's eyes . . . She forgot that this was the enemy, a young man trained to take life. She forgot that long months of worry over Niall with the subsequent loss of her tiny son had been brought about by the Nazis and their greedy war. She saw only a critically injured human being, lying as Niall had lain, in a foreign land without consciousness to aid the instincts of self-preservation.

A wildly staring Matthew only had time to mutter, "My God, what way did he survive?" before he rushed behind a bush to vomit.

Shona removed her warm wool cape and was gently tucking it round Anton's body when shouts from the shore heralded the arrival of Fergus and Bob.

"I'll be going to fetch them," said a ghostly Matthew and ran unsteadily to the boat.

At first, when Fergus saw the slim figure of his daughter kneeling by the injured German, he was filled with anger. He had been at dinner when Grant burst into the kitchen with the garbled message, interrupting his discussion with Bob about the ludicrous situation that had arisen on the island because of Behag's misleading message. The news had reached every corner of Rhanna and it was a near certainty that the subject was being analysed with thorough enjoyment over dinner-tables everywhere.

Babbie, rising soon after Shona's departure, had taken herself off on a walk to Portcull to fetch some groceries for Kirsteen. In Merry Mary's shop the atmosphere was charged with excitement.

Little Merry Mary was an Englishwoman who for many years had been labelled as an 'old incomer' which she regarded as an honour. After more than forty years she was now regarded as a native and with her quaint tongue and equally whimsical ways she might indeed have sprung from Hebridean soil. Limp ginger hair hung over a bright, inquisitive face from which protruded a square nose, dubiously decorated with a large brown wart. Unknown to its host it had been an object of great interest to the island children over the years; the first child to notice its demise being promised a monetary reward from every other youngster on the island. Like everywhere else Rhanna suffered from inflation and likewise did the value of Merry Mary's wart.

Happily she was as unaware of her wart as she was to the mischievous attentions paid to it, and in her delightfully jumbled shop that morning her tongue was wagging busily, entirely oblivious to all but the latest events on the island. The tiny shop was crowded, tongues clicked, heads nodded, curious looks were directed frequently towards the Post Office.

Erchy the Post came strolling out of the establishment, a nonchalant whistle on his lips. He walked very casually over to Merry Mary's but his composure failed him at the last moment and he almost fell in the door.

"Well! And what is she saying for herself?" came the inevitable cry of unconcealed curiosity. Under normal circumstances the islanders gave the impression of being disinterested in gossip even while they listened avidly. If a stranger was in their midst a gently malicious tale would cease and the interest quietly transferred to something mundane. But events that morning were of a great magnitude and no one paid the slightest attention to Babbie gazing at the array of glass sweet jars with what seemed to be undivided curiosity. Babbie had spent most of her childhood in an Argyllshire orphanage where she had picked up a fair Gaelic vocabulary from an ancient gardener. Although it was a vastly different Gaelic to that of the Hebrides she nevertheless got the gist of the conversation. One or two of the younger islanders lapsed frequently from Gaelic to English which was a great advantage.

Erchy ran a hand through his sparse sandy hair and looked faintly bemused. "She is not saying a word! Not a single word. It is like the shock has taken her tongue. Poor auld Robbie is begging her to speak but the bitch is just standin' at the counter with her lips tighter than the backside of a day-old chick. 'Tis lucky she is human enough to have calls o' nature like the rest of us and Robbie got a chance to tell me the news ..."

He paused importantly while sounds of encouragement echoed round him then went on. "Well, Robbie was thinkin' there were three German airy-planes over the island last night. Righ said it was a Heinkel three and Robbie thought he said three Heinkels and told Behag so. Well, you see, she reported that parachutes were droppin' everywhere and help was to be sent urgently. It was Totie Little of Portvoynachan saw men landing over at Aosdana Bay before dawn this morning and she told that writer, Dugie Donaldson. For a whily everyone was running round in circles dodgin' the lads from the boat till they found out they were Commandos come to rescue the island. A lot o' them have gone away again but a few have stayed to help with the Jerries. Time is precious to these lads and there's goin' to be a fine stramash over the whole affair."

"They will take the contraption away from Behag!" said someone in awe.

"Totie will be gettin' it," put in Morag Ruadh, the nimble-fingered spinner who also played the ancient church organ which Totie had itched to play for years. "Totie always has her eye on other people's occupations," she finished with a toss of her red hair.

"Ach well, she is having a clever head on her shoulders," hazarded Mairi McKinnon, Morag's cousin.

84

Morag's eyes blazed. "And what are you insinuating, Mairi? There is *some* brains in the family!"

Morag had a spiteful tongue, more pronounced since her dithering, simple younger cousin had, by means more innocent than calculating, got herself pregnant which in turn had got her swiftly to the altar, a fact not easily borne by Morag Ruadh, at a loss to understand why she had never arrived at that revered spot herself.

Tears sprang to Mairi's guileless brown eyes. Her happy life had been shattered since her adored William had gone marching away to join the navy and she was easier hurt than she had ever been.

Kate McKinnon, fresh-faced and full of her usual energy despite her nocturnal activities, rushed to defend her daughter-in-law to whom she had grown very close after an initial spell of resentment. "Ach, leave her be!" she scolded Morag Ruadh. "Can the cratur no' make a simple remark without you jumpin' down her throat?"

"Simple right enough," muttered Morag, but Kate's boisterous voice drowned all else as she addressed Mairi earnestly. "And how is your poor father, mo ghaoil? It was a bad state he was in when I was last seeing him."

"Ay, well, he's right enough now," faltered Mairi, recalling to mind the picture of her father being trundled past her window in a wheelbarrow at midnight. She had merely thought he was being delivered home by his crapulous friends and no one had told her otherwise till the operation was over because she was useless in an emergency. "The doctor made a fine job of him but we were thinkin' that someone would be over to see was he better this morning but neither the doctor or Biddy has come."

At that moment, Elspeth Morrison, the gaunt, sharp-tongued housekeeper of Slochmhor, pushed into the shop. Her life had been embittered by her childless marriage to a fisherman who had met his end through drink. Her saving grace was her dour devotion to the doctor and his family and she jealously guarded her position in the household.

"The poor doctor is exhausted being up all night," she imparted haughtily. "He is in no fit state to be gallivanting after people who bring illness upon themselves! A fine thing indeed to be operating on a man pickled in drink and the stuff so scarce it is a mystery how he managed to get so much of it inside himself !" Here she looked meaningfully at Kate who was looking at bobbins of thread with great interest. "Biddy is the one should be seeing to Todd," went on Elspeth. "Knowing her she will have had her fill o' sleep. The doctor was sayin' she decided to bide the night at Todd's because she was feart to go back over the Glen with the Germans about but she should have checked in at Slochmhor to see was she needed this morning . . ." She snorted disdainfully. "The doctor wanted her to call in at the Manse to see how was the Germans. I wouldny blame Biddy if that was maybe why she is makin' herself scarce !"

Mairie, looking uncertain of her facts, murmured, "Ay, well, she was not near the place this morning and Father worrying a bit about his stitches too tight."

Elspeth put her sharp nose in the air. "And tight they would have to be to keep all that liquid from oozing out . . . he will be uncomfortable for quite a whily," she ended unsympathetically and the subject of Todd's health having been exhausted the shop turned eagerly to fresh speculation over the fate of Behag Beag.

CHAPTER SIX

The Commandos

Babbie made her way back to Laigmhor, mischievously imparting all the gossip she had heard. It only confirmed what Fergus already suspected and by the time he heard his son's tales of 'monsters and ghosts' on Sliach he was in no mood to believe in further ridiculous rumours. Nevertheless there was still the question of the two missing Germans and, though they would soon be found by the efficient Commandos, he felt he couldn't take any risks till the whole affair was sorted out.

Old Bob was annoyed at the disruption the German bomber had wreaked in his normal working routine. At sixty-eight he was gnarled and tough through a life-time of working in every kind of weather the winds brought to Rhanna. He revelled in the hard work his job as shepherd brought him but it was a time-consuming task which left little room for interruption.

When Fergus pushed away his half-eaten food and began the struggle into his jacket, Bob wiped his mouth with a horny hand. "The bairns are havering, man!" he said gruffly. "We have no time to be chasing fairy tales!"

Fergus looked at his black-eyed son and solemn-faced Donald standing with his hands folded behind his back. Before Fergus could speak Kirsteen intervened. "I know when Grant is lying," she said quietly. "And I don't think Shona would have sent him to tell a fairy tale."

Grant looked up at his father. "Shona said the monster was a parachute ..."

"And the kelpie on the wee island was likely a German," added Donald breathlessly.

It was enough for Fergus. "You get on with your work, Bob, I'll go over to Sliach and see what all the fuss is about!"

But Bob suddenly felt ashamed. He knew Fergus wouldn't ask help of any man unwilling to give it and if it wasn't for Kirsteen's kindness his midday fare would be nothing more than bread and cheese washed down with milk. He scraped his chair back and strode to the door to push his feet into muddy wellingtons.

"I'll get along with him, lass," he told Kirsteen. "Thankin' you for my dinner."

She gripped his knotted brown hand briefly. "Thank you, Bob," she said simply, but he knew what she meant. He made to follow Fergus but she stopped him by calling in rather awed tones. "Shouldn't you take a gun? It – might be dangerous."

"Ach no, Matthew will have his! If the German has come down on Sliach it's more likely prayers he will be needin'."

"Can I come with you, Bob?" Grant asked anxiously, the idea of chasing Germans far more appealing to him than an afternoon with school books. "I have a fine gun I made myself."

Seeing Kirsteen's rather harassed look Babbie put down the dish cloth and began to peel off her apron. "I'll take you to school . . . the pair of you," she said firmly. "We'll go to the harbour for a wee while first and chase the seagulls."

Grant snorted, feeling himself far too manly for the pastimes he had revelled in only recently, but Bob was hurrying away, calling on Dot who was rounding up a dismayed squadron of hens.

When Bob saw the young German airman he knew it was well that he had come because Fergus with his one arm and a visibly shaken Matthew would never have managed to get Anton into the boat.

But at first Fergus had no intention of doing such a thing. His dark eyes snapped and the muscle of his jaw tightened. It was one thing for the men of the island to deal with the enemy, it was entirely another to see his daughter tenderly administering to one of them. She was frantically tearing strips from the hem of her white petticoat to make them into bandages.

Rage consumed him. A German lay on Rhanna soil and his daughter was behaving as if his life were a precious thing that had to be preserved. His hand flashed out to grip her roughly by the shoulders and haul her to her feet. "Get away from him!" he ordered harshly. "Bob and myself will see to him!"

Tears of anger glinted in her eyes. "Will you, Father – will you see – to this?" She pulled back the blood-saturated cloak to reveal the terrible wounds.

"Dear God, help him!" muttered Bob, swallowing hard.

"God . . . and Lachlan!" she cried passionately. "He needs attention quickly or he'll die . . . if he doesn't anyway," she added so sadly that Fergus put his arm round her and whispered huskily, "I'm – sorry, mo ghaoil – it was just – things that bother me sometimes." He raised his voice. "Matthew, row like the devil then get along over for Lachlan! Tell him to bring his trap as far as your house!"

Matthew, glad of something to do, almost fell into the boat and splashed away hurriedly.

Fergus looked down at Anton. "Is . . . there anything you can do for him, Shona?"

Wordlessly she laid a broad strip of petticoat over the gaping viscera. Bob and Fergus gently lifted Anton's body till a thick wad of material was fixed in place. It was immediately soaked in blood and Shona stepped out of what remained of her petticoat and bound it over the bloodstained pad.

"My, but you're a bright lass," said Bob admiringly. "There's more in your head than was put there by a spoon."

"I can't do any more." Her voice was filled with frustration. Her experience of nursing was of a limited nature though her few months' training had equipped her with an efficiency that was at times a surprise to even herself. Her legs were shaking and she felt sick with reaction. Silently she sent up a prayer that Lachlan hadn't been called to another part of the island. She looked at Anton's face. It was drained of colour and the congealed blood on his forehead leapt out from the whiteness in a vicious riot of purple and red.

It was very quiet. The cold green water lapped the little island. A lone Redthroated-Diver paddled hurriedly by, uttering its melancholy mewing wail, annoyed that its chosen nesting territory had been violated by humans. Over the crags of Ben Machrie a great bird soared majestically.

Bob's hand rasped over the stubble on his chin, his eyes raking the misted azure of the sky. "Damt eagle," he muttered uneasily. "It's roamin' up there like it's waitin' for the lambs comin'."

But his unease wasn't incurred by the sight of the eagle whose home lay in the remote mountain ledges. His eyes kept straying to Anton lying like one already dead and his grip tightened on the bone handle of his shepherd's crook.

Fergus leaned against the bole of a tree and lit his pipe with a show of calm but his mind was racing. He tried to keep from looking at Anton but couldn't, the anger in his heart now replaced by a pathos he could barely understand. It wasn't right to feel like this about a German and he struggled with his thoughts. What was right? To hate because it was the proper thing to do in war? The night before he had looked at Jon Jodl and had felt only pity. They were all victims of circumstance. This dying youngster was just another victim in a world created by the greed of his so-called leaders; another pawn in the deadly, intricate game of war.

There was something else too that leapt into Fergus's mind, rearing up from the depths of the past. He was remembering his terrible battle with the deadly waters round the Sgor Creags, the frail speck of his life struggling with a sea that wanted to crush his body to pulp. His left arm had been mangled beyond repair. Lachlan had amputated it while he lay in a world of hellish delirium; completely without his senses he'd had to depend on the help of people who loved him most.

The wounded German was unconscious and dependent, but if he wakened at that moment who could there be who was familiar and beloved enough for him to ask, "Will you help me?"

Fergus blew a mouthful of smoke into the hazy blue air. For a moment it hung suspended then gradually dispersed and it seemed in that moment that all the prejudices that had swayed his thinking went with it.

Shona twisted round in a gesture of impatience and caught the look of deep tenderness in his black eyes.

"You're a fine nurse," he told her quietly. "You did a grand job. I'm sure he'll be grateful to you."

"I don't want his thanks, Father, just a chance of life for him, that's all. I wish Lachlan would hurry."

Dot was barking impatiently from the shore. She had followed Matthew through the woods but realising her master wasn't coming behind she had come back to look for him. The sound of her yelps echoed into the corries of the Ben then rebounded back over the loch to be lost over the shaggy moors.

"I'll kill that damt dog!" cursed Bob as the eerie ghost bark bounced again and again off the face of the mountain. In normal circumstances he would have roared at Dot to be quiet but hard and tough as he was he felt himself to be in the very presence of death and his watery eyes gazed broodingly at the unrestrained antics of the lively dog.

Time is eternity when filled with urgency but barely thirty minutes passed before the tall, slim figure of Lachlan burst through the thicket of pines on the opposite shore. The sight of him clutching his black bag and the air of reassurance that seemed to enshroud him brought sighs of relief from the men and a welcoming cry from Shona. He jumped quickly into the boat, pushing it off from the shore to come gliding through the calm green water.

His presence on the tiny island brought both peace and hope to the hearts of everyone there for just to look at McLachlan was to know love. His tanned face was finely drawn, his mouth firm and sensitive. But it was in his eyes that anxious souls found peace; in the deep brown pools lay the compassion of his heart, the last thing that many of his patients saw before letting go of life.

He looked at the neat layers of Shona's petticoat and patted her arm. "You've done well, mo ghaoil," he approved quietly before starting on a swift examination of Anton's broken body.

Fergus stood against the tree and watched Lachlan's long, sensitive fingers. He had removed his coat to cover Anton and his shoulder blades showed through his pullover. He was thin and still boyish with his dark curling hair that always strayed over his forehead when he bent over. So Fergus remembered the doctor Lachlan who had tended him so devotedly.

For a moment Fergus held his breath. How he loved the man who was both doctor and companion to him. But it hadn't always been so. Fergus's first wife, Helen, had died giving birth to Shona and in his grief Fergus had blamed Lachlan. It was many years later, at the time of Fergus's accident, that the two men had healed the rift between them. Something caught in Fergus's throat. How bitterly he regretted those lost years. He had wasted so much precious time that could have been richly spent with the man who healed with skill and an unstinting devotion.

Lachlan was removing Anton's leather helmet and Fergus knocked his pipe out against the tree to go and kneel by the doctor. "Does he have a chance, Lachlan?" he asked softly.

"It's difficult to say till I get him back to the house. I've sent Matthew over to fetch Biddy, and Phebie is getting the surgery ready." He passed a hand over his brow and looked worried. He was always doubtful about his abilities as a surgeon. Working on an island with limited facilities he'd had to deal with many emergencies over the years and the healthy patients who had come through surgery carried out in crude, makeshift conditions were a testimonial to his capabilities. But he was completely without ego and it was perhaps the lack of it which endeared him to so many. "He ought to be in hospital," he continued. "With complete asepsis and every modern surgical technique . . . but I'll do my best."

The pause had come with the removal of the helmet. The young man had already reminded him of Niall with his youthful features and firm chin; now, the crop of fair curling hair completed the illusion. Gently he ran his fingers through the thick hair. "He's got concussion, but the helmet saved him from more serious damage. It's the shock I'm worried about . . . he's lost so much blood." He looked at the little boat rocking peacefully. "In my haste I brought only my bag – could you – all of you – take off any clothing you don't need and pad out those planks a bit?"

Wiry old Bob was coatless but he pulled off a tattered cardigan and stood in his shirt sleeves without the hint of a shiver. Fergus removed his jacket and felt the goose pimples rising, but he moved to the boat and began to lay the pitifully inadequate coverings on the bottom. Bob came at his back armed with a bundle of dead bracken which he pushed under the clothing.

"You have a head on you, Bob," commented Fergus and he too began to gather moss and bracken. In minutes a soft bed was made and the arduous task began of getting Anton into the boat. It was no easy task for, though slim, he was tall and muscular. Bob and Lachlan grasped his shoulders, Shona supported his middle in an effort to keep the wound from opening further, and Fergus took his ankles in the strong grasp of his right arm. He went on to the boat first and his stomach lurched as the frail little craft tilted alarmingly. For a moment he hesitated and looked down. There was no gradual shoreline from the tiny, rocky islet – the land dropped down immediately into deep black depths. He shuddered because water had frightened him from boyhood. The land was his backbone, water something to be admired so long as his two feet were firmly on the ground. He stumbled against a thwart and the little boat responded by bucking alarmingly.

"Steady, man," said Lachlan quietly and the moment was over. Soon Anton was lying on his bed of mossy bracken but taking up most of the confined space.

"Only two of us will get in wi' him," muttered Bob, blowing his nose into a grimy hanky with a nonchalant air. "It's how we'll be managing on the other side that worries me."

No one looked at Fergus, for never by a word or glance had any man suggested that the loss of his arm was an inconvenience to him. But he was always quick to sense unspoken thoughts and he said roughly, "Get along over, I'll wait here."

Shona slid a thin arm round his waist. "I'll wait with you, we can keep each other warm."

He looked at her anxiously. She had divested herself of most of her warm clothing to cover Anton, and Fergus felt a rush of protectiveness. He pulled her close and she felt the warmth of his body burning into her, the very nearness of it dispelling the chilly tremors that were bringing her out in goose pimples.

Bob pulled swiftly at the oars. In his days of tending sheep and cows he had seen many a sickening sight but they were of things within his experience. The sight he had recently witnessed was without those bounds and his tough old stomach churned, making him row the harder.

Dot saw him coming and her barks grew in volume, but her sense of devotion was lost on her disgruntled master who lunged at her with his boot the minute he jumped ashore. She tucked her tail well between her haunches and slunk into the bushes.

"Come back till I toe your arse, you bugger!" cried Bob in frustration but his dog had no intention of coming back to such a fate and the old man turned his attention to helping Lachlan. Both men were grimly aware of Anton's open wound and were only able to ease him over the planks a few inches at a time. The task was made no easier by the swaying of the boat and Bob stopped to wipe watery mucous from his nose.

"It's no damt use, Doctor!" he spat. "We'll never manage the lad between us! I'd best go back for McKenzie! We need another pair o' hands!" Which last remark was proof of Bob's invincible faith in Fergus. But before they could move, Dot began making a nuisance of herself again, whimpering in the bushes and making excited half-yelps. The distraction was too much for Bob and he roared, "Shut up you brute or I'll skin your hide . . . !"

The rest of the utterance was never to be because the dog suddenly shot out of the undergrowth, ably assisted by the muzzle of a murderous-looking Tommy gun held by a man attired in khaki battledress and a tin helmet from which sprouted sprays of fir branches.

'Your dog was causing a bit of a nuisance," he told Bob pleasantly, then he turned to Lachlan. "You look like you could be doing with a bit of help?" Before Lachlan could answer he called into the trees. "Out of it, lads! We need some muscle here."

Magically there appeared from bush and tree half a dozen young men all sporting a variety of natural camouflage. Without a word they went straight to the boat and lifted Anton out as if he were thistledown. Bob immediately climbed back into the boat to row to the island for Fergus and Shona leaving Lachlan to introduce himself.

"Pleased to meet you, Doctor," said the thick-set, heavy-jawed young man whose gun had sent Dot yelping. "I'm Dunn, the officer in charge of this charade." His teeth showed in a flash of amusement. His eyes travelled to Anton. "I see you have found another of the bomber crew?"

Lachlan nodded slowly. "Yes, he's very badly wounded and needs immediate attention. My house is a fair distance from here but I've brought my trap to the clearing on the edge of the wood. We'll have to carry him to it . . ." He spread his fine hands in a gesture of despair. "I'm worried about the bumping he'll get on the way down. The track is a rough one."

Dunn grinned reassuringly. "Don't worry, Doctor, we'll get him back to your house." He turned to the others and there was a swift exchange. Before Bob was half-way over the loch the men had removed their battle-jackets, fashioning them into a strong, pliable stretcher into which they placed Anton. There was no regimental dividing line between officer and men. They worked together as an efficient team and Lachlan looked on admiringly. Soon they were all making their way through the dark, silent woods with a subdued Dot slinking at Bob's heels. Fergus had wrapped his jacket around Shona who was carrying her blood-stained cloak over her arm.

Dunn looked at it and his professional mask fell for a moment. "He's lost a lot of blood. Do you know how he came to injure himself?"

"Probably on the mountain – coming down," she said quietly. "There's a lot of jagged rocks on that side of the mountain."

"And you've only just found him?"

"Ay, the children heard moans from the island."

"So he's spent most of the night in the open?"

"And most of the morning. He's suffering badly from exposure."

"A real tough-skinned Jerry!" Dunn's words were harsh but Shona knew they were only a cover.

They had reached the clearing and Dunn nodded towards the trap. "You get in, Doctor, and lead the way. It's better that we should carry him, lessen the risk of rattling him around."

Fergus fell into step with Dunn who was at the head of the stretcher party. "It's been a wild goose chase for you," said Fergus in his deep lilting voice. It wasn't a question, but a blunt statement of fact.

The officer appreciated it, and laughed. "Wild geese would be a bloody sight easier to catch than the ghosts we've been chasing. We were told the island was invaded by German paratroops and were sent over to investigate – can't be too careful – never know what the bastards will be up to . . ." he checked himself and continued pleasantly. "We've got on to Naval Patrol to let them know it's a bit of a false alarm . . . some of us are staying for a bit though . . . there's still another of the bomber crew to locate and it seems your Home Guard are having a bit of trouble running him to ground. We met some of them over on the north side of the island but they didn't seem too keen to hang around there."

Fergus smiled at this but Bob's weatherbeaten countenance creased into a frown. "No one in their right senses will be staying round that damt place for long!"

It was a cryptic remark, one typical of the superstitious older generation and Bob, being one of the best Seanachaidhs, was renowned for his ability to arouse curiosity in the least imaginative beings, but the officer merely smiled politely and said nothing.

Bob's gnarled fingers curled tightly round his crook. "The

de'il deals wi' his own," he snarled, defensive yet assertive about his beliefs. "It is a consecrated place yonder at Dunuaigh. The monks will no' be likin' the intrusion that is goin' on wi' folks of all nationalities trampin' over their restin' places!"

Shona smiled impishly. "But Bob, there is only one German likely to be wandering and no doubt wishing he could be found."

" 'Tis enough! 'Tis enough!" barked Bob and he stamped away to begin his belated work, calling impatiently on Dot who went scampering after him gladly enough.

Tina was standing at the door of her cottage. She raised a languid arm in the manner of one acknowledging a carnival procession, her only betrayal of surprise manifested by the slightly breathless utterance, "You have caught the German laddie then?" Which singular observation rendered the sturdy presence of the Commando troops as of little import. "If any o' you are seeing Matthew send him home for his dinner," she added in slightly accusing tones, then turned to scoop Eve from the water barrel into which she was gleefully climbing.

Shona ran ahead and climbed into the trap beside Lachlan who immediately tucked a rug round her legs. "You take care mo ghaoil," he told her. "We must have a nice rosy lass waiting for Niall when he gets home."

She laughed, tucking her arm through his. "Don't worry. Kirsteen has stuffed so much food into me since yesterday Niall will think I'm a prize turkey when he sees me. A good excuse for him to thraw my neck!"

Their laughter drifted back to Fergus who had just heard from the officer about the raids over Clydebank the previous night. First-hand news could be had from the accumulator-powered wireless sets owned by those interested and affluent enough to possess one. Fergus had one in his parlour but the morning had been too rushed for anyone in the household to think about switching on. The officer went on to say that it was believed the bomber which had crashed on Rhanna was one of a group which had taken part in the raids then, having been hit, had lost all sense of direction.

"Oh God, no!" breathed Fergus. "The doctor's son stays in Clydebank, he and my daughter are sweethearts! Good God! Is there no end to it?" It was a cry from the heart and Dunn looked at him in sympathetic enquiry. "Niall was injured at Dunkirk," explained Fergus. "Lachlan, his wife, Shona – all were wild with grief because they believed him to be dead – but he came back with a wound that meant no more fighting for him . . ." He smiled wryly. "It would seem the war has caught up with him anyway. How am I to tell his parents that?"

Dunn cleared his throat "Would – you like me to do it?"

Fergus hesitated. The stretcher party went marching carefully down the grass-rutted track. It was very peaceful there among the fields with the crushed grasses releasing an almost forgotten scent of summer. The dairy cows, released from winter byres, showed their pleasure in soft little half-bellows which they blew into each other's ears. The frost of the morning had disappeared and there was a gentle heat in the haze of the sun, a delicate promise of the green, Hebridean spring to come. Banners of blue smoke curled from croft and farm, rising to hang in tattered shrouds against the misted purple of the mountains.

Down below Lachlan turned his dark head, his face a pale blurr of enquiry and Shona, her hair a fiery beacon in the sun, turned also, wondering why Fergus and the officer had stopped. Fergus wondered wildly what to do. How would Shona feel having an echo of the past brought back? Phebie would react typically, with a quiet display of normality hiding her deepest fears . . . and Lachlan, the doctor in him rising up out of his despair to try and save the life of a German . . . but how would Lachlan the man feel afterwards? How would they all feel till news of Niall filtered out of the confusion of an air raid? Shona . . . again Fergus hesitated. She had come home to Rhanna for a holiday, to rest that tightly strung little body which Fergus was still inclined to think of as belonging to a child. But even though she had been home such a short time he was seeing a change in her. She had gained a lot of poise, her emotions were under a tighter reign. Once, Rhanna and all it meant had been her only horizon, now there were others which seemed to have broadened her whole outlook on life.

He straightened his broad shoulders. "I'll tell them," he said abruptly and ran down the rutted track to catch up with the trap. Lachlan heard him out in silence, a faint flush high on his cheek bones the only sign of his inner fears. Shona, her deep blue eyes wide, stared at her father as his firm lips formed halting words into some kind of meaning. She wanted to put her hands over her ears, to scream at her father to be quiet, to shut her mind from the facts. It had been easier in childhood when little fantasies had helped her over the many hurdles of her young life. But she wasn't a child any more, there were no little illusions to help her now.

In a dream she heard herself saying, "No one will be knowing the facts yet. It – will be some time before we hear any news?"

"I'm afraid so," murmured Dunn, coming up behind Fergus. "Everyone is too shattered and harassed to make much sense of anything. I believe it all started last night and the all clear didn't come till just before dawn this morning. Everything will be in a turmoil but I'll get some enquiries through if I can . . ." He smiled kindly and went on. "Mr McKenzie tells me the young man has had experience of battle and is at present with Civil Defence so I'm sure he knows how to look after himself."

What he didn't add was that there was a strong likelihood the German bombers would return to Glasgow and Clydebank that night but he felt he had already said enough on the subject. The stretcher party had halted some distance ahead and Lachlan turned to Shona. "Go home, mo ghaoil. I'll understand."

She put her small hand over his and shook her head vehemently, the tears in her eyes making them look like blue stars. "No! You'll need all the help you can get! If I sit at home I'll just dwell on all the things that might never happen!"

Fergus took her other hand and crushed it tightly. "You take care, Ni-Cridhe," he told her softly. She caught her breath. 'Ni-Cridhe', the Gaelic endearment for 'my dear lassie'. It wasn't often he expressed himself so freely in public and she knew that he was feeling something of her pain. It was his way of telling her how much he cared.

"I'll take care, Father," she breathed gently.

"We'll expect you in for tea," he nodded and, turning abruptly on his heel, he strode away.

A curious crowd had gathered outside Lachlan's, ample proof that Matthew's tongue had been busy. When the stretcher party hove into view everyone began to talk among themselves as if by doing so they were proving that their presence in a remote spot in Glen Fallan had no bearing whatsoever on the latest events. So absorbed did they appear that it seemed an impossibility their interest could lie in anything that was happening outside their own little circle. As Lachlan came by in the trap, heads lifted one by one in a great display of surprise.

"It is yourself, Doctor," acknowledged Kate McKinnon innocently. "We were just thinkin' over the things o' last night and wondering where the other two German lads were hidin' but I see you have another one there."

With one accord they all turned to look upon the deathly pale face of Anton being marched past their vision.

Lachlan got down from the trap and said with a deceptively charming smile, "And you have all left Portcull to have a little chin-wag in the middle of Glen Fallan?"

Old Joe's sea-green eyes betrayed nothing. "Ach no, not at all, Doctor," he rebuked gently. "We are waiting for the lads to come over the Glen to see will they have news for us."

"Ay," put in Erchy the Post who, with his satchel slung over his shoulder and one foot on the pedal of his bike, had the air of someone who had been rudely interrupted in the middle of a busy day. "That is a fact, Doctor. Also Matthew was asking us to wait and tell you that Biddy is not at home."

"But I know that!" cried Lachlan. "She spent the night at the Smiddy!"

Fingal McLeod, a tall lanky young crofter who had lost a leg to a fox snare, nodded wisely. "Well, well now, that is likely why she is no' at home."

"But I told Matthew she would be at Todd's," said Lachlan.

"Ach well, that's where she'll be right enough," murmured Erchy.

Lachlan was growing exasperated. The islanders could be trying and unhelpful when they had a mind, and it was obvious they were in no mood to be helpful now.

Shona felt her temper rising. It was a trait over which she had to exercise control but just then it erupted in a mixture of anxiety and grief. "Well!" she cried hotly. "One of you get along over to Todd's and fetch Biddy!"

"Matthew will be over there now," said Fingal soothingly.

Shona tossed her auburn head and her eyes sparkled with rage. "You are just like a bunch of old women! The laddie you are all gaping at so eagerly may die! Lachlan can't do everything himself and I'm not fully trained to help properly! For God's sake! He's a German, I know, but he's also a human being!"

Lachlan had disappeared into the house leaving Elspeth listening at the door. Her strangely immobile face was gaunt with outrage at the very idea of a German, wounded or otherwise, being allowed to cross the doctor's threshold. In Elspeth's mind, Slochmhor and everyone therein owed all to her efficiency as a housekeeper, and she felt it was her right to exercise her opinion as to what went on there. When Phebie had asked her to help prepare the surgery for an emergency case she had agreed willingly enough, scrubbing and cleaning till the air reeked of antiseptic. Not until the Commandos crossed the doorstep with Anton did she realise that for the past hour she had been preparing the way for a German airman and she was speechless with indignation. But at Shona's words she found her tongue quickly. A shame-faced Erchy was straddling his bike ready to rush off but Elspeth's tones stopped him in mid-flight.

"Wait you there, Erchy McKay! It is the King's business you should be about! You have no right to be gallivanting off when you are on duty!"

She was coming down the path into the crowd and Erchy stopped, his kindly face both bewildered and angry. He was about to tell her that the 'King's business' was only a part-time job on an island that only received mail three times a week, but before he could speak another figure came flying along on a bike, pedalling swiftly along the bumpy Glen road. It soon proved to be Babbie Cameron, her wind-tossed hair a fiery beacon, pale freckled skin whipped to a delicate rose. The bike had been left in a ditch by Murdy the night before and she had simply borrowed it. It was a rusted heap with a wobbling front wheel and Babbie now discovered it had no brakes. She catapulted into the crowd, sending everyone scattering, giving an undignified haste to Elspeth's spindly legs in a scuttle for safety. Babbie's feet rasped along the stony road in an effort to stop the machine. Gallantly the menfolk rushed to her aid, having to make no excuses for hands that had to grab at forbidden fruits in order to avert a catastrophe. Babbie was an attractive sight standing against the backcloth of Sgurr nan Ruadh. While she panted for breath the men fussed and Elspeth glowered.

"Sorry everyone . . . and thanks," smiled Babbie, adroitly removing Fingal's hand from her left thigh. She turned to look at Shona. "Your father popped in to tell us about – things . . . I thought I might be needed."

Shona felt like hugging her there and then in the middle of the Glen. Instead she put out her hand. "You're just in time, Babbie – the doctor will be waiting." And with her head held high she marched with Babbie up the path to Slochmhor, an outraged Elspeth forced to make way for them at the gate.

"I'll be telling Biddy to look in on her way home," called a rather subdued Kate. "She will not be liking it if she feels left out."

"As you like," returned Shona from the door. "Though 'tis a pity you were not thinking about it sooner."

The villagers ambled back to Portcull in a somewhat embarrassed silence, Fingal and Erchy breaking away from the others at the hill track leading to Nigg. Erchy's satchel already contained two rabbits which he had collected from his snares half an hour earlier.

Erchy pushed his bike into a clump of bushes and grinned at Fingal. "Let us go about the King's business then," he said in a hideous falsetto. Both men roared with laughter, made all the merrier at the prospect of an afternoon poaching Burnbreddie.

"We might find the other Jerry waiting to ravish her ladyship," snorted Fingal ecstatically. He halted for a moment to sit down on a mossy stone. "Wait you, Erchy, I will have a wee look to see have I got everything we need."

Carefully he unscrewed the bottom half of his peg leg, peered inside, then satisfied as to the contents fixed it back in place. "Old Peggy is fully equipped," he grinned. "I have an extra flask of Tam's whisky in there too. We will no' go thirsty."

In the surgery at Slochmhor, Lachlan too was finding every reason to be grateful to Tam. Earlier in the day he had pressed a generous bottle of whisky into Lachlan's hands. Nodding and winking he had warned, "Don't be telling a soul now, Doctor. 'Tis for your nerves when you have to be doing these awful things like Todd's appendix."

Lachlan had put the bottle to the back of the cupboard thinking it unlikely that it would be needed in the near future. He smiled wryly at the small glass in his hand. Todd's appendix was nothing to what waited for his attention now. Anton lay scrubbed and ready . . . ready for what? Life or death? The responsibility lay with Lachlan and the thought made his hands shake.

One of the Commandos, a sturdy man with a strong stomach, had volunteered to stay behind and help. He popped his head round the door. "Ready, Doctor?"

Lachlan gulped down the whisky and spluttered, "Yes, I'm ready." He smiled. "I don't make a habit of this, Private Anderson."

Anderson looked at the whisky bottle with interest.

"Would you like a drop?" asked Lachlan, amused despite himself.

"I don't mind, sir, I really don't mind."

He gulped down a generous mouthful, straightened his shoulders and followed Lachlan briskly into the surgery.

CHAPTER SEVEN

Invalids

Biddy stirred and struggled out of the longest sleep she had ever had. Her mouth was dry and her aching head was spinning so alarmingly she hastily closed her eyes again to shut out the sight of the whirling, cobwebby roof. She felt sick and for a moment couldn't sort out one thought from another. The smells of the Smiddy came to her, horse manure and leather, fragrant hay and rusting iron. Bits of hay had worked their way into her clothing and were making her very uncomfortable. Carefully she moved an arm in an experimental gesture. Well, one limb was still intact anyway. Slowly she shifted the position of her cold, cramped body and immediately a searing pain shot through her ankle.

"Damt bugger!" She swore through gritted teeth, the pain bringing her sharply to her senses. For a moment she lay, unable to believe it was daylight and that she must have spent the night in Todd the Shod's barn. Painfully she raised herself on an elbow to grope for her glasses, but they eluded her searching fingers. Screwing up her eyes she peered round the big shed but there was no sign of life. The visiting horses had been collected earlier by their owners. Biddy ensconced in a pile of hay which was almost smothered by a jumbled heap of ironmongery, had escaped notice.

Robbie had called in at the house to see how Todd was bearing up and to offer to keep the Smiddy horses in his own shed until things were back to normal. Mollie McDonald had been very appreciative of the idea because she knew she was going to have her hands full with Todd without having to see to the horses as well. Already Todd was wallowing in the attention his operation was bringing. He was of an easy-going disposition and Mollie knew from experience he would hold on to his convalescent period with a gentle air of martyrdom for as long as he thought he could get away with it.

So the Smiddy, normally filled with the sounds of horses and hammering, was deserted in the drowsing quiet of the midday hour when most people were at dinner.

Biddy's first feelings of surprise soon turned to extreme indignation. What kind of place was it where people went about everyday affairs without a thought to the nurse who had tended them so devotedly for years? Biddy was feeling far too neglected to allow rationality to gain the upper hand. In the excitement of the previous night everyone's routine had been broken and no one was quite sure where anybody might be, but she wasn't taking any of that into account. The cold of the night had played havoc with her circulation. Her extremities were like lumps of lead, especially her feet which were nearest the side door. Fortunately, in his haste to get to the Headquarters, Todd had left the forge only partially damped and this had kept the shed at a fairly warm temperature.

"Damt Germans!" Biddy was venting her wrath on anyone or anything that came to mind. "I'll kill the buggers if I catch them!" Then she raised her voice, uttering appeals for help which flowed with such lusty frequency that the pigeons in the loft fluttered up in a cloud of dust and made a hasty exit.

Mollie McDonald came in, a red-faced bustle of amazement. She stood in the doorway, taking in the sight of the old nurse, toothless and without spectacles, lying among hay and junk, and her mouth fell open. Mollie instantly misconstrued Biddy's plight. It was well known that Biddy was fond of 'a wee tipple'. She carried a hip flask wherever she went and fortified herself whenever she felt the need. It was purely for 'medicinal purposes only' she told anyone who questioned her but few did. Hers was a job that called her out at all times and in all weathers and so devoted was she that no one blamed her for 'having a wee snifter to warm her auld blood'. Indeed, the islanders saw to it that her flask was never dry and frequently topped up her 'Firkin for the fireplace'.

But Mollie was in a mood that morning to blame the 'Uisge-Beatha' on a great many things. Her good nature allowed her to overlook many of her husband's little misdemeanours but the manner of his arrival home the night before had caused her some embarrassment. But that was mild compared to the humiliation later, with the doctor and Biddy talking in whispers about Todd's drunkenness. Now here was Biddy, hideously glassy-eyed and stupefied, obviously suffering from a massive hangover. Mollie folded her arms and clamped her lips together. Biddy had found her specs and was hastening to put them on in order that she might hear better the words of sympathy that would surely follow her discovery.

"Well now, Biddy McMillan!" Mollie's voice was taut with disapproval. "A fine thing this is indeed and you with your reputation to uphold. It's a reputation for an alcoholic Cailleach you'll be earning and no mistake. I knew last night there was something funny goin' on wi' Todd an' his cronies but never – never did I imagine that yourself of all people to be in on a thing like that. You're worse than auld Annack Gow and that's sayin' something for she was never sober when Jock was alive if I'm mindin' right!"

Biddy was speechless. Small inarticulate grunts escaped her toothless mouth. With her glazed eyes and wiry grey hair hanging in limp strands over her lined, yellow face she might indeed just have wakened from an inebriated sleep.

Mollie snorted and continued softly. "Ach, but it is terrible just. The world is goin' to ruin! Germans and soldiers all over the island an' our very own nurse lyin' drunk in my Todd's place o' business. 'Tis no wonder you were not over seeing to him this morning." She clucked reproachfully. "Biddy, mo ghaoil, if you had to sleep it off could you not just have stayed in the house to be decent-like?"

Biddy removed her specs because she could hardly believe what she was hearing. Her ankle was throbbing, she was frozen to the marrow and instead of sympathy she was receiving abuse.

"Is it blind you are, Mollie McDonald?" she gasped through tears of exhaustion and self-pity. "It is the doctor I am needin' this very meenit! I feel like I am dyin' wi' exposure and my ankle is broken! Get help quickly you silly woman – and put the kettle on for a cuppy."

But before Mollie could hasten away Kate McKinnon appeared and she too stared at Biddy. "What way are you lyin' there for, you daft Cailleach?" she twinkled mischievously. "It's no wonder Matthew couldny find you! They are needin' you over at Slochmhor."

Biddy's howl of derisive indignation split the air asunder.

"Needin' me! God! It's the doctor I am needin' and quick! Now, will you stop hangin' about like a couple o' spare farts and get me in that damt house before I die!"

Fortunately Kate and Mollie were strong women. Between them they carried Biddy into the house amid a shower of abuse, instructions and complaints.

An astonished Todd, wallowing in self-pity over his post-operative discomforts, found his martyrdom seriously undermined by the advent of Biddy who was placed near him on an adjoining sofa. Mollie hastened to swing the kettle over the fire while Kate went out to look for someone to take a message to Slochmhor. Knowing the position there, she was doubtful of help arriving quickly, nevertheless she grabbed a small boy who was slinking about under the bridge with a fishing rod, playing truant.

"Get goin'!" she ordered when he sniffed rebelliously, but he scurried away quickly when she added. "Disobey me and I'll march you to old Murdoch by the skin o' your lugs!"

On the sofa Biddy was groaning loudly with pain in between gulping hot tea laced with brandy. "It's broken, I know the bugger has broken itself!" she proclaimed loudly, addressing her swollen ankle.

Kate helped herself to tea from the huge pot, then sat down on the edge of Todd's sofa to eye Biddy thoughtfully. "It's an assistant you should be having, Biddy," she began sternly, pausing to let the inevitable barrage of protest subside before going on. "I was just thinkin' the thing last night when I heard you had to sprachle out your warm bed to see Todd here. It's too much to ask o' an auld chookie and now you are having this accident and maybe endin' up wi' piles and piddle trouble wi' the cold gettin' up your passages all night."

Biddy wrapped a patchwork quilt round her knees and glowered into her tea. She knew Kate was right but she wasn't going to admit it because to do so, even to herself, was a signal that she really was getting beyond nursing the island single-handed. There had been an assistant several years before but she hadn't stuck the post more than a month and this fact she sourly pointed out to Kate who made a gesture of impatience with her big, capable hands.

"Ach, c'mon now, mo ghaoil! Is it any wonder the poor soul

sceedaddled like a fart in front of a turd? You never gave her a chance! Criticised everything she did . . . in front o' her patients too. I mind her saying to me, 'I am not able even to give an enema but that old bitch is peering over my shoulder to see am I putting the tube in the right passage.' Near to tears she was telling me that, and myself knowing she was good at it too for she gave me one thon time I was laid up wi' my back."

Todd had been mending the handle of a goffering iron with what appeared to be single-minded intent but when he looked up, the smile on his craggy face showed otherwise. "It will not be a man causing a mistake like that," he observed with an avidness that was out of keeping with his supposedly delicate condition. The profundity of the statement seemed to surprise even himself. He spat on to the peats from the conveniently placed sofa and watched the ensuing results with every sign of enjoyment.

For a few moments the sizzling of roasting saliva filled the kitchen, then Biddy said with slow deliberation, "It is well you are not yet knowing what we had to sew up last night, Todd McDonald. Ay me, the Lord giveth and the nurse taketh away . . ."

Kate spluttered into her tea, Todd's guileless blue eyes glazed over and Mollie, coming back with a bowl of cold water from the rain barrel for Biddy's ankle, stood in the doorway, her loosely hinged jaw once more falling to its lowest extent.

"Ay, ay," continued Biddy wisely. "It can happen! These scalpels is sharp things and your belly that round a wee slip no' an easy thing to avoid – but, ach – don't worry, Todd, at your age it won't be mattering too much and it will never be noticed! Lachlan is a great hand wi' the embroidery and I am having a wee keepsake o' yourself to be remembering you by. It's fine for an old body like myself that never was having a man to occupy me, as you have told me yourself on more than one occasion," she sighed regretfully. "I can be lookin' at it and thinkin' Ay, poor auld Todd, he was aye generous wi' himself right enough." She fixed him with a fond gaze. "Just think, you will go down in posterior like that other cheil . . . Napoleon I think it was. There was always a rumour they preserved his in a wee boxie."

She stirred her third cup of tea with a great show of calculated sorrow. Todd was sitting like a ramrod, his rigid torso looking as if it were nailed to the back of the sofa.

Mollie looked at him with concern. "You were sayin' yourself, Todd, you were surprised you havny been needin' to pee since the operation. Have you – had a wee look yet?"

Todd's face had grown bright red and he was glaring at Biddy with malevolence. "It is no' an assistant you are needin', Biddy McMillan! It is a replacement! I am going to write to the medical board and ask for one to be sent right away!"

Kate threw herself back on the sofa in a fit of laughter and Todd yelled in pain as her weight pinned his legs.

"Ach, but you should see your face, Todd!" she screeched. "It is yourself will be needin' the replacement and maybe Mollie another husband, for who would be wantin' a man that's nothing more than a castrated ram!"

Mollie's mouth quivered but she managed to scold sternly, "It's your tongue should be cut out, Kate McKinnon! Todd is all the man I need. Poor soul, he is no' able to take any more shocks, he had enough last night to last him a whily." She turned to Biddy. "Now then, Biddy, Kate and myself will be seeing to that ankle o' yours."

"It's broke I tell you," protested Biddy but Mollie quelled her with a stern eye and she allowed her shoe and one of her black woollen stockings to be removed. Mollie's lifetime of administering to a hypochondriac husband hardened her sympathies and she was inclined to think that everyone exaggerated their ills.

"Ay, you've only twisted it," asserted Mollie with a nod.

"I tell you it's broke," said Biddy faintly, who knew by experience that her ankle was only badly strained.

Todd's post-operative pallor took on a distinctly rosy glow during the removal of Biddy's stocking. It was one thing for a Gael to make jokes about the female form but quite another to have a feminine leg exposed to his vision, even though the limb in question resembled a badly warped spurtle.

"Here," he protested. "This is no place for a woman to be doing such things."

Kate got to her feet with a mischievous grin. "Ach, the poor Bodach is right enough! Him bein' a virgin mannie now won't be having the thrill of a woman's leg any more. He'll be celebrating like thon monks in the monkeries!"

"Damt women!" Todd exploded while Kate, with a great show

of solemnity, fixed a blanket between the sofas so that it formed a screen.

For a time silence reigned, broken only by Todd's unrestricted flow of spit frying on the peats and Biddy's staunchly suppressed moans as Mollie bathed her ankle. The women were in a subdued state of mirth because Kate had produced a half bottle of whisky from her ample apron pocket and it was passed quietly round. Mollie's dainty little sips were typical of the majority of island women but Kate and Biddy had no inhibitions and gulped from the bottle with avid enjoyment.

Todd sighed forlornly behind the blanket, then mumbled something indistinct. Mollie was softening and put a hand to pull back the blanket but the hard-hearted Kate stayed her and said gaily, "We are no' understanding a word you are saying, Todd McDonald! You will have to speak up."

"I am saying," he bellowed in desperation, "that I am wondering why it is I am not yet needin' to pee! My belly is sore and I am hungry and a damt bad day it is when the Germans get more attention than the islanders. I am wantin' the doctor to see why I am no' still havin' the use o' my bladder!"

At that the women could contain themselves no longer and their yells of mirth filled the kitchen. Biddy had forgotten her throbbing ankle and she gasped, "Is it gropin' for it you are, Todd, and never finding the damt thing?" She struggled upright and in an effort to gain purchase grabbed at the blanket which fell in folds to the floor. A crimson-faced Todd stared at the three screeching women with something akin to terror, his hands beneath the blankets frozen into immobility.

"Ach God!" screamed Kate. "The best laugh ever! He is searching for it right enough and no' lookin' sure if he's found it yet!"

"Never mind," supplemented Biddy, taking off her glasses to wipe her streaming eyes. "It is there right enough but if you are still not sure, well, it is just not all men are lucky enough to be made like bulls. Anyway, you mustny worry about not having the urge to relieve yourself. It happens after an operation and you will be dehydrated with all that drink you had last night."

Mollie held up the bottle. "Maybe a wee drop o' this will get him goin', the soul."

Todd put out an eager hand but Biddy stayed him with an ominous warning about the dangers of alcohol after abdominal surgery. He opened his mouth but no sound came; his big, homely face crumpled and he looked like a forlorn small boy denied a treat.

Mollie's soft heart could take no more. "There, there, my poor man," she soothed. "I'm going to heat some broth and we'll all have a wee Strupak. The doctor won't be yet for a whily so we might as well enjoy him. Mairi will be over later wi' the bairns to see how you are, so that will cheer you up."

The thought of his dithering, faithful daughter, bustling about with soulful goodwill, did nothing for Todd's flagging spirits and he sank into a state of petrified gloom, his brooding eyes fixed dolefully on the window which afforded a view of the harbour where a tranquil blue sea lapped the silvered white sands. A fishing trawler was puffing into the bay with the usual following of gulls darting and drifting according to the whim of the air currents.

Soon the harbour was full of the unhurried bustle that the Rhanna folk applied to everyday tasks. Old Joe, perched on a lobster pot, with his pipe sending busy little blue-grey clouds into the face of a sea-stained crony, looked like a snowy-haired gnome. Every so often he stabbed his pipe into the sky in a circular motion, taking the heads of his listeners round with it while the tale of the German bomber unfolded. Canty Tam, always to be had wherever there was a crowd, gazed vacantly but smiled with satisfaction at the goriest details. Ranald had been half-heartedly scraping barnacles from the upturned bottom of a boat when the trawler sailed into the harbour and he had thankfully abandoned the irksome task. He now prodded his paint scraper into the sky, making exaggerated circles to demonstrate to a young fisherman how the bomber had thundered over the village before its final wild flight to the mountains. There were a few moments of pipe-sucking, thoughtful silence with all eyes fixed on the upper corries of Ben Machrie where trailing wisps of vapour drifted in and out of high secret places.

"It must have been quite a sight," was the eventual general verdict and Tam McKinnon, arriving back from Nigg where he had spent the morning repairing a croft roof, nodded seriously.

"Terrible just," he stated lugubriously and his cronies nodded in sad agreement though, with the exception of Righ, not one of them had witnessed the event. But Righ was fast asleep in the lighthouse cottage and Tam was able to embroider his tale, helped by the nodding heads and sympathetic 'Ays' of the others.

Canty Tam smiled secretively at the sky, addressing it with a grimace of conviction. "And was my mother not after telling me you was all drunk last night?" he accused the lacy cloudbanks pleasantly. "She said to me only this morning while I was supping my porridge, 'You keep out o' that Tam McKinnon's house, my lad, for he is after doin' things that will bring the Peat Hags on him'." He brought his gaze from the sky to grin at a vexed Tam. "She told me lots more but there was no need for when the bells were ringin' last night I saw you all comin' out o' your headquarters an' you was drunk! That German airy-plane was already on the island then!"

There was a howl of derision from the fishermen that brought blushes to the faces of the Home Guard.

"Och, c'mon now, lads," soothed Tam earnestly. "Surely you are no' believing that foolish cratur. We might have had one or two wee drinks but needing them indeed for we were out all night lookin' for the Huns!"

But young Graeme Donald, a grand-nephew of old Annack, smiled with quiet radiance into the salt-washed faces of the other fishermen. "Are you hearing that now, lads? Everywhere else whisky is scarcer than virgins and here is our Tam bathing in the stuff. Great Aunt Annack might be a Cailleach but, by God! She has some nose on her face for sniffing out the hard stuff! She told me the time was near ripe for Tam's whisky an' it's here, lads! We just arrived in time!"

His words were met with a great whoop of approval that sent the gulls screaming from the harbour walls.

"I was goin' to tell you lads," assured Tam plausibly. "What way would I be wantin' all that whisky to myself? There's more than enough and I was just thinkin' comin' over the track that a shilling a pint wouldny be too much to ask . . ."

"Sixpence!" cried a hard-bitten old sailor. Tam looked sad but he was already leading the way to his house followed by an eager, thirsty mob.

Todd watched from his couch and his face brightened, thinking that he was about to be inundated by well-wishers but the minutes ticked on and he sighed, his idea of a long convalescence now looking less attractive.

A black shape flapped into view and stopped at the gate to look with sorrowful reproach at the tawny slopes of Sgurr nan Ruadh. Dodie was in a pitiful state. His grey-green eyes were sunk into his face like currants in a wizened treacle dumpling, and the grey-black stubble on his chin heightened the illusion of a fungus-covered reject. Having spent a harrowing, sleepless night, he had also spent a grief-stricken morning in a search for his beloved cow. His long, loping gait had carried him for miles and his huge wellington-encased feet, though used to a lifetime of hard work, were not without the usual painful properties of corns and callouses and now ached relentlessly. Tears coursed down the weatherbeaten indentations of his sunken cheeks, mixing with the frothing mucous from his nose. The frayed cuffs of his ancient mackintosh were soaked where he had drawn them frequently across his face.

Dodie was the last person Todd wanted to ceilidh with and for a long moment he considered the possibility of ignoring the presence of the island eccentric standing so pathetically at his gate. He knew, as did every other islander, that Dodie would never enter a house unbidden but hospitality was ingrained into the hardest of hearts; strupaks and ceilidhs extended to all whose lives were interwoven on Rhanna.

Todd shifted uncomfortably. The womenfolk hadn't noticed Dodie, they were so taken up with chatter. Todd observed Dodie's weary, drooping figure and suddenly felt terribly ashamed. Compared to the lonely, spartan existence endured by Dodie with little complaint, his life was one of gay companionship and homely comforts. But just as he was about to instruct Mollie to let Dodie in, a girl riding a bicycle whizzed up to the gate, braking so hard she almost fell over the handlebars.

Babbie propped Lachlan's bike against the gate and was immediately accosted by Dodie whose distress was such that he forgot to be embarrassed by the presence of a strange, young female.

"Have you seen Ealasaid, miss?" he sobbed, his carbuncle

wobbling wildly. Babbie's short time on Rhanna had allowed no time for her to become acquainted with the eccentricities that abounded on the green, surf-washed island. Someone less level-headed might have been scared out of their wits by Dodie's black-clad slobbering figure but Babbie was both sensible and soft-hearted. Her professional eye saw Dodie's terrible distraught condition and she curled her slim fingers round the big calloused hand resting on the fence. In normal circumstances he would have taken to his heels at such an intimacy but now he didn't even notice.

"When did you last see Ealasaid?" she asked gently. Her green eyes were flecked with amber giving them the translucent look of a clear sea freckled with seaweed. They were odd eyes, dreamily masking a million secrets yet they sparkled with soft lights of laughter and kindness. She was standing in front of Dodie and her red hair, which breathed of sunshine and all the bright fire of autumn, made the slopes of Sgurr nan Ruadh look dull in comparison. The pallor of her delicate, freckled skin was startling in its fiery frame yet oddly in keeping; her mouth was too generous for her to be beautiful but her smile so radiant that to observe it was to know enchantment.

The influence of her calm, sweet voice reached Dodie's disturbed mind. She had answered him in Gaelic and though it was not of the island he understood it just the same. In a whisper he said, "I let her out yesterday, it being such a fine day. I thought she would stay with the others in the pasture but she is a wanderer, just. I have never set eyes on her since and I'm feart the Germans will get a hold o' her. She has my milk you see and I'm needin' it bad for I have had no breakfast without it."

The resplendent rumbling of his empty stomach reminded him afresh of his plight and he scrubbed his hands into his sunken eyes.

Babbie searched her mind for words of comfort. She had only been able to understand some of Dodie's rather garbled explanation. She knew nothing of the type of existence he led but she recognised deprivation when she saw it.

"Please don't worry," she urged quietly. "All the Germans have been caught but one, and the Commandos are over on the moors looking for him now. I'm sure your wife will come home soon. Perhaps she stayed the night with a friend. I know one or two people did that last night."

Dodie stared aghast, his cheeks stained crimson at the very idea of owning a wife. It was well that Mollie appeared at the door just then for in his fright he was about to take once more to his heels.

"Come you in," called Mollie kindly, addressing Dodie but with the usual Gaelic hospitality including Babbie in the invitation.

"I was coming anyway," said Babbie, turning to undo her bag from the bicycle. "The doctor asked me to come over to have a look at the nurse and to see Mr McDonald."

Dodie had galloped thankfully into the cottage and Mollie smiled politely. "Of course, yes . . ." she hesitated. "You'll be Shona McKenzie's friend. I was hearing she was home for a nice wee rest and she was bringing a young lady for resting too." Mollie had a very whimsical way of expressing herself and a habit of cocking her head expectantly. Babbie sensed the unspoken questions and her smile cast its full radiance on Mollie.

"That's right, Mrs McDonald, I am here for a rest. My name is Babbie Cameron and I'm a fully trained nurse. The doctor is just finishing off up at Slochmhor. Phebie and Shona are helping out so I have been spared for a wee while."

Mollie had already fallen under the girl's spell and she beamed fondly. "My, how kind of you and you here for a holiday too. Come away in for a cuppy . . . a Strupak we calls it in these parts."

"I know that already, Mrs McDonald, and I'd love a cuppy."

"Ach, call me Mollie. We like to be informal here. The only time we are ever seeing our surnames is when we are reading them on our gravestones!"

Dodie's garbled explanation for visiting the cottage assaulted everyone's eardrums for a few moments but it was to Kate he addressed most of his apologies. "I was after seein' you up by the muir this very early mornin'," he moaned, fidgeting at the recollection, "and I was wondering if you or Tam had seen my Ealasaid thereabouts. I heard too you were in Glen Fallan a whily back and wondered was she there. She likes that nice green patch o' grass near the burnie . . ." He hesitated then finished in a gallop. "I was no' after seein' a thing wi' you and Tam this mornin' and no' knowing you were there till after I saw you!" Kate's face was red with suppressed mirth but she managed to mutter a few sympathetic remarks though none of them constructive.

Mollie took Dodie's arm and led him to the solid, wooden crofter's bench under the window which she opened discreetly. "I'll make you a nice strupak, you look like you could be doin' wi' something." She eyed his lumpy face with concern. "You're gettin' thin, Dodie. Are you feedin' yourself right?"

He seemed embarrassed by the question and stuttered quickly. "Ay, ay, right enough."

"I noticed you limping, Dodie," observed Babbie with deliberate carelessness for she had already assessed that the old eccentric was sensitive to personal remarks but her next words proved she didn't know him well enough. "If you take off your boots I'll have a look to see if you have any blisters."

Dodie looked positively terrified by the suggestion and slid slowly to the end of the bench. Todd let out a snort of mirth that hurt his stitches but didn't stop him muttering. "None of us is yet ready to go to the Lord with asphyxiation."

"I have not introduced anyone," intervened Mollie hastily. "This lass is Babbie Cameron, Shona's friend of a nurse and these . . ." She indicated Biddy and Todd. ". . . is the patients. If you'll be excusin' me . . ." She hastened away in search of the tea caddy because Todd looked positively aghast at the idea of a young girl 'looking at his condition'.

Biddy, after a short, indignant gasp, folded her hands on her stomach and lapsed into a grim silence.

"Which of you first?" asked Babbie cheerfully, setting down her bag to remove her coat. Beneath it she wore a green tweed skirt and a thick green jersey which enhanced the red fire of her curls. She was slim to the point of being skinny but though the sweater was in itself shapeless it couldn't entirely hide the curving swell of her soft breasts. Rhanna men liked their women 'well padded' and no matter how beautiful the face or figure of a slim woman she rarely merited a second glance after the first swift appraisal. It was a different matter if the slimness was enhanced by properly placed padding. In these circumstances a neat waist was an enticing place to hold on to before the hands started to explore further. Babbie fitted this category. Her bottom was well rounded, her breasts beautifully shaped.

Todd's eyes gleamed. He was changing his mind once more about the duration of his convalescence. "You had better do the Cailleach first," he said off-handedly. "At my age I am better able to endure things without complaint."

Biddy could contain herself no longer. Her foot was still throbbing; her ankle swollen to elephantine proportions. She needed no one to tell her she was going to be laid up for a while. But she had conjured up visions of an island mourning the suspension of her loving care. A temporary nurse would have to be sent for and everyone would see then how devotedly she dedicated herself to her patients. Now here was a slip of a lass, full of breathless smiles and caring words and if Todd's eager smile was anything to go on then the menfolk of the island would certainly be in their element. Biddy felt cheated and took no pains to hide her feelings.

"It's the doctor I'm wantin'," she said fretfully. "What qualifications would a child like you be having I'd like to know?"

Babbie's green eyes sparked but she answered evenly. "First of all I'm not a child, Miss McMillan. I was twenty-three on my last birthday and I have been an S.R.N. for three years, which means I'm also a fully qualified midwife. Furthermore . . ."

"Ach, stop boastin'," interrupted Biddy gruffly. "I'll take your word for it but you'd best see to the Bodach first. I'll be keepin' for a whily. I've survived this long after lyin' half dead all night while the doctor attends to Germans," she ended with an air of blatant martyrdom.

Todd was looking very aggrieved at being referred to as a 'Bodach' but he comforted himself with the thought that Babbie wouldn't have the Gaelic and would therefore be unaware he was the old man the word implied.

Babbie's firm little chin tightened even further at Biddy's words and she took matters into her own hands. "I think I'll look at you first, Miss McMillan. It can't have been very good for you spending the night out of doors at your age. Your ankle looks very swollen. No doubt you have sprained it."

"Strained!" asserted the flabbergasted Biddy.

"We'll see, but I'm sure I'm right." Babbie turned away quickly to hide the sprite in her dancing green eyes. "Could we have some sort of screen between the couches?" she wondered and Kate, thoroughly enjoying the lively exchanges, rushed once more for the blanket.

"Sprained right enough," diagnosed Babbie a few moments later. "What a good thing Mollie had the presence of mind to bathe it in cold water." At this point Biddy almost choked with indignation but Babbie went on coolly. "The doctor will have to confirm it certainly but meantime I will strap it up . . ." She squeezed the ankle gently. Biddy winced but remained aloofly silent, her eyes diverted from the charm of the girl's quizzical but sympathetic smile. "No ligaments torn, I'm sure," she went on. "But you're going to need a lot of rest. Do you have someone at home to look after you?"

"She lives alone in Glen Fallan," supplied Kate because Biddy's lips were pulled into her mouth so tightly they looked as though they would never open again.

"Oh." Babbie was nonplussed for a moment but Mollie, seeing a way of hastening Todd's recovery, said quickly, "Never a need to worry, my lassie. It will be a whily before Todd will manage the trek up to his own bed so Biddy and himself can while the time away together. It's what neighbours are for."

An audible groan broke the silence on the other side of the blanket and Biddy said grimly, "I will no' be staying here wi' that Bodach moaning all the time and watchin' my every move. Forbye – I have Bracken to see to and I have forgotten my teeths."

"Ach, I'll fetch your teeths," assured Mollie. "And we'll bring the cat down here. She'll be fine with our two."

A few inarticulate snorts issued from behind the blanket which finally emerged as a plea for the privacy a sick man was entitled to.

"Now don't be worrying about that," dimpled Kate. "I'll be coming in to help Mollie look after her two patients and if there's anything private needin' done we'll just whip up a curtain . . ." She turned to Babbie. "Are you good at givin' enemas, mo ghaoil?"

Babbie saw the mischief in Kate's eyes and she answered solemnly, "I'm an expert – always was, even as a greenhorn."

"A green what?" whispered Todd.

Kate fell into a rocking chair, narrowly missing an oblivious tabby cat. "What more could you ask for, Todd?" she choked ecstatically. "A nice young nurse to give you enemas and Biddy to peer under the blanket to make sure it doesny go in the wrong hole!" Laughter was robbing her of speech but she managed to gasp. "If you make too much noise we'll just tell all the folk on Portcull you're having a wee practice on the bagpipes!"

Babbie's examination of Todd was swiftly efficient but her youthful presence and undoubted femininity had overcome his earlier enthusiasm for her attention; he retained an embarrassed silence throughout.

"Everything is fine, Mr McDonald," she assured him firmly, sensing his unspoken doubts. Her green eyes held his for a moment and she placed her cool little hand on his arm. "Is there something troubling you?"

He gulped, opened his mouth, closed it and stared at a spider on the ceiling.

Mollie peeped round the blanket. "He is no' needin' the use o' his bladder, nurse," she said bluntly.

Babbie stopped in the act of raising her teacup to her lips and tried to decipher Mollie's quaint expressions. "He'll be needing to use it sometime, Mollie." She smiled mischievously. "Unless of course you're thinking of giving it away . . . Todd."

It was too much for Todd; his reserve dropped like a stone. "I canny pee, you daft lassie. Never a drop though I'm feelin' my bladder is burstin'."

She nodded. "This happens after an abdominal operation but it's nothing to worry about . . . just take plenty of fluids . . ." She paused because she had heard of his drunken condition the night before. "Non-alcoholic of course, and if that doesn't work, we'll try a catheter."

"In the right opening of course," mumbled Biddy irrepressibly and poor Todd was almost glad of the advent of Mairi who dithered and fussed over him till he really began to feel as important as his condition warranted. Dodie too came in for much of Mairi's attention. Her friends referred to her as 'a clockin' hen' because she enjoyed coddling and mothering people. With her adored William away at sea she had a surplus of affection and though she was able to spend a lot of it on her two long-suffering children, she still had plenty to spare.

Dodie let her cluck and fuss. She was the only female he would really tolerate without embarrassment. Somewhere in the depths of his simple, introverted mind was a sensing of her own lack of worldliness which made him respond to her with a touching, child-like trust.

"I'll away, then," smiled Babbie, going to the door and looking back at the cosy room with the peat fire glowing in the hearth flanked by the sofas on which reclined the disgruntled invalids.

"They'll be sendin' a spare nurse," intoned Biddy grumpily. "Just till I'm back on my feets," she added hastily.

"There's no immediate need," said Babbie patiently. "I've already told the doctor I'm willing to stand in for a while."

"Oh, but it will have to be done through the authorities," imparted Biddy. "Seein' you're just here for a holiday, it wouldn't be right to give the job to you. Anyways, you couldny stick it for more than a day or two, for these folks is no' easy to look after with a stranger. They're used to me and my ways."

For a moment Babbie leaned against the doorpost and wondered how she was going to face the days ahead. But already she had fallen in love with the island and its people with their contrary mixture of moods. She straightened up and said in Gaelic, "You pretend to be a tough Cailleach, Biddy McMillan, but your heart is softer than a sponge . . ." She smiled. "As for you, Todd McDonald, you'll never be a Bodach as long as you live!"

She walked quickly outside and shut the door, leaving behind such a babble of amazed exclamations that it took her all her self control not to shout out with laughter.

CHAPTER EIGHT

'Ealasaid Did It!'

It was getting on for evening when the Commandos ran Carl Zeitler to ground. The moors shimmered in a thick blanket of mist that seemed to stretch to eternity. It was an odd feeling. Rhanna was just a tiny island, isolated far out in the Atlantic, yet certain weather conditions made the great undulating shaggy blanket of the Muir of Rhanna reach out to drape over the world. During the long sparkling days of the Hebridean summers the illusion was heightened even further. The deep blue of the ocean, glimpsed between distant outcrops of perpendicular cliffs, was the cradle on which the heather-covered mattress lay, with the heads of the mountains rearing up into shrouds of gossamer mist. Then the land and the sea became as one with nothing between them and eternity.

The members of the Home Guard had long ago abandoned the moors for the comfort of more amiable pursuits. In the hours of daylight their interest had been sharp enough, with each man feeling a throat-catching excitement at the idea of being the first to capture the elusive German. But the twilight brought strange looming shapes to play on the whispering amber grasses. Cloud patterns danced on the aloof ruddy face of the winter moon and the shadows loomed over the moor.

The imaginative mind, fed from the breast on myths and folklore, saw the flapping cloaks of spooks and peat hags gliding over lost lonely places. The thin voice of the sea riding in on the breeze came only to breathe the life of the past into the eerie shadows. These were the nights of the witching island moon when fancy ran free and the crofters only left the comfort of their homes to see to their beasts or to walk a short distance to ceilidh in another warm house. The mist had rolled in from the sea in thick folds to drape itself over the island like a shroud. The search was now concentrated in the forsaken vicinity of the Abbey ruins and one by one the islanders slunk off into the mist as silently as their stoutly-booted feet would allow.

The Commandos had had a long tiring day, but that they were able to take in their stride. Having come to an island expecting to round up a whole flock of German invaders they had been disconcerted to discover that the whole thing was a false alarm and had quickly dispatched a message back to base to the effect that the mission would be accomplished much sooner than expected. Their irritation had evaporated quickly in the peaceful environment of Rhanna. Without being able to help themselves, each man had felt a reprieve from the serious and dangerous duties of the war. Despite a lack of military skills the islanders had somehow managed to net three Germans. The story of Tam McKinnon's capture of Ernst Foch was thoroughly appreciated by the Commandos and a mood that was almost festive descended upon them. Their search of the plane was carried out with the utmost efficiency and there appeared to be no sinister reason for its arrival on a remote Hebridean island. Dunn was sufficiently satisfied to report his conclusions back to base.

Only one German remained to be taken and on a small island like Rhanna that seemed an easy enough task. But they soon discovered how wrong they were. The terrain of Rhanna, while having a distinct character of its own, was nevertheless reminiscent of many of the Western Isles. The usual hazards of wide open spaces presented no problems to the Commandos. They knew about peat hags and peat bogs; they were familiar with the ebb and flow of the tides and, with the added advice gladly given by Righ, had already explored many of the deep dank caverns that yawned into the cliffs surrounding a greater part of the coastline. What they weren't so prepared for was a people so incurably addicted to the mythical legends of the moors that certain parts of it were taboo unless entry was essential. But the gregarious islanders always accompanied one another on such expeditions. The search for the German had been considered necessary and, on the whole, had been undertaken with curiosity. But the nearer the search got to the Abbey ruins the more enthusiasm began to wane. Lusty cries of merry banter became more subdued till eventually everyone spoke in whispers and took frequent peeps over their shoulders. Much of it was exaggerated but the effect was such that even the Commandos lowered their voices to eerie whispers.

"Is it the German you're afraid of?" mouthed Anderson to Torquil Andrew, a strapping figure of a man whose Norse colouring and piercing blue eyes made him a great favourite with the women.

Torquil didn't answer for a moment. He drew a big strong hand over his shaggy thatch and his blue eyes contemplated the craggy grey stones of the Abbey hunched together like old men sharing whispered secrets. "Na, na . . . tis no' the Germans," said Torquil without a hint of discomfort. "Thon's the place o' the ghosts and they don't like being disturbed."

"But it's an old ruin," persisted Anderson.

Torquil looked at him with pity and said heavily, "And all you know, eh? Yon's the hill o' the tomb, man. Underneath these hillocks is caves full of coffins. Walk on the turf above and waken the dead beneath!"

"And you all know where the openings of these caves . . . or tombs – are?"

"Some ay, some no'," was the general agreement.

"But they're all grown over and mustny be disturbed," whispered old Andrew, one of the best Seanachaidhs (reciter of tales) on the island, possessed of an imagination that turned the most mundane event into a thing of magic. He looked hastily over his shoulder and added, "The mist is gathering. Look now! It's creeping in over the sea and the Uisga Hags will be hidin' on the rocks near the shore. Sometimes they come right ashore in a mist and before you know where you are they are lurin' you out to sea where you will be after drownin'."

"The – Uisga Hags?" came the inevitable query.

"Ay, ay, the green water witches," explained old Andrew patiently. Thoughtfully he gathered a large gob of spit into his cheeks which he inflated several times before spitting to the ground with an expertise that left no traces on his lips. Staring at the frothy strings dangling on a grassy tussock he went on in deliberately dramatic tones, "They're the spirits o' witches cast out o' the island hundreds of years afore, an' they have just hung aboot haunting us ever since. Beautiful mermaids they be one minute but if you are out at your lobster pots an' dare to take your thoughts away from your work one look into the wicked green eyes o' a mermaid witch an' you're done for. There she changes into a wizened crone wi' whiskers an' warts an' she carries you off to the bottom of the sea to show you off to the other hags." His rheumy blue eyes twinkled mischievously. "Hard up for men they are down there on the bed o' the ocean an' the first thing they do is take your trousers off. It's the surest sign a man has been taken by the hags when his trousers float all limp and empty to the surface o' the sea!" It was the cue everyone needed to let out a subdued bellow of laughter, for there, on the open moor, with the wraiths of haar curling into the hollows, the tale and the tone of old Andrew's voice sent shivers up the spine.

But the Commandos were in no laughing mood when not long afterwards the islanders drifted away in twos and threes and were soon lost in the mist. The soldiers were now sure they had narrowed the search to Dunuaigh, but without knowledge of the hidden caverns beneath the heather they knew to search there would be useless and for a time they had stumbled about the Abbey ruins and searched thoroughly the cloisters of the crumbling chapel. But they were tired and hungry and wearily decided to head for Croy to see if they could borrow some form of transport to get them back over Glen Fallan. But half-way along the narrow little track to Croy they were apprehended by a white-faced Angus, the groom of Burnbreddie. He was seated at the wheel of a motor car but seeing the Commandos in front he slid to a halt beside them to stare in the manner of one stupefied by fear. "It is glad I am to have found you," he imparted hastily. "You have to take the motor car an' go along to the big house for dinner. Her leddy-ship is getting everything ready . . . the silly old bugger," he added under his breath.

"Thank you – but we half-promised Mr McKenzie to go back there for a meal," nodded Dunn politely.

Angus stepped cautiously from the car. "Na, na, you mustny do that. Her leddyship wouldny be pleased. I am going over to Croy to borrow a horse an' will ride down to Laigmhor to let McKenzie know you will not be comin'. He'll understand. We all know what her leddyship is like when she has a bee in her bonnet."

"We could drive down there and tell him ourselves, then you could ride back with us," offered Dunn.

"Na, na, I'll go quicker on the back o' a horse. I'm used to the beasts." He stood there, acutely aware of the smell that emanated from him in waves. That morning he had dosed himself with a generous measure of cascara to aid the function of his bowels, never dreaming that old Madam Balfour would order him to clean the car and drive to the top of the island to pick up the Commandos. The road to Croy was no more than a horse track over high cliffs with the sea thundering into caverns forty feet below and old Angus's cascara had worked faster than normal putting him in a very perplexing condition. Red-faced with embarrassment he nodded back towards the car and lied quickly. "I was taking a calf over to Croynachan yesterday and it shat the seat." Without waiting for an answer he sprachled away with startling agility in the direction of Croft na Beinn where he hoped to borrow a spare pair of trousers from Archie Taylor. He knew his plight would be met with a mixture of dismay, amusement, and the warm sympathy the island folk imparted to each other in times of distress. Later on the tale would be added to the store of anecdotes specially reserved for ceilidhs but at that moment Angus was beyond caring about the future. He was astute enough to know that he could lay the blame on Burnbreddie's doorstep and there it would remain forever, fantasised out of all proportion.

He had given the Commandos some hasty directions and on the journey over to Burnbreddie, with the sea surging and reverberating into hidden caves far below, Anderson commented, "No wonder the old boy crapped himself. I don't fancy too much of this myself!"

Madam Balfour of Burnbreddie, fairly bristling with importance, impatiently awaited the arrival of the Commandos. On hearing of their advent on the island she immediately plunged into preparations for a slap-up dinner which meant that all the best china was brought out for the occasion.

"But the men might not come, Mother," pointed out a half-amused Rena. "They are soldiers with all sorts of schedules to keep. I hardly think a dinner appointment might fit into their plans. From what I hear, their mission is to get the Germans off the island as quickly as possible. They won't have time to indulge in society chit-chat."

But her mother-in-law's prim little mouth tightened. "They *are* human beings, my dear girl, and must eat like the rest of us . . . besides . . ." A well-worn note of martyrdom crept into her tones. "We must all do our duty to our soldiers. I would hope that if my poor Scott was in a like situation he would be treated like the gentleman he is." She sniffed and a glimmer of tears sprang to her beady grey eyes. But Rena had witnessed such tears too many times to feel any sympathy and she said firmly, "I heard from Annie that Fergus of Laigmhor is providing for the Commandos."

"Hmph! That man!" The words were malicious because Madam Balfour had never seen eye to eye with strong-minded Fergus. "He has a cheek to take anyone into his home with the shameful reputation he has to his name . . . all those illegitimate children . . . it's a disgrace!"

"Mother!" Rena's voice was full of warning because she admired proud Fergus and she was also extremely fond of Kirsteen. "Stop exaggerating! If you're referring to little Grant you're the one who should be ashamed! We all know what happened there!"

"Oh, do we? That's all you know, my dear. There's a whole line of bastards in the family. What about our ladyship, Shona McKenzie? No more than a child herself giving birth in a cave like a common tinker! Of course, what can you expect on an island like this? They're hypocrites! The lot of them! Did you know about Alick? Just a schoolboy he was when he got a girl into trouble. If the silly girl hadn't miscarried there would have been another bastard for you. Hot-blooded gypsies! No control! That's my opinion of the McKenzies. It's a wonder poor Mirabelle doesn't turn in her grave. What she saw in them I'll never know . . . and my dear James – he thought the world of Fergus McKenzie. I have often wondered about that. James was such a gentleman – but of course you know all about that, Rena, Scott will have told you about his poor father . . . ah me . . . one remembers a generous heart."

She dabbed at her eyes and Rena could barely hide a smile. Her husband had regaled her with endless tales of his drink-sodden, womanizing father whose erotic appetites and thirst for alcohol had undoubtedly contributed to an early death.

Despite Rena's protest Madam Balfour got her way. It had been a long time since she had indulged in the social niceties which had once been a common occurence at Burnbreddie. The car was resurrected from the garage where it had lain unused since Scott's departure.

It was one of two cars on the island; the other was owned by Lachlan who had been talked into buying it by a doctor acquaintance who was shocked to find his colleague still using outdated modes of transport. After much persuasion Lachlan had acceded to the suggestion of a car but he felt embarrassed and out of place in a vehicle that made all eyes turn. He began to find the car more trouble than it was worth. Machines of any sort were regarded with amused suspicion on Rhanna. Few of the men were mechanically minded, including Lachlan himself who found it easier to manipulate a horse or a bicycle than he did a contrary starter-motor. With the coming of war, fuel was difficult to obtain and the car lay in a shed, used only for the most urgent cases on the farthest corners of the island.

The young laird, a keen horseman, seldom used the car which had been purchased at his mother's insistence that 'people of our standing ought to have a car'. To her it was a status symbol. Unlike Lachlan, she revelled in the attention when her son drove her round the bumpy island roads. With his going she could find no one else willing to drive the vehicle. Angus, the aged groom, used to a lifetime of caring for horses, resented the space the car took up in the stable buildings. He had been shown how to drive, 'aying' his way through the course of instruction then tucking the knowledge away in the furthest recesses of his mind in the hope he would never have to use it. Now here was 'her leddyship' disturbing the tranquillity of his mind with her latest whim, ordering him to drive a contraption that he hated with all his placid being.

During his absence Madam Balfour made merry with powder and rouge, changed into an absurdly outdated evening gown, then stormed down to the kitchen to rap out orders in her high-pitched imperative voice. Annie McKinnon, younger daughter of Kate, flounced about with a vigour that made the kitchen utensils clatter noisily. Although she could speak English in the charming

126

lilting way of every islander using it as a second language, she infuriated Madam Balfour by conversing only in the Gaelic. If the mood took her she surprised the old lady by mischievously throwing random English words into her conversation. Madam Balfour fumed and swore vengeance but Annie was a good worker and these were hard to come by on an island where people drifted dreamily through life and time was assessed by the seasons rather than the hands of a clock.

In the end Annie was the only one thoroughly at home with the guests. At first Madam Balfour was thrilled to discover two Englishmen among them. She babbled out reminiscences of her girlhood in London but she was speaking of an era that was of little import to anyone there. Her affectations only served to redden the faces of the English boys who suffered some teasing looks from their mates. Rena somehow managed to keep a conversation going but it was Annie, bouncing in and out with plates, who brought grins of appreciation from the men. Addressing them in perfect English she made sparkling remarks, she flirted and smiled, all the while avoiding Madam Balfour's disapproving eye.

After dinner the hostess led the way into a large oak panelled apartment which she grandly referred to as 'the evening room'. The Commandos sat uncomfortably on huge, well-stuffed sofas, balancing tiny cups on tiny saucers, and made polite, stilted conversation. Madam Balfour tried every tactic she knew to get the talk flowing but as her questions were mostly designed to ferret they were met with carefully guarded answers. She grew highly excited describing the 'near catastrophe' of the previous night, airing her imagination long and loudly that decent people weren't safe in their beds anymore. She went on at length about Behag Beag and her misinterpretation of the situation on the island.

"Of course the woman is a crank," she sniffed disdainfully. "I'll never understand the powers-that-be allowing such irresponsible people to carry out such frightfully important work. The whole episode was a shambles! Half of the so-called Home Guard were drunk when the plane came down. There's talk that they are brewing their own whisky now! Oh, I wouldn't put it past them! These people would drink all day if they could. They detest work, you know. No ambition, none at all . . ."

'Their own whisky," murmured one of the English boys thoughtfully. It was the first glimmer of interest shown by the men since their arrival and Rena hid a smile.

Soon after that they made their excuses and prepared to leave. "You poor, dear boys," mourned Madam Balfour when they were all assembled in the hall. "You must be so tired. Don't you think it would be wiser to call off your search till morning? There's plenty of room here. I would be only too pleased to . . ."

Dunn took her hand kindly. "You musn't worry about us. We're used to getting about the countryside in all conditions . . . we have plenty of torches . . . and . . ." He peered through the window. "It looks as if the mist has lifted a bit now anyway. Thank you for all your hospitality."

"A pleasure I'm sure," fluttered the old lady, her veneer falling away for a moment in gratitude for Dunn's thanks. For a few seconds a lonely old woman took cantankerous Madam Balfour's place but, just as quickly, she was herself again saying insistently, "You simply *must* take the car. It will save your poor feet and the headlights will be a help . . ."

"Mother, they'll never track anyone down in a car!" said Rena in exasperation. "This isn't a city, it's an island!"

"It's for the war effort," came the irrelevant reply. "We must all share what we have. The car will get them around much quicker."

"Straight into the Atlantic," murmured Rena and the men smiled rather sheepishly.

Annie came into the hall, wearing a green woollen cape that contrasted delightfully with her dancing black curls. "Did I hear someone mention a car?" she dimpled. "My, I could be doing with a lift down to Portcull. My man will be wantin' his tea and I might get lost in the mist."

Dunn smiled at Madam Balfour. "We'll accept your kind offer – er – your ladyship. Can't have a young lady getting lost in this weather. After we have delivered her safely we can cut inland through the Glen Fallan road till we get to the moor."

The old lady was speechless as the men, muttering polite thanks, turned and went down the steps with a mirthful Annie at their heels.

"Annie!" Madam Balfour found her voice.

"Yes, my leddy?"

"You pretend not to speak English, yet all evening you have spoken nothing else!"

Annie's brown eyes opened wide in surprise. "But, my leddy, they were not understanding the Gaelic!"

"Neither do I, Annie, yet you use no other language with me."

"Och, my leddy," dimpled the roguish Annie, "it is just that I am thinkin' you will be learning it better that way. I'll be bidding you goodnight . . . and thanking you for the loan of the car!"

The door closed and Madam Balfour fumed. "I am going to give that girl notice! I won't stand her cheek another day!"

"Of course, Mother," said Rena who had heard the threat a hundred times. She turned and went upstairs to tuck in her two little sons, leaving Madam Balfour to flounce back to the evening room where she poured herself a good measure of brandy which she kept 'for her heart'.

The delighted Annie pressed herself in between two soldiers on the roomy back seat of the Austin. "It's grateful I am," she said breathlessly. "That old Cailleach would have kept me there all night." She looked round the interior of the car appreciatively but said doubtfully, "It's a nice machine for a car but I don't like the smell of that petrol stuff and there's nothing left afterwards to make use of. With our old horse you just shove hay in one end and it comes out manure the other!"

The men found Annie an entertaining companion and laughed gaily as the car jogged down the winding driveway of Burnbreddie. Once past the little clachan of Nigg the road twisted higher over cliffs that dipped basalt columns into the swirling sea far below. At times the way was so narrow it seemed a certainty that the offside wheels would career out into thin air. Natural corrosion had eaten away the soft crumbling earth on the clifftops and it was only a matter of it being held together by a tangle of roots.

Dunn would have liked to leave the road and drive on the stony turf to the nearside but a deep soggy ditch, coupled with groups of cud-chewing sheep bedded down on the roadside for the night added to the other hazards. Rhanna sheep gave no precedence to anything on wheels. The island was theirs to roam as they liked and the noisy motor car was just another intrusive object to bleat at with disdain.

Dunn weaved the car around the potholes, tried not to think of the horrific drop to the sea, wound his way round the groups of unyielding sheep, and told himself he was of the stuff that was trained to face anything. But when the mist swooped down again, thicker than ever, rising higher till he couldn't see the cliffs and the only things visible were the strange yellow orbs of the sheep's eyes glinting in the headlights, he began to wonder about his nerve. Annie appeared not to notice the hair-raising hazards of the journey. To her the Commandos were beings with super-human qualities and with that simple philosophy in mind she chattered gaily. The mist lifted slightly and in the distance the bell tower of the old Kirk loomed and beside it the tall chimneys of the Manse.

"Ach, these poor Germans," imparted Annie earnestly. "They'll be gettin' their punishment right enough. My God, but yon minister will be havin' them on their knees prayin' for their souls to get into Heaven. I am hearin' he wants to have a ceilidh for them – him that doesny even know what the word means. He was after tellin' Torquil Andrew of Ballymhor that he wants the Jerries to carry a picture of Scottish hospitality to the prison camps they will be goin' to."

The Commandos were making slightly inarticulate sounds as Annie blithely prattled on. A ceilidh for the Germans! They knew then that they had come to another world, one that knew little of the conventions that stifled the individuality of the so-called sophisticated communities over the ocean. Even while they were amazed they couldn't help exchanging smiles of delight.

A warm little blob of light shone through the mist and Annie exclaimed, "Ach, would you look at that! Dokie Joe never draws the curtains. I keep mindin' him of the blackouts but I would be as well tellin' the sheeps."

Dunn stoped the car and Annie jumped out, but turned her merry face to impart cheerfully, "It's grateful I am. And don't be worrying – you are not the only ones nearly shat the seat coming over that damt road!" She roared with laughter at the men's discomfited looks then instructed, "Wait you here a wee minute. I have something will put the bile back in your belly."

She was back in minutes in a swirl of mist and a tang of peat smoke. She proffered a small bottle. "Here, each take a good swallock. I will not be leavin' this spot till you do."

The soldiers 'swallocked' obediently and there followed a few well-controlled splutters followed by a short, surprised silence.

" 'Tis the Uisge-Beatha!" giggled Annie. "That means the water o' life . . . a real taste o' malt from the Fallan itself."

Dunn felt a glow travelling down into his belly. "It's grand stuff, Annie. Did you make it yourself?"

"Ach, that would be telling. You should know better than ask that." She lowered her voice. "If you catch that other German and get over to the Manse with him you'll be havin' a taste more of it. You will never get off the island in this mist. It will do no harm to wait till mornin'. The Jerries won't be running away and yon poor bugger at Slochmhor looks like he might be dyin' at any minute . . . if the Lord spares him. The minister told Torquil only to be askin' teetotallers but there being few of those on the island we'll be havin' a merry time." She began to move away but called over her shoulder, "We'll be seeing you later then!"

The Commandos discussed the logic of Annie's words as they drove into Portcull and finally decided it would indeed be foolish to leave the island in present weather conditions. The haar was growing thicker by the minute, rolling banks of it swathed the countryside, swallowing sights and sounds into its damply voracious throat.

Dunn wanted to report the latest developments via the Post Office transmitter and he stopped the car at Behag Beag's cottage. He rapped the door but there was no answer and he stood in the silence, feeling the raw cold of the sea seep through his clothing. Occasionally a meek little puff of wind blew the mist into swirling wisps, revealing the blurred face of the moon peering in sullen anonymity through the hazy curtain. It was during such a break that Robbie's round face hove into view. At sight of Dunn his eyes widened and a look of embarrassment settled on his homely features. "Ach, it is yourself, lad!" he greeted with affected affability. "Can I be helping you at all?"

With much sympathetic nods and 'ays' he heard the officer out then put a stubby finger to his lips. "She's no' talkin' to a soul," he intoned dismally. "All day I am hearin' nothing but silence.

I used to think it would be heaven to hear her mouth shut now I am thinkin' she's even more hell wi' her lips closed. The air is noisy wi' her silence! If it's into the Post Office you're wantin' you'd best get Righ. He has a set o' keys him needing access to the contraption."

But Dunn would have none of that and said firmly, "I am certainly not going all the way up to the lighthouse in this weather. Your sister has a duty to perform and I will see that she does it!"

The authority of the words almost took Robbie's breath away but he summoned enough to say meekly, "Indeed, just, but I was seeing you wi' a wee wireless contraption of your own. Could you no' be using that to send out a message?"

"It isn't quite adequate for my purpose, Mr Beag. Will you please tell your sister that the Commando officer wants to see her?"

"Ay, yes, well . . ." Robbie floundered helplessly then he straightened his shoulders and pushed open the door. "In you come then and be telling her yourself."

Behag was sitting in the kitchen, her scraggy figure outlined against the grudging light from seedy flames that were curling half-hearted tongues round the damp peats. On her knee sat an equally rigid black cat. In a corner of the range a fire besom was propped and, to anyone with a flicker of imagination, it wouldn't have been difficult to picture both woman and cat climbing aboard the broom and whizzing into space to the waiting witchery of the island moon.

Robbie made a dash to the scullery where he splashed cold water into a basin. He had heard about the Manse ceilidh and saw a chance to get out of the house for the night. Far better to spend the night Psalm singing than to sit by a grate where even the very peats seemed to spit out their disapproval while he polished his guns and 'listened' to Behag's silence.

Behag neither moved nor spoke at the intrusion into the cottage, but her clamped lips grew tighter as Dunn started to speak. He was firm but was also possessed with a fine tact. In a few words he dispelled Behag's guilt and made her feel an important ally in the war game.

"I would like you to accompany me to the Post Office, Mistress Beag," he finished courteously. "To be truthful, I am not acquainted enough with the machine to get the best from it." He smiled charmingly. "It is not exactly the most up-to-date transmitter but I am sure that is no deterrent to a woman like you . . . you are in a very important position you know, Mistress Beag . . . you and the Coastguard are probably our two best assets on the island."

Behag was blossoming like a wilted plant revived by water. Her jowls, which had been sunk in several wizened layers on to her neck, unfolded one by one into taut furrows as she slowly tilted her head heavenwards. In a silent flurry of gratitude she thanked the Lord for allowing her to keep her dignity despite all the gossip and the taunts she had endured in silence all day.

"Of course I'll accompany you," she said tightly, then added irrelevantly, "The peats is damp," which was her way of apologising for the cheerless hearth. The black cat was deposited without ceremony on to the floor and she scurried to get the keys of the Post Office.

Robbie looked up from drying his face on a towel which bore the family crest of Burnbreddie, scrubbed and rubbed by Behag till it was only just discernible. "I am playing a game of chess with poor auld Todd tonight," he lied obliquely. "So you will no' be needin' to wait up wi' my supper, Behag."

She gave him a look that would have quelled the stoniest of hearts and he sighed, knowing that the 'silent treatment' was going to last for a very long time. Later, when she could justifiably lift up her head again, the population of Rhanna was destined to hear repeatedly the story of the gallant Dunn, 'an officer and a gentleman, just', who, when her very own kith and kin had forsaken her, gave her the strength to carry on. But for the moment it was enough that her spindly legs carried her swiftly to the Post Office. There, with great attention to detail, she lovingly explained the workings of her machine. Dunn yawned in the darkness, listened for as long as he could bear, then with a great urgency instilled in her his need of haste in the matter.

On the drive through Glen Fallan he regaled his men with the tale. "I fully expected the old witch to whisk me away on her broomstick," he finished, adding, "Poor old Robbie is only her brother but more henpecked than any husband I know. Apparently it was because of him she blew her fuses last night! He's scared to go into the house now."

Anderson leaned forward. "I don't know about you chaps but I'm all for getting this German geezer double quick. We could have a bit of fun at this Manse ceilidh . . . try a bit more of this water of life stuff. The doctor gave me some earlier and Annie has whetted my appetite for more."

Dunn nodded. "Suits me, but I want two ticks in at Laigmhor to apologise for dinner and you can hop along into the doc's to see how Büttger is."

Fifteen minutes later they were on their way once more. Despite the mist and the bumpy road they were in a cheerful mood. When they could take the car no farther they left it beside the wreck of the German bomber and continued on foot. The light from the moon now filtered down in nebulous uncertainty but it was enough to show the men they were on safe ground. They were breasting the oddly rectangular plateau of Dunuaigh when a series of hideous bellows penetrated the blankets of vapour, splitting the silence asunder. The men stood listening, unable to control the heart-pounding flow of adrenalin that poised them ready for action. Some way distant the Abbey ruins lurked, grey towers humped broodingly up through the sea of mist.

"No wonder the islanders give this place a wide berth," hissed Brown, his fingers caressing his gun. "That sound came from under us . . . where the monks' tombs are supposed to be."

"Oh, c'mon, Brown!" gritted Dunn. "You ought to know better than that. Let's all get down there – carefully."

As they scrambled their way to the base of Dunuaigh the unearthly bellows came again.

"It's a bloody cow!" mouthed Brown in tones of relief. "I'm sure it's a bloody cow!"

"Bloody or otherwise we'd best have a look," returned Dunn leading the way through snagging bramble and gorse. The light from their torches bounced back at them from the amber eyes of a group of sheep who bleated balefully at the disturbance. A few moments later all was silent again but for the sigh of the sea moaning low through the heather scrubs. It was all so peaceful it put the men off guard for a moment. None of them was quite prepared for the terrible cacophony of raucous roars, grunts and snorts which erupted just about seven feet from where they were crouched.

"Christ!" rasped Brown. "That's the second time tonight I've nearly parted company with my guts!"

The sounds came from within a ramshackle tin hut that had been built into the hillside and was sometimes used as an extra shelter by the tinkers who came every summer to the island. A discernible flow of guttural German abuse now accompanied the cow concert and the Commandos knew they had found their man. It took much heaving and pushing to open the door of the shed because Ealasaid was leaning against it in her amiable bovine fashion, tufts of her wiry hair pricking out of the many knot-holes in the rotting wooden planks the tinkers had used to hold the hut together.

"Get me out! Get me out!" screamed Zeitler who had reached the stage when he wouldn't have cared if his rescuers had been Martians.

But five minutes elapsed before Ealasaid condescended to heave her bulk away from the door giving the Commandos the chance to ram the barrels of their guns through the opening. But Zeitler was in no condition to resist capture, he was glad to see the men and his pale eyes bulged with relief. The stench in the hut was unbearable for Ealasaid had not only urinated liberally; she had also relieved her bowels in the uninhibited way that cows have. In the cramped quarters of the hut Zeitler had been unable to escape the results and his flying boots were thickly coated in dung.

His haggard face was showing the effects of the harrowing hours he had put in since his landing near the Abbey ruins on the Muir of Rhanna. He had soon sought the shelter of the hut. His idea had been to stay in the hut till the moment of his inevitable capture and wrapping himself in his parachute he had fallen asleep on a rickety, planked bench. Awakened by the sound of tramping feet he had thought the time of capture was at hand but a peep through a hole in the tin cladding revealed the rotund silhouettes of several cows muching at a small patch of juicy grass among the heather roots. The cold light of dawn shone on plump, blue-veined udders and Zeitler suddenly knew where breakfast was coming from. But he knew nothing of cows and their ways. The hill cattle were not only self-willed, they were cunning with it and watched the inexperienced Zeitler with disdain while they flicked nonchalant tails and glared balefully from long-lashed eyes. Every time he lunged at one it pranced out of reach with unexpected agility, resuming grazing with what appeared to be placid intent of purpose, belied only by a watchful eye rolled in Zeitler's direction. It was Ealasaid who finally succumbed to the guttural coaxings issuing from the ridiculous figure now kneeling in the heather. Ealasaid was thinking of her morning feed of fresh hay which her faithful master fortified her with while he stripped her udder. Zeitler looked as though he was proffering some tasty tit-bit in his big hands and Ealasaid took a pace or two forward. Encouraged, the German held the palms of his hands temptingly forward and the curious Ealasaid could contain herself no longer. She broke into a trot and Zeitler's face broke into a grin.

But the temptingly proffered hands held nothing but a rather nasty unwashed odour and Ealasaid blew her nostrils disdainfully over them. Zeitler caught her shaggy mane but she shook herself free and butted him playfully with her huge head. Each time she did so he retreated in fright till eventually he turned tail and ran to the shed. Behind him galloped Ealasaid, reaching him in time to butt him on to the bench where he sprawled his full length. Ealasaid reversed, her heavy rump clattering the door shut and it had remained so all day, literally jammed tight by the cow's great bulk.

In the course of the day Zeitler had bawled himself into exhaustion and slept fitfully on the bench while Ealasaid sprayed him with dung and urine. In desperation he managed to grab one of her teats and direct jets of creamy milk down his throat and in the process many of the badly aimed squirts washed over his face and soaked his clothing. But Ealasaid had a daily yield of three gallons. As the day wore on she became increasingly uncomfortable and exceptionally hungry. At first her soft little moans could barely be heard but two hours prior to the arrival of the Commandos she had maintained an incessant bellowing that had nearly driven Zeitler out of his mind. He almost fell into Dunn's arms muttering over and over, "Danken Gott! Danken Gott!"

"That cow," indicated Brown with a nod. "Isn't that the one the old hermit described to us this afternoon?"

He was referring to an encounter with Dodie, who, with Erchy acting as interpreter, had sobbed out the story of his lost cow. Dunn looked at Ealasaid. "You're right, Brown. Get your rope round its neck and we'll take it with us. Might as well collect the whole baggage. The old bloke's house is up past Nigg I believe."

"Aren't we going back to the car?" asked a weary Anderson. "It would be quicker to drive back over the Pass."

"It's a fair walk back to Croynachan," pointed out Dunn. "It will be easier to nip over to Burnbreddie and borrow a horse and trap from the Duchess. I'm sure she'll be delighted to help the war effort and no one is going to steal her car. To be honest I don't fancy driving about in this muck, a trap will be safer."

"Over that road again!" groaned Brown.

"Never mind," consoled Dunn. "The old dear might offer to lend us her groom as well – that's if he hasn't died of a heart attack!"

As it happened Madam Balfour had been lifted out of the doldrums by three large brandies. She welcomed the Commandos profusely, showered extravagant praise upon them, flared her nostrils in repugnance at Zeitler and finally sent word to Angus to escort the Commandos safely to the Manse.

Sniffing and grumbling, Angus hitched the horses to the trap and tied Ealasaid's rope. He hadn't bargained for another meeting with the Commandos and hid his embarrassment in dour words but as they were trundling down the driveway he began to chortle with subdued joy.

"I'll be gettin' to the ceilidh after all," he explained with a gleefully wicked grin. "Now that I have an excuse to be goin' to the Manse," he added hastily. He glanced at Zeitler huddled in the back seat. "We'll be showin' the Jerries a bit o' life right enough but I'm hopin' this one will be changing his clothes and scrubbing the dung from his feets before he gives us a Highland fling. He smells terrible just!"

The words were uttered without the hint of a blush and though Anderson strangled a snort Angus ignored it, turning a dignified attention to the horses which he handled with a loving expertise. Just outside Nigg they left the cliff road, taking the hill track to Dodie's house.

"Aren't we taking the cliff road to Portcull?" asked Brown.

"Na, na, the hill is safer in this haar. A wee ways longer mind but better than the cliffs. Anyways, we are handing the cow into old Dodie. He lives along the way, here."

"And the hill track takes you back along to Portcull?" asked Dunn faintly.

"Ay, that's right. But what way do you ask? Annie would have taken you by here earlier."

"We went by the cliff road," said Anderson bitterly.

Angus shook his grey head indulgently. "Ach, but she is a terrible lassie, just. The wee bitch should have told you but the cliffs is quicker to Portcull if you aren't after landin' in the sea. She'd be wantin' to get home quick an' get ready for the ceilidh."

Dodie's face was a study of transfixed wonder when the trap arrived at his door and his beloved Ealasaid was unhitched.

"My bonnie lassie," he muttered huskily, and scrubbed the tears of joy from his eyes. He loped forward and entwined his long arms round her hairy neck. "You bugger, I could kill you so I could," he moaned happily. "Look you, my poor beastie, your udder is about burstin'. Come now and let Dodie get dinner for us both."

Old Angus repeated the story told to him by the Commandos and Dodie erupted into a state of delirious joy. "Ealasaid did it!" he whispered in awe. "She caught an enemy all by herself! Ay, my God! My Ealasaid should get a decoration right enough! I'm hearing they give them to people they calls heroes. Ealasaid is a hero!"

In a haze of joy he led the cow away and for the rest of his life it was his belief that the credit for Zeitler's capture lay firmly at the door of Ealasaid's byre.

138

CHAPTER NINE

The Manse Ceilidh

The Rev. John Gray had never in all his years on Rhanna felt quite so fulfilled or so important as he had done since the two Germans, Ernst Foch and Jon Jodl, were delivered into his care the night before. He had always felt uncomfortably out of his depth when carrying out his pastoral duties among a people who sensed his lack of confidence and also his slightly superior attitude towards them. He had always given them the impression that he regarded them as heathens whose only sure salvation lay in a conscientious Kirk attendance coupled with a selfless devotion to 'The Book' and its teachings.

But his methods of trying to bring God to the people were hopelessly out of keeping with the simple faith of the Hebridean people. His theological sermons were away above the heads of the majority of parishioners and matters weren't helped by his stern refusal to learn the Gaelic which was the only language that many of the older inhabitants understood. He had of course picked up the odd Gaelic word and an intelligent man such as he could easily have learned it all. But he felt that to do so would be to encourage the easy-going islanders to take a step back in time. What he failed to see was a proud little community of Gaels struggling to hold on to a culture that was their inheritance. In the name of progress too much had already been taken away but no one could rob them of their individuality. They had met the so-called civilised world half-way, but had no intention of stepping over the border to be swallowed into anonymity for ever more.

So the Rev. Gray laboured on under his delusions and the barriers between himself and the people of Rhanna remained firmly erect. Lachlan, anxious about the condition of Jon Jodl, had called in at the Manse late that morning. It was an oddly disquieting sensation to see two Commando guards at the door, the guns slung over their shoulders glinting dully in the hazy sun.

But the interior of the Manse was quiet and peaceful. The smell of broth wafted from the kitchen and a plump cat sat washing its whiskers in the hallway. Ernst Foch and Jon Jodl were ensconced in the drawing-room with the minister who was conversing with them in reasonable German. On the table the big family bible lay open and Lachlan felt a quiver of sympathy for the Germans. They were obviously receiving the 'hell, fire and water' treatment but neither of them appeared dismayed by the fact. Both were clean and polished looking and had obviously benefited from a hot bath, which must have entailed a great deal of work because the low-lying position of the Manse made it unsuitable for a natural supply of piped water.

Jon courteously let Lachlan examine him. The dazed look in his eyes had been replaced by one of quiet peace; a warm flush on his thin, boyish face had dispelled the cold pallor of the early morning.

"Ask him how he feels, John," Lachlan instructed the minister.

There followed a few guttural exchanges, then the minister turned a beaming face. "He says he is well and very happy. God is finding a good disciple in this boy – eh, Lachlan?"

But the doctor shook his head. "No, John, I don't think so. He has withdrawn into a little fool's paradise, that's all. The shock of last night is still there under the surface but I think when he landed on Rhanna he saw it as an escape from the hell of war. He got out of it just in time I think – some can take it – others . . ." He spread his fine hands and shook his dark head again, the look in his brown eyes quelling the protests the minister was getting ready to throw out.

Instead Gray said querulously, "You think the Lord had nothing to do with it then?"

Lachlan gave him a strange look. "God has to do with everything. Why else do you think the boy landed on a Hebridean island just when his mind was ready to snap?"

"You're right, Lachlan! You're right!" came the joyous boom. "Oh, dear God! If only I could get through to the people here the way I've got through to these boys, ah, happy days then!"

"Ach, stop havering, man!" cried Lachlan, showing a rare flash of temper. "You're talking to these men in their own language! When have you ever bothered to do that to the islanders?"

The minister's face showed a mixture of emotions but it wasn't anger that made him flush red and quickly change the subject. "Will you stay and have some dinner with us, Lachlan? Hannah is preparing it now. You look done in, you know. The people here take you too much for granted."

"It wasn't the people of Rhanna who kept me up all night," Lachlan replied meaningfully. "Thank you for the invitation, but Phebie will have my dinner ready. I thought to have time to call in at the Smiddy to see how Todd is but I will have to leave it till afternoon now."

The minister cast his eyes heavenwards and shook his head sadly. "Ah yes, Mr McDonald – a terrible business – drunk I believe . . ."

"What about this chap?" interrupted Lachlan, glancing at Ernst who was sitting quietly with his hands folded on the table, his large, squarish head sunk on to his chest. "Has he been saying much? He was as healthy as a horse when I examined him last night."

The minister beamed proudly at Ernst. "I can honestly say that this boy has listened to everything I have been saying – taking it all in. Repentance . . . one can always tell when repentance takes the place of rebellion. Both he and Jon are naturally concerned about their comrades. Jon in particular keeps asking about his commander, Anton Büttger. They know there was no one left in the crashed bomber but they worry still about their companions. It just shows – their hearts are in the right place – eh, Ernst?"

He gave the wireless operator a hearty swipe on the back which made him jump, his heavily lidded eyes hooding the contemptuous look he threw at the minister who had bored him into despair. Ernst came from a good Christian family and had been brought up with faith in God instilled into his boyhood mind. But in his latter years his devotion to the Führer had swamped his thoughts till the advent of his wife and son had reawakened in him his early ideals, killing off his worship for the Nazi leader. In his present, bewildered mood, Ernst would have welcomed a few gentle reminders about the Heavenly Father but he was unable to take the heavy stuff that had been poured into his ears since breakfast. He was too weary to listen. Imprisonment loomed on his horizon and he knew it would be a long time before he saw his family again. In silence he had let the minister's words wash over him till he sank into a comatose state of gloomy oblivion.

Mrs Hannah Gray popped her head round the door to announce that dinner was ready and Lachlan took his departure. Hannah Gray was a much less overpowering personality than her overbearing husband. Her years with him had taught her that silence was the best form of defence against his forceful outlook on life. She felt a great sympathy for the Germans and they responded to her kindness with courteous gratitude.

The idea of the ceilidh at first dumbfounded Mrs Gray but the more she thought about it the more excited she became. During her years on the island she had often longed to throw a ceilidh in keeping with tradition, but her husband wouldn't hear of it, telling her sternly that such events were only excuses for uninhibited drinking bouts and an invitation to the devil to wreak havoc in drink-weakened minds.

Mrs Gray made do with giving Strupaks; but her visitors were stiffly formal and always looked poised ready for flight. By contrast, whenever she dropped into a neighbour's croft, a Strupak was a gaily informal affair. She had never ceilidhed in the long, dark nights of winter, and when passing a cottage gay with laughter and song, she had often longed to join the merrymakers but knew that her presence would only embarrass them.

Now, a ceilidh of her very own! The very thought sped her steps to the kitchen which was soon fragrant with the smell of baking. "It must be referred to as more of a praise meeting," the minister had warned her righteously but when Torquil Andrew appeared at the kitchen door with the sack of potatoes she had asked to buy from him she gaily told him the news.

"A ceilidh, Torquil." She beamed happily. "Here in the Manse – tonight. Tell your friends about it . . . but . . ." She put a warning finger to her lips and screwed her face into a conspiratorial grimace. "You know Mr Gray doesn't like the drink so . . . only those who don't."

Torquil's handsome face broke into a wide grin at the idea of a whiskyless ceilidh. Laughing loudly he pulled the small dumpy Mrs Gray into his bronzed arms and waltzed her round the kitchen. "A ceilidh, Mrs Gray! Just what we could be doing with. Mind though – some might no' like the idea o' drinkin' tea, wi' the Jerries. But I'll be gettin' a few folks together, never you fear, mo ghaoil."

He went off to spread the news and Mrs Gray turned back to peer with pleasure into the oven where a batch of scones were rising in fluffy puffs. "It will be a fine ceilidh," she whispered into the depths of the oven. "And even though John will make everyone sing hymns I'm sure it will be a success just the same."

But not even Mrs Gray was quite prepared for the unprecedented triumph of her first ceilidh. It started quietly with only a handful of islanders shuffling through the door to look in uncomfortable silence at Jon and Ernst sitting meekly together on a huge wooden settle.

"My, it's a course, course night!"

"Cia mar a Tha!" (How are you?)

The first arrivals muttered embarrassed exchanges in a mixture of English and Gaelic, then arranged themselves in silence around the big cosy room.

"A dreich night," observed Merry Mary sadly, unwilling to relinquish the safe topic of the weather conditions.

"Ay, ay, right enough," came the sage agreements but after one or two similar observations the company grew unnaturally quiet, the focal point for all eyes being the crackling coal fire which everyone stared at with undivided attention.

Mrs Gray looked round in dismay. But for the two Germans, old Andrew and Mr McDonald, better known as Jim Jim, the company was made up entirely of elderly women, and Mrs Gray knew that a good ceilidh needed a fair number of each sex to liven proceedings. She looked at old Andrew who sat with his fiddle cuddled on to his knee. He appeared faintly out of his depth among such an odd company, fidgeting first with his bow, then with a pipe-cleaner which he poked into the depths of an ancient briar, extracting a great amount of an obnoxious tarry substance that was deposited carefully on the bars of the fire.

Jim Jim was sitting about three feet from the hearth, a distance that was no deterrent to the well-aimed flow of spit which he shot across the intervening space at regular intervals. The sound of it roasting on the coals filled the room and the gathering stared at the popping bubbles with what appeared to be an avid interest.

Mrs Gray leaned over to Isabel McDonald and said in an anxious whisper, "I wonder what has happened to Torquil and the other men. He seemed delighted when I told him about my ceilidh. What if no one else comes?"

Isabel McDonald looked at her in wonderment. "Ach, mo ghaoil! It's the way o' things. The younger ones will ceilidh at each other's houses first! They always do. When they gather up enough o' a crowd they will be comin' round here sure enough – or maybe staggering more like!"

Mrs Gray looked at her in horror. "Oh, but John will never . . ."

At that moment the Rev. Gray came running downstairs and into the room. "What . . . nobody singing yet?" he bellowed lustily. "Where is Morag Ruadh? She should be at the piano by now!"

Isabel McDonald knew that her red-haired, quick-tempered daughter was passing her time at the door with two Commando guards. For long, Morag had been a source of worry to her elderly parents because though past forty she had, as yet, failed to find herself a suitable marriage partner. Morag, with her red hair and nimble body was not an unattractive woman but she laboured under a delusion that she alone was responsible for the welfare of her ageing parents. This had embittered her outlook on life to some extent and her scathing tongue quickly scared off any would-be suitors. Contrary to Morag's beliefs, her parents were longing to be free of her spicy tongue and they were quick to encourage the attentions of any men that chanced their daughter's way.

"Morag has been kept back tonight, she will be along later, Mr Gray," said Isabel glibly. Inwardly she prayed. "Forgive me, God, for my sinful lies but Jim Jim and myself are no' able to take Morag all our years. It is wrong I know, Lord, to let a man up your skirts out o' wedlock but this looks like the only way Morag will ever catch one. Let this be the night of such a sinful happening so that the poor bugger who does it will feel obliged to marry her. Forgive us all and keep us pure, Amen.'

The minister's voice thundered out imperatively. "Where is everybody? We must have more men for the singing. Bring in the guards! There's no need for them to be out there now!"

Jim Jim looked at him and said in tones of slight reproof, "There I must disagree wi' you. You mustny be forgettin' there is still another Hun to be caught. You wouldny like a big German charging in here to us defenceless people and shootin' us all down like dogs. Would you now?"

"Pray God, of course not, but ..."

"Then leave the sojers be the now. You can be bringin' them in when the other lads bring in the Hun, we'll be needin' guards then wi' three Jerries about the place."

"Well, all right ... yes, surely, you're right, Mr McDonald."

Jim Jim sat back amid nods of righteous approval from the gathering while outside one Commando remained at the door and the other walked casually with Morag Ruadh into the Rev. John Gray's fuel shed. Morag Ruadh was in an unusually abandoned mood. Earlier in the evening she had complained to Kate McKinnon of feeling 'a cold coming down' and Kate had made her drink a generous amount of the Uisge-Beatha. After the first mouthful and the first spate of indignant outrage at what she told Kate was 'an evil trick, just' she had thirsted after more of the water of life, whereupon a liberal Kate had sold her a pint for just ninepence. Arriving home Morag informed her parents she was going into the scullery to 'steam her head'. With a great show of preparation she put Friar's Balsam into a bowl of hot water then repaired to the privacy of the scullery where she spent a solitary hour alternately 'steaming her head' and tippling from the cough bottle which she had carefully filled with whisky.

Now she was ready to throw caution to the winds. She was neither drunk nor sober but had arrived at that happy state where no obstacles loomed in the horizons of life and all things were possible, even for a forty-two-year-old spinster. Her gay mood showed in a softening of her ruddy features. She looked almost pretty with a green homespun shawl reflecting the green of her eyes and showing to advantage the bright gleam of her fiery hair. It mattered not to her that the Commandos were years younger than herself. They were men, exciting men at that, so different from the withdrawn, easy-going, males of the island. She giggled and gave the guards sips of whisky from the innocent-looking brown cough bottle. The men were glad of the diversion. The superb tasting whisky was a welcome change from the endless cups of tea provided by the kindly Mrs Gray and the surprising heat of the home-brewed malt quickly melted any doubts the men might otherwise have felt at being obviously seduced by a middle-aged spinster.

Morag looked at the black tracery of the elm branches lurking in the chilly mist. With an exaggerated shudder she drew the folds of the shawl closer round her neck. "Look you, it's a bitty cold out here," she said softly, her legs beginning to tremble in a mixture of anticipation and surprise at her audacity. She lowered her voice to a hoarse whisper. "It's – it's warm in the fuel shed over yonder. A nice bundle of hay there too . . . just to be resting in for a whily."

She drifted away into the mist and the older of the two men handed his gun to his companion. "Me first, Thomson," he said with a chuckle. "She's asking for it and I've got it. By God, I'll put a smile on her face that will stay there for the rest of her days."

"Age before beauty," grinned Thomson. "Don't soak it too long though because if something younger turns up I'm for the fuel shed too!"

While Morag was arranging herself enticingly in the hay, the minister was loudly bemoaning her delay in arriving. "We must have Morag Ruadh for the piano!" he cried, running an impatient hand through his thick mop of grey hair. "I asked her to come early! What can have happened to her? Morag has never let me down yet." He swung round to Isabel who was gazing sleepily into the fire. "Can something have happened to her?" he demanded.

"It is to be hoped," murmured the old lady, hastening to add loudly, "Do not be worrying yourself, Mr Gray. Morag was feeling a cold coming down and you know she is always feart of gettin' stiff hands and feets, her a spinner needin' all her fingers – and there is the organ too of course. Morag would never forgive herself if she was never fit for the organ on the Sabbath. She has already steamed her head, now she will likely be rubbing herself with linament to keep supple. She'll be along right enough in her own time."

"Well, we'll have to do without the piano!" The minister frowned round at the motley company. He felt very disappointed. His big idea of showing the Germans a real display of Scottish hospitality wasn't getting off to a good start. He had visualised a devoted Morag Ruadh stolidly accompanying an enthusiastic crowd singing rousing songs of praise all evening. Instead there was only a handful of dejected-looking islanders who were being unnaturally polite to each other. They were also inclined to murmur to one another in Gaelic which made the minister even more frustrated.

Jon Jodl suddenly startled everyone by getting swiftly to his feet. His thin, boyish face was alight as he addressed the minister in excited German. The exchange brought a smile of delight to the Rev. Gray's face.

"The boy's a musician!" he boomed joyfully. "And he has offered to play for us. Be upstanding everyone and give thanks to the Lord, then we will start with the 23rd Psalm – and I want to hear every voice raised to the Almighty . . . in English."

"Balls," muttered old Jim Jim but his wife nudged him in the ribs and hissed a warning "Weesht, weesht!" but he paid no heed, standing up to sing, defiantly, the 23rd Psalm in Gaelic. The well-known strains drifted out into the frosty night and the Commando guard began to hum under his breath while he strained his eyes into the ghostly darkness surrounding the Manse.

Earlier in the day Dunn had told the Commandos on guard duty that the capture of the fourth German would almost certainly be accomplished before nightfall but night had fallen hours ago and there was no further sign of the search party. Thomson swung his arms and looked towards the peat shed, wishing he hadn't been so hasty in giving Cranwell first option on Morag. Being seduced by a middle-aged spinster on a frosty March night was infinitely preferable to standing around in the cold doing nothing. "Hurry up, Cranwell," muttered Thompson impatiently. "It's my turn!"

But Cranwell, in a daze of heated excitement, was in no hurry to leave the warmth of the fuel shed. In throwing caution to the skies, Morag Ruadh had also thrown off much of the inhibitions that had restricted her life to date. She had seldom allowed herself to take alcohol but then she had never tasted anything quite like Tam McKinnon's home-brewed malt. It lay in her belly like a glowing furnace, numbing her brain to all the conventions that had kept her life on such a strict rein. Now she was only aware of the desires of her body which were so strong that she wasted no time on pretty preliminaries.

Cranwell's passions were thoroughly roused when, on entering the shed, he saw Morag sitting on a pile of hay, eagerly unbuttoning her blouse to expose the enticing swell of her breasts. The light from the moon filtered hazily in through the wooden slats that weren't blocked by mounds of peat and coal. Several hens had bedded down in the hay for the night and they clucked in sleepy disapproval at Cranwell's entry.

"Mind where you put your feets!" Morag's warning came in a slurred hiss. "You'll be having these damt hens clocking like the hammers o' hell . . . may God forgive me," she added piously and hicked loudly.

It wasn't the most romantic of settings but romance was the last thing in Cranwell's mind. The diffused glow of the moon was kind to Morag, hiding any blemishes that might have been apparent in the cold light of day. Lying in the hay, her full, white breasts protruding voluptuously from her dark array of clothing, she looked as tempting as a Greek goddess to the woman-hungry Cranwell. He stumbled towards her and she wildly began to undo openings in his clothing. His violent movement towards her disturbed a nearby hen. It gave an indignant screech and fluttered its wings into his face. "Gently now," mumbled Morag Ruadh who was tugging so violently at parts of Cranwell's body that he gasped in surprise. She spread her legs and he buried his face into her breasts, holding his breath in anticipation of the exquisite moments to come.

It was at that moment that Jon Jodl struck up the opening for the 23rd Psalm and Morag suddenly stiffened beneath Cranwell.

"What is it?" His voice was a groan. "Don't stop me now for God's sake! Here!" He uttered an exclamation of alarm. "You're not a . . . don't tell me you're a . . ."

"Virgin!" Morag finished the question for him, her tones full of bitter scorn. "Indeed no, I am not!" she continued spicily. "I have had my moments, Mr . . . Commando." Inwardly she fumed at his very supposition of her chastity simply because her moments had been all too few and so long ago she was unable to place them in the mists of time.

"Then why do you hesitate?"

"Ach well, it is the singing o' the psalms. I am wondering who is playing the piano for I promised the minister I would do it –

I play the organ on the Sabbath, you know." She finished proudly.

"Never mind that," he returned with a smothered laugh. "I have a fine organ here you can be playing with."

"Indeed, that is terrible just . . ." she began but he was doing things to her that made her forget all else and she gave herself up to the 'lusts of the flesh' that she had so often condemned as a weakness in others. When it was over and Cranwell had fallen away from her like a satiated tick, she sat up to take another gulp from her brown bottle. "There is a bucket o' water in the corner," she stated softly. "I will just a few minutes bathing myself then you can be sending in your friend."

In the ghostly light Cranwell stared but before he could speak, Morag said with a wicked little laugh. "It's shocked you are, you a man who ought to be too tough to be shocked. Don't be worrying yourself Mr Commando . . . I am not in the habit of lusting after men. When tonight is over I will go back to being the Morag Ruadh everyone knows – a lady who spins and weaves cloth and who plays the church organ on the Sabbath . . . but before that I will be making the most of my opportunities. One! Two! Three! It makes no difference because I will have to answer to the Lord just the same and I can only burn in hell once!"

With trembling knees Cranwell made his way back to Thomson. "Your turn, mate," he choked. "She's freshening up for the next session – be warned – you've never experienced a woman like her!"

Thomson stared. "Does that mean bad – or good?"

"Good! Bloody good! She nearly raped me before I was halfway through the door!"

Thomson threw his gun at Cranwell and reached the fuel shed as the notes of *Rock of Ages* wafted out from the Manse. Several hymns and psalms later he was back in his place, shakily lighting a cigarette when old Angus drove the trap up the steep brae to the Manse door. On his way through Portcull, Angus had picked up one of two of his cronies and a great deal more were wending their merry way on foot.

"Keep clear o' the big Jerry," Angus warned several sparkling maidens who were trying to jump into the trap. "His feets are covered in dung and you'll no' be likin' that on your dresses!"

Everyone seemed to arrive at the same time, disrupting the

'praise meeting' that the minister was enjoying with rare enthusiasm.

Seated at the piano, Jon Jodl was revelling in the opportunity afforded to him and he was oblivious to the envious scowls thrown at him by Ernst. Jon cared not what he was playing so long as he had the command of an instrument. When the laughing crowd piled into the room he was playing a gay little melody which brought forth smiles of appreciation from the new arrivals. In the hubbub Carl Zeitler was whisked away to the wash tub in the scullery. There, watched over by two soldiers, his urgent need for hygiene was speedily undertaken. Mrs Gray, glad to get away from the hymn singing for a while, presided over gallons of water heating on the range in the kitchen while in the scullery the men divested Zeitler of his repulsive-smelling layers of outerwear. Sounds of merriment came from the drawing-room and Mrs Gray smiled to herself. It was going to be a good ceilidh after all.

"I will just heat this – er – gentleman some food," she said politely, glancing at Zeitler's brooding face. "After we have cleared up in here we can join the others." She looked up at Thomson and Cranwell whose faces were rather haggard in the light of the lamp. "Poor lads," she murmured sympathetically. "You look done in . . . but never mind, there's enough hot water for you all to have a nice wash. I've made lots of lovely food so nobody will starve."

Torquil Andrew came into the kitchen, a pretty dark-haired girl hanging on one arm and a basket of food on the other. "Some bannocks and scones," he explained with a flash of his white teeth. "I told Mother I was coming over to the Manse to sing hymns and she was that pleased to think I've changed my ways she started baking right away."

"Oh, Torquil, you shouldn't," beamed Mrs Gray in delight while in the scullery Zeitler was making strangulated sounds of protest because someone had left the door open and he sat in his zinc tub for everyone to see.

After Torquil there came a stream of people all bearing a little offering of some sort. Mairi handed over a pot of croudie cheese. "It will be nice on the bannocks – the way Wullie likes it," she explained sadly before her brown, rather vacant gaze, came to rest on Zeitler. "My, my," she said with mild astonishment. "You would never know he was a German without his clothes – I suppose it's just you expect that funny wee Hun sign to be everywhere on them – even their bodies!"

The earlier arrivals breathed sighs of relief when the familiar faces of the more rumbustious islanders appeared through the door. In the excitement everyone forgot inward promises of abstinence in all things the minister might consider improper. Despite the restrictions caused by rationing the generous islanders passed round packets of cigarettes while the older men lit smelly pipes. Old Andrew who, in the first part of the evening had done everything with his pipe except smoke it, thankfully accepted a good fill of 'baccy' from old Joe and reached for his fiddle to tune it. The Germans accepted cigarettes and, after introductions, smiled in some bemusement at the various nicknames bestowed on them. A shining Zeitler was brought through to join the company, one or two children sneaked in by the side door and the once silent and empty room was filled to capacity.

"Good! Good! We're all here now!" boomed the Rev. Gray, looking round the gathering with some dismay because he hadn't expected such an enthusiastic turnout for a praise meeting. "Now we shall really raise the roof with our singing!"

The door opened once more to admit a serenely contented Morag Ruadh who came on the arm of Dugald Donaldson. Dugald, determined to follow up the activities of the German invaders, had cycled over the rough moor road from Portvoynachan, his pockets bulging with notepads and pencils. Morag, having allowed herself some time in the fuel shed to 'gather herself up', emerged to meet Dugald at the Manse door and had surprised him thoroughly by hanging on to his arm and chattering with unusual animation.

Cranwell nudged Thomson. "Look, surely that's not another one!"

"These island women have stamina," replied Thomson. "I'm just about balled up. Twice, Cranwell, twice in the space of half an hour and she still looks as fresh as a daisy!"

"Good, good!" approved Tam McKinnon at the minister's words. "Erchy has brought his bagpipes and we'll have Andrew playin' the fiddle. 'Tis a pity poor auld Todd is laid up for it's handy to have two pipers at a ceilidh. When one gets out o' breath you can just hand the pipes over to the other while the bag is still full of air."

The minister looked at Tam with disapproval. He had told Mrs Gray only to ask teetotallers to the ceilidh and here was Tam McKinnon who, it was rumoured, was actually brewing his own whisky. In fact, on looking over the new arrivals, the minister saw only those who were notoriously fond of 'the devil's brew'.

"You cannot sing hymns to the bagpipes, Tam!" he said sternly.

Erchy grinned mischievously. "No, but she'll play them. Wait you and you'll hear what I mean." He patted his pipes affectionately. "Just right she is for a good blow. I've given her some treacle to keep her supple and a droppy whisky to give her a bit of life."

It was Erchy's habit to fondly give his bagpipes a female gender but while everyone else smiled appreciatively the minister's frown deepened. "I have no idea what you are talking about, Erchy, but there will be no whisky-drinking women in my house. Now ..." He turned to Morag Ruadh and smiled ingratiatingly.

"Morag is here at last and only too ready, I'm sure, to relieve this young man at the piano – isn't that right, Morag?"

Before leaving the fuel shed Morag had consumed the remainder of her whisky and she was now seeing the world through a rosy glow. She smiled charmingly at the minister, confounding him by replying, "Indeed, I will not! I'm for the skirl o' the pipes and a good bit of a story from Andrew and Joe. 'Tis a night o' fun I'm after."

The minister's jaw fell and everyone else looked at each other in astonishment.

"It's no' natural, no' natural at all! Morag Ruadh is no' herself," was the general verdict. Jim Jim and his wife looked at each other.

"Here," said the latter, "was you thinkin' earlier that Morag was actin' a bit funny?"

Jim Jim nodded. "Ay indeed, Isabel. I had a mind I was smellin' the drink off her, but knowing Morag I thought it couldny be. My God, would you look at the smile on her face. She's been havin' a bit fun out there and well she looks on it too. I never thought o' Morag as bein' bonny before but tonight she has the look o' a new woman."

The blast of the bagpipes filled the room and with a mad 'hooch' Morag was the first to get to her feet, turning to pull Dugald after her.

Isabel nudged her husband. "Look at that now. She and Dugald Ban are right friendly all of a sudden."

Jim Jim removed his pipe from his mouth to make a faultlessly aimed spit at the coals, despite the swirling skirts that flounced wildly to the tunes of the pipes. "Well now, there's a thing," he said thoughtfully. "A fine thing, just," he continued with a gleam in his eyes. "Dugald Ban would just be right for Morag and him wi' his ambitions will maybe become one o' they famous people with plenty money."

He withdrew into the depths of his armchair to contemplate a future enriched by the many little comforts that a comfortably married daughter could provide, and as soon as the red-faced Erchy stopped to gather breath, he spoke in a voice so mysterious that all eyes in the room turned towards him. "I am after thinking of a very odd story told me by Black Ewan that time I was over in Barra helping wi' the mackerel shoals."

At the very mention of Black Ewan the atmosphere in the room was charged with a subdued excitement. Black Ewan of Barra was well known throughout the Western Isles for his strange powers of second sight and his spine-chilling tales that went hand in hand with his 'seeing eye'.

"Now, now, we'll have no tales of witchery in this house," protested the minister but he might well not have spoken because a chorus of encouragement met Jim Jim's words.

"It was a gey queer tale but true – true according to Black Ewan," pursued Jim Jim, pausing to let his words take effect in the intervening hush. Erchy's heavy breathing and the coals crackling in the grate were the only things that filled the silence for a few moments.

"Go on now, Jim Jim," encouraged old Joe, his curiosity getting the better of his resentment at Jim Jim taking the limelight away from himself and Andrew, the two recognised seanachaidhs in the room.

"Well, it was about the time o' the Great War," continued Jim Jim slowly. "And you mind Black Ewan was out at sea wi' the Naval Patrol vessels?"

"Ay, ay, that was the time he found the barrel o' rum floatin' in the sea," supplemented Ranald with a beaming smile, "and was so drunk on it his mates tied him to a chair in the wheelhouse because it was the safest place for him."

"Look you, that has nothing to do wi' my story," said Jim Jim scathingly. "It is about one o' the lads on the boat who was always boastin' about the amount o' women he managed to have and never after marrying any o' them."

With a little apologetic cough he avoided the minister's stern eye and Annie McKinnon took the opportunity to break in mischievously. "My, my, that sounds like my Dokie Joe before he was after wedding himself to me!"

"Ay well, if it was Dokie he must be gey auld for this cheil was nigh on forty and that was more than twenty years ago!" Jim Jim was growing agitated by the interruptions and he carried on swiftly. "Black Ewan warned the cheil to stop his mischief and with his seeing eye he foretold the man was going to seduce the daughter o' a witch. If he wasn't after marrying her he would have a fate that no mortal could foretell it would be so evil. Well, it happened right enough and worse than anyone could have imagined. Out at sea, with no land expected for miles, an island just appeared out of nowhere. On it was marooned a lovely young maiden, hair black as night and eyes like the black peats on the moor. All the men on the vessel were terrified but no' the seducer. He landed on the island an' promised himself to the maiden if she succumbed to him. Well, she did right enough, the bad bad lassie, but then he was all for leavin' her to go back to his ship. Just then a fearful hag rose out o' the sea, green wi' slime and black wi' warts. She screeched out an evil curse on the seducer that was terrible to hear. He remembered his mother tellin' him 'Never look into the eyes of a Green Uisga Caillich and their curses might no' work', but he was so taken aback he stared straight at the hag. There and then he was turned into a lump o' black rock, all twisted like he had died in agony. On the top was a black skull with two empty sockets where his eyes had been."

Jim Jim paused for breath and a round-eyed Ethel said wonderingly, "Och my, the poor mannie, it must have been sore on him."

"Ay, but that's the kind o' thing that happens to men who go round seducing innocent women then leave them in the lurch," nodded Jim Jim with a meaningful look at Dugald Ban, named so because of his mop of white hair.

Morag Ruadh threw back her head and gave a shout of laughter. "Ach, Father, you'd best stick to damping the peats with your spit for you're no use at all as a story teller . . . as Joe and Andrew will be after tellin' you from the look on their faces."

"Ach, but it was good, it was good, Jim Jim," applauded Angus who was ensconced behind the couch taking furtive sips from a bottle that was a duplicate of Morag Ruadh's.

CHAPTER TEN

"Slainte!"

The Rev. John Gray peered through the gathering haze of smoke in the room and felt a pang of real dismay. Somehow his usual authority over his flock was holding no water and the thought came to him suddenly that, other than home visits, Sunday worship, and the annual Sunday school picnic, this was the first time he was meeting the people on a social footing and he didn't quite know how to handle the situation. Many of the younger men were openly flirting with the young females, while the older men were handing round little brown bottles such as might be found in any medicine cupboard on the island.

Tam McKinnon caught the minister's look and broke into a fit of exaggerated coughing. "And isn't this mist an awful thing, just?" he spluttered innocently. "We are all having a tickle in our throats and just saying we hope we were not going down wi' the 'flu." He held up his own cough bottle and looked at it affectionately. "A grand mixture right enough, just the job for a tickle in the throat. I am feeling better already."

The minister turned to his wife who had just succumbed to Torquil's charming persuasion to take a sip from his bottle. She had swallowed quickly, thinking the 'medicine' would have an unpleasant taste. The first fiery sensations of the Uisge-Beatha glowed in her throat, making her crimson-faced in an effort to stop gasping. But it was no use. She broke into a torrent of coughs just as her husband informed her it was time to get tea going.

"Tea? Yes dear, of course," she spluttered, then she bent low to Torquil's shaggy head. "You young devil!" she hissed. "That was whisky you gave me."

His keen blue eyes snapped with mischief. "Is that a fact now, and here was I thinkin' it was medicine. Ach well, a spirited woman like yourself is surely no' goin' to turn up her nose at a wee drop o' the good stuff . . . here . . ." He proffered the bottle again. "That's a terrible cough you have there, try some more medicine . . . I'll help you make the tea and later on we'll have that dance you promised me."

Mrs Gray was no more immune to Torquil's charm than the rest. Her cheeks turned a pretty shade of pink at his words. Taking the bottle, she sipped daintily, then daringly downed several good swigs.

"The tea, my dear," said the minister. He looked at the brown bottle in her hand with enquiringly raised brows; she patted her throat and coughed.

"A tickle, John," she explained gently. "Just a little one, but better to take action before it gets worse. I'll go now and make the tea."

Torquil followed her into the kitchen. In his wake came several womenfolk. The tea-making was accompanied by much merriment, a slightly intoxicated Mrs Gray proving no dampener on the fun. It may even be said that she was an eager participant in the keen competition to gain Torquil's attention. Gone was all the reserve she had upheld through the years as the wife of the Rev. John Gray; now she was Hannah Gray, a woman in her own right. She let Torquil squeeze her waist and when he refilled his bottle from a generous hip flask, she drank in his gentle words of persuasion along with the whisky from the bottle he held to her lips. "I shouldn't, Torquil," she protested faintly and took a hearty swig. The rest of the womenfolk were likewise fortified and when the cups of tea eventually sat steaming on the table each one was laced with a good measure of whisky.

Mrs Gray staggered into the drawing-room with a tray of tea. Behind her tripped a merry procession bearing plates of food. The room was in a happy uproar. An exhausted Andrew had handed his fiddle to Jon Jodl whose long, delicate fingers extricated tunes that were unknown to the island but were so irresistibly gay they invited hands to clap and feet to tap. The Commandos and the Germans had all partaken freely from the brown cough bottles and an air of comradeship existed between everyone. Only the Rev. John Gray remained soberly reserved and his mood wasn't improved by his first sip of tea.

"Hannah, this tea tastes terrible," he said tightly but Hannah was beyond caring, giving him what the islanders called a 'glaikit grin'.

"Well, John, if you don't like it . . . away through and make yourself more," she told him flippantly, but he was of the breed who believed the kitchen was only a woman's domain and he had no intention of domesticating himself now. Several minutes later he held out his drained cup and with great dignity requested a refill.

"Ach, you enjoyed that," grinned Kate, going off to fetch the teapot into which Tam had poured a half pint of whisky. "There now." She handed the minister the replenished cup. "It is tastin' a wee bit funny but the water is that peaty the now it canny be helped."

Ernst Foch sat by the fire and stared moodily into the flames. His feelings of geniality were being replaced by a dark depression which made his thoughts very bleak. "Helga . . ." He murmured the name of his wife softly but Zeitler, sitting nearby, heard and his pale blue eyes bulged widely.

"Helga! Helga!" he said mockingly. "That dear little wife of yours is far away now, Ernst. You have to think of other things, you must keep up your faith in the Führer. We are here because we fought for the Fatherland! We have to remember that is all that matters."

"Go to hell," said Ernst but Zeitler wasn't listening. His own words had inflamed his mind afresh to the Nazi doctrine and he stood up suddenly, clicked his heels together and looked round at the gathering. Through an alcoholic haze he saw the amazement in every face as he yelled lustily. "Will you all stand up with me to salute the Führer and his cause?" His arm shot out. "Heil Hitler!"

Prior to the outburst the gathering had been in some discomfort as the minister, utterly enthralled, went into raptures listening to Jon Jodl playing the gypsy air, *Zigeunerweisen* on Andrew's fiddle. The rather sombre opening strains made the fun-hungry revellers look at each other in dismay while the minister, his face somewhat flushed after consuming four cups of tea, nodded his ardent approval and murmured, "The boy has taste! A fine musician indeed. He has a future ahead of him! The war can't last forever!"

He leaned towards Kate and gave her a conspiratorial wink. "Good tea, my dear, very good! I must say there's something to be said for peaty water! By jove, it has really warmed me up and I am hoping you can squeeze me another cup from the pot."

Kate obligingly 'squeezed' the pot and put her lips close to his ear. "There now, it's as dry as a fart in a corpse!" she imparted in a bubble of merriment.

"Mrs McKinnon!" exploded the minister but the ghost of a smile hovered at the corners of his mouth. "Would you care to dance with me, my dear?" he added as Jon broke into the wildly stirring *Czardos*. A hotch-potch of an Irish jig made the floorboards jump beneath the rugs because everyone had reached the stage when everything with a rhythm to it made the feet itch to dance.

But Zeitler's roar brought everything to an abrupt halt. Everyone stared, suspended in a state of transfixed wonder.

"Sit down, Zeitler!" said Jon, his thin face taut with apprehension.

Although Dunn couldn't understand the German exchanges he sensed trouble and got slowly to his feet. Ernst licked his fleshy lips. His first instinct had been to go for Zeitler but instead he turned his wrath on Jon whose obvious enjoyment of the evening was somewhat galling under the circumstances.

"Gut Gott, Jon, you are finding your courage at last!" he sneered. "Somewhat late though to be of any help to the Fatherland! Is it the limelight that goes to your head? Mama would be proud if she could see you now . . . her little boy all grown up!"

Dunn sighed. It had been a long weary day. The gaiety of the ceilidh had lulled the senses away from reality but Foch and Zeitler were bringing it speedily back. The minister was making pacifying noises but Ernst continued to throw jibes at Jon whose face had resumed its formal pallor.

"I warned you, Ernst," he said quietly. "I told you – up there – I'd thrash you. Say one more word and I'll . . ."

"You'll what – kill me?" goaded Ernst. "But you haven't got Anton here to wipe your nose, Jon, and Mama is very far away. How can you possibly stand on your own feet?"

Jon got up quickly, his eyes blazing in his drawn face. "Get outside and I'll show you what I mean!"

"Can you tell us what they're saying?" Dunn enquired of the minister who looked at him with glazed eyes and frowned in perplexment. "They want to fight . . . they go on about fighting after all my talks with them about peaceful living!"

"It's a private war I think," muttered Dunn. "Foch has it coming to him by the look of things."

Ernst had risen to his feet. "You don't have the nerve," he told Jon dourly, though apprehension was in his eyes.

Jon lunged forward, sending his chair flying backwards. He grabbed Ernst by the back of the collar and bulldozed him to the door. There was a hurried scraping of chairs as everyone rose to make way.

"We'd better stop them!" said Cranwell but Dunn shook his head.

"If they don't get it out of their system now they'll just do it another time. It must have taken a lot of shit-throwing to rouse a chap like Jon. He was like a happy kid playing that fiddle, now he's as dangerous as a wounded animal. We'll get outside and make sure he doesn't kill Bullhead," he grinned wryly. "Poor buggers, they're as much victims of war as we are."

After the first feelings of dismay the islanders were delighted at the chance to witness a fight between the Germans. The warmth of the house was abandoned for the cool frosty air outside. The Rev. John Gray wrung his hands and took another mouthful of tea before venturing outside. "What are we to do, Hannah?" he asked his wife whose eyes sparkled in a crimson face. "The ceilidh is in ruins – oh dear – it will be the talk of the island for years!"

But his wife was beyond caring about gossip. She hadn't enjoyed herself so much in years. All too often in her supporting role as the wife of a minister, she had listened, consoled, sympathised, often pushing down natural urges of her own in case she would be talked about. Tonight at any rate her defences were down, she was an entity unto herself, a whole instead of 'a better half'.

"John," she said calmly. "I don't give a damn. I'm having a wonderful time – I must throw ceilidhs more often." She took the bottle that Tam had given her, from her pocket. "Slainte!" She called out the Gaelic 'Good health' loudly, sipped heartily from the bottle, then turned outside.

"She's drinking! Hannah has gone to the devil!" the minister told the empty room and wondered why he wasn't as shocked as he ought to have been. He was warm and dizzy and seemed to glide out of the house like a piece of thistledown.

A circle of spectators had gathered round the two Germans and cries of 'Get into him, Mac' were ample proof that the young musician had already earned the affection of the people. But the children that Ernst had befriended early in the evening gave him lusty peals of encouragement. They were in the minority, but their shrill voices competed ably with the adults. Gaelic and English filled the air, bottles and pipes were brandished.

The moon had thrown off its shrouding mist and now rode brilliantly in the sky. Pale, ghostly beams shone into the mountain corries, flooding them with light. A frothing burn gleamed on Sgurr nan Ruadh, a sparkling jewel among the dark heather; Loch Tenee glinted below, a deep basin of frost-rimed silver reflecting the surrounding trees in a perfect mirror image. It was a beautiful night with the bright twinkle of stars splintering the heavens in a milky profusion. It was also bitterly cold with a glittering hoar frost clothing bracken and heather on the hill slopes. Nearer the shore the air was too laden with salt for the frost to settle properly, nevertheless it was a night for indoor pursuits by cosy hearths.

But the crowd gathered on the lawn by the Manse gave not a second thought to the weather as they avidly watched Jon's wildly flaying fists. Dugald was making frantic observations into his notebook by the subdued light from the Manse windows, while the others drank from their bottles, shouted encouragement and generally behaved like spectators at a boxing match.

Jon was no fist fighter but fury gave him the strength of a lion. At first the thick-set Ernst had all the advantages on his side. His meaty fists found their mark over and over, sending Jon sprawling on the wet grass. Ernst stood over him panting, knuckles bunched to strike the minute Jon got to his feet. He had gone down for the third time, now he sagged on all fours, trying to gather himself for another clash with his opponent's iron-hard fists.

"I can't do it," he thought bitterly. "Ernst is going to win and everyone will laugh at the foolish weakling, Jon Jodl."

"C'mon now, Mac!" urged the crowd. "Get up, man!"

Ernst wiped a smear of blood away from his mouth which Jon had clipped by pure chance. He looked at the dark patch on the back of his hand and the sight of it enraged him further. "What are you doing crawling around there, Jon?" he mocked. "Playing leapfrog? I think even Anton would laugh if he could see you now. Mama – dear old Mama – would cry and kiss all your little sores better. Mama is too blind to see that her little boy is more yellow than a buttercup!"

The words imbued the exhausted Jon with a final burst of strength. His heart pounded; his head was light, but he urged his sagging limbs upwards. Ernst wasn't prepared for the hail of punches from his opponent's wildly flaying fists. Many of them missed their mark but the majority hit home. Ernst felt the dull thudding blows raining down and put up his arms to defend himself. But it was useless. Jon was gasping and sobbing but the power of his emotions forced his aching muscles to keep going. Ernst sagged to his knees, his arms folded over his head. Blood from a split lip mixed with saliva and lathered down his chin, a gash on his eyebrow was rapidly closing his eye.

The Commandos intervened then, forcibly tearing Jon away. The crowd cheered, then rushed forward to thump him on the back in congratulation. Old Angus flourished his bottle. "A drop o' the bonny malt will put the life back in you, son. Take a good swallock."

Jon swallocked and coughed.

"Slainte!" The men held up their bottles and solemnly toasted the bleeding Jon with the Gaelic 'Good health'.

Jon staggered against the Commandos who were holding him upright. He raised his bottle to the crowd. "Slainte!" he cried feebly.

The Rev. John Gray shook his spinning head. "What are they saying, Hannah, my dear? I don't seem to be making much sense of anything!"

"You wouldn't understand anyway, John," she said softly. "Now, I must go and boil up some water. There's a few broken heads that will need bathing..."

She broke off. A tremendous uproar was coming from the screen of bushes at the back of the Manse.

"Mercy!" cried Kate. "The hags are at work tonight for sure! The de'il is everywhere at once!"

"It is the moon at work," said Morag Ruadh cryptically. She glanced up at the cold face in the heavens. "Strange things happen when the moon is full – ay – very strange," she added softly and with a secretive smile softening her mouth she followed on Kate's heels.

Kate gave a startled exclamation when she saw her son, Angus, engaged in a pitched battle with the big, square-headed Zeitler. With her back to a tree, sobbing quietly, was Ethel, dress torn, her hair a matted tangle of pine needles.

"What happened, lass?" cried Kate, running to fold her muscular arms round the girl.

"I was just going to the wee hoosie," sobbed Ethel, "when that big Hun came up at my back and threw me on the ground. It was terrible just! He was trying to tear my clothes off. I kicked him wi' my feets but he was stronger than McKenzie's bull – ay, and just as lustful . . ." She paused, unable to explain further but Kate was never at a loss for words, no matter the situation.

"The dirty pig!" she fumed. "I'll kick the balls off him, that I will! We should carry him to the sea and throw him in! By God, that water would soon freeze the rooster off him! He'd never use it again – no' even to pee! Tam, get in there and help Angus kill him!"

"He's doin' fine by the look on things," answered Tam hastily.

"But what about his heart, Tam? And his back? He'll kill himself!"

"Ach no, Angus wouldny kill himself. That would be daft just. No, no, he'll kill the big Jerry instead."

The Commandos were pulling the two men apart but it was no easy task. The thick-set, lumbering Angus had rendered Zeitler almost unconscious but for him that wasn't enough.

"I want to *kill* the bugger!" he yelled, butting his head at the intervening soldiers like an enraged bull. "He – he tried to seduce my Ethel!" The significance of the words shocked him into silence for a moment and he stared at the bloody Zeitler, seeing again the scene that he had witnessed on his way to the bushes to relieve his bladder.

During the fight between Ernst and Jon everyone had been too taken up to pay much attention to Zeitler, who, despite his ordeal with Ealasaid, was refreshed after his bath and a generous hot meal. He was possessed of voracious appetites of one kind or another which he fed with scant regard to others. His blood lust had been indulged with the advent of war but it had meant the repression of other things that made life sweet. Opportunities were all too few for amorous encounters if such a term could be applied to brief interludes bought in the back-street. The sweet, fresh appeal of the island girls was so different from the calculating females of his particular experience that he had spent a good part of the evening wondering how to go about winning one for himself. The fight had created the diversion he needed and he'd slunk after Ethel with single-minded intent. Her cries for help had gone unheeded in the general uproar but he hadn't bargained for the ensuing tussle with the gentle-looking Ethel. In her terror at being attacked by the very German whose arrogant bearing had been the source of much comment all evening, Ethel had used her 'feets' to great advantage. With more energy than intent she had kicked Zeitler in his most vulnerable parts, rendering him incapable of anything but agonising self-pity. He had doubled up on top of her, his crushing weight making her yell afresh for help. It was then that Angus, a furious tornado of muscle and rage, threw himself at the helpless Zeitler.

Despite her recent ordeal Ethel was enthralled. "Just look at my Angus." She beamed in radiant admiration. "Och, but he's a bonny fighter." She paused to look round at the gaping crowd. "No one will be saying things about him again . . . unless of course to praise him,' she finished virtuously before going over to gather her victorious husband into her arms and murmur lavish words of praise upon him.

"Ay, ay, Ethel's right," applauded Tam. "I raised my sons to be like myself . . . and I'll thank you to stop sniggering, Annie, my girl, or you'll get a warmed lug, married or no."

Brown was looking in dismay at Zeitler's puffed and bloody face. "How the hell will we explain this lot?" he asked Dunn. "Say that we were having such a merry time at a ceilidh we simply turned our backs on the prisoners who proceeded to roam about, brawling with each other and attempting to rape women?"

"Hardly, Brown, we'll simply tell the truth. If it all sounds too far-fetched for words it's just too bad. Get this Casanova inside and lock him up. I knew he was trouble when we sniffed him out in that hut – all head and no brains!"

"Sir." Anderson addressed Dunn. "Could I be spared for a few minutes? I'd like to pop along to the doctor's to see how the German Commander is doing."

Dunn nodded. "It might be a good idea. I suppose in a way you have a personal interest in him. You did a good job this afternoon. Off you go but don't be all night. I'd like us all to turn in early if possible. We have an early start tomorrow."

"Are we sleeping – here?"

"Yes, Anderson. Mrs Gray offered us her remaining spare room with plenty of blankets to go with it."

"Good old Mrs Gray," grinned Anderson and went off down the hill.

Hannah Gray was in the kitchen seeing to the casualties. "A fine assortment of broken heads," she said cheerfully, swabbing at a purple bruise on Ernst's face. Several of the women were fussing round Jon who was white-faced and very quiet. Ernst looked over at him and his bulldog features softened. He spoke in rapid German and held out his hand. Jon raised his head slowly, hardly able to believe his ears. He had just given Ernst a thorough beating; now he was being offered apologies and the hand of friendship. Uneasily he proffered his own bruised hand. Ernst took it in a firm grip, his fleshy lips stretched wide.

"You fight well, Jon. My face will tell me so for days . . . but I deserved it." He looked up at Tam and said carefully, "Uisge-Beatha?"

Tam's mouth fell open and Torquil said, "I think he's asking for some o' your whisky, Tam."

Tam grinned delightedly. "Well, damn me – and using the Gaelic name for it! These Jerries are clever right enough . . . here, Bullhead." He held out his hip flask because all the cough bottles had run dry. "Take a real good swig – you ugly big bugger," he added in rapid Gaelic and everyone roared with laughter.

Ernst took the flask, but passed it to Jon. "You first, my friend."

Jon took the flask and raised it high. "Slainte!" he cried and the islanders took up the cry.

"The best bloody ceilidh ever," said Torquil to Mrs Gray.

She looked startled. "But, Torquil, what about all the fights we've had tonight? You don't often get such happenings at a ceilidh."

Torquil showed his white teeth in a cheeky grin. "Och, mo ghaoil, it's daft you are. It was the fighting made the ceilidh – though of course it was terrible what happened to poor Ethel," he added hastily. He glanced at Angus ensconced on the coal box with Ethel sitting at his feet looking up at him in wide-eyed adulation. Torquil grinned again. "No' so terrible for our Angus, eh? He'll be a hero for the rest o' his days – at least to Ethel."

The Rev. John Gray was snoring on a hard wooden chair; hands clasped over his chest, legs stretched like pokers – he was in danger of sliding off his perch. "The Lord is my – Psalm twenty-six – I have trusted also in the Lord; therefore I shall not slide – tea terrible . . ." he muttered insensibly.

"To hell wi' psalms," chuckled Robbie. "Away you go over to the Headquarters, Tam, and be bringin' up some more o' your cough mixture. It's early yet and I'm no' goin' home to have Behag sniffin' at me like a ferret and shoutin' at me wi' her eyes."

"Ay, I will that," responded Tam willingly, whereupon Kate set about collecting the bottles. Tam stuck out his large square palm and cocked his eye at the company. "Cross my hand wi' silver and I'll be bringin' back full bottles."

"Ach, you're worse than my Aberdeen cousin!" exclaimed old Angus. "He looks for change out o' a farthing."

"Well it's more than a farthing I'm after," smirked Tam and though everyone grumbled they handed over their money willingly enough.

Tam closed his laden hand and winked at Mrs Gray. "You won't be saying a word in the wrong ears, mo ghaoil?"

"Tam McKinnon!" she said sternly. "If people want to buy your cough mixture it is nothing to do with me." She put her hand in her pocket. "And I'll be having a drop too. I think Morag must have passed her cold on to me. I'll never get the chance of medicine like yours again."

Tam looked at her with reverence, "Mrs Gray, this will not be your last ceilidh on this island," he intoned in a respectful whisper. He stretched out his hand with her coppers in it and dropped them back into her pocket. "Be putting them in the Kirk plate for me on Sunday," he said benevolently, then turned to follow the sound of Kate's clanking bottles outside.

In the little guest room at Slochmhor, Anton Büttger lay like one who had already passed through the Valley of the Shadow. The soft lamplight shone on fair curls crisping out from the layer of bandages encasing his head; thick eyelashes lay on high cheek-bones and a fine little stubble of hair shadowed the hollows of his cheeks making his face look thinner than it was.

A faint dew of sweat gleamed on his upper lip and Babbie stooped to bathe it gently away. Despite his fever his hands were still clammily cold and again she put them under the blankets, stopping for a moment to check the bandages that swathed his middle. Shona plumped the pillows on the shake-down bed set in a corner of the room, and tried to dispel the numbness that surrounded her thoughts like a cloying shroud. She had listened to the tea-time news about the raids over Clydebank and Glasgow. It was a depressing account of devastation, of a chaos from which no order could yet emerge. A lot of people had died, a lot more injured and there was simply no way of knowing if Niall was among the living or the dead. More raids were expected that night – tonight . . . Shona shuddered and looked from the window to the moon breaking through the mist layers to ride high and clear in the sky. It was 10.30. At that very moment the German bombers might be sweeping over Glasgow, crushing out the lives of innocent people, wrecking the lives of those that were left. A picture of Niall darted into her mind, tall and handsome with his sun-tanned limbs and boyish smile, his corn curls glinting in the sun, his firm lips close to her own . . . She could almost feel them brushing her face . . . She started and pulled away the net curtain that had blown softly against her cheek.

The keen air from the moor whispered in through the slightly opened sash, laden with the sharp clean smell of the frost-rimed bracken on the hill.

She turned and looked back at the room – at the bed occupied by the young German airman – and her memory took her back over the years when, as a little girl, she had lain in the same bed. It was during the terrible time that Mirabelle had died, and

Hamish too, the big laughing Highlander who had been grieve at Laigmhor. He had died on the treacherous rocks of the Sgor Creags in the same sea that had crushed her father's arm to pulp. It had all happened at once and she had spent her nights at Slochmhor, a frightened little girl, unable to sleep.

Niall had come to her then, an awkward boy of twelve, his thin arms enclosing her with his boyish comfort. "I'm just through the wall from you – we can tap out messages to each other." His words tossed back at her over the years and a sob caught in her throat.

Babbie looked up quickly. "Are you all right, Shona?"

"Yes, I'm fine." She composed herself quickly and added, "How – is he? Will he pull through do you think?"

Babbie shook her bright head. "Only time will tell that. He's young – strong – the doctor did a wonderful job. You're lucky to have such a man on the island."

"Yes, I know, he puts up with a lot but he seldom complains."

"Some would say he was wasted here."

"Wasted? He probably does more healing in this wee island than many doctors do with all the modern aids of the big hospitals." She looked at Babbie quizzically. "Can you really see Lachlan swallowed up in a big city practice? Here he is somebody, he stands out . . . do you think that's as daft as it sounds?"

"I know what you mean," said Babbie softly. "He's special. I watched him today, Phebie too, working like Trojans to save a German even though they were worried to death about their son." She left the bed and went over to Shona, her mysterious green eyes dark with sympathy. "You too, Shona, you worked like a fury though your heart was with Niall."

Shona took a deep breath. "I didn't want to think. I've discovered that's the worst punishment of all. It's the not knowing that's worst. It's like being in a dark tunnel, never knowing whether you're crawling towards the light – or going back into the darkness."

"Yes, I know, it's the most terrifying feeling on earth . . . yet somehow – in some strange way, one gets used to the dark." Babbie spoke almost to herself. She sounded so strange that Shona looked at her sharply.

"What a queer thing to say, Babbie." She forced a laugh. "If the old islanders could hear you they'd be getting the shivers and saying you were a spook wandered from the tombs at Dunuaigh."

"Sorry, I have a habit of saying silly things. The nurses at the home told me I gave them the shivers and now I'm doing it to you." She was herself again, apologising in characteristic fashion, the radiance of her smile lighting her weary face.

"It's bed you need," said Shona firmly. "I hope you manage to get some sleep, you look exhausted."

"Don't we all? It's been a long day. Don't worry about me, you know what I'm like once I get into bed."

Shona laughed. "I'll be sorry for the man you marry, you'll never get up on time to see him off in the morning."

"Ach well," Babbie smiled ruefully. "I'd better stay an old maid then, I'm heading that way now – twenty-three and not even an engagement ring to show for it."

"A real grannie," giggled Shona, feeling oddly cheered by the older girl's careless good humour.

Babbie turned to her small suitcase and began to look out nightwear. She had been adamant about moving over to Slochmhor to be immediately at hand. Lachlan protested even while he desperately wanted to accept help. He was exhausted after a night with little sleep and a day spent battling to keep the angel of death from taking the young German. With Biddy laid up, things were even more complicated, so after a lot of persuasion on Babbie's part he gave in and Shona had helped her move her things from Laigmhor.

"You don't know what you're letting yourself in for," Lachlan warned. "Even though the lad can barely lift a finger the island will have you labelled as a lassie with loose morals, ay, and a hundred times looser because the lad is German."

Babbie laughed gaily. "But Biddy would have done the same thing surely?"

"Ay, but there's a queer difference between you and Biddy! At her age she's not likely to do much damage, now is she?"

They had both laughed, Babbie carelessly because in her compassion for the sick she cared little for the wagging tongues of the healthy.

Lifting a green nightdress from her case she looked at it in disgust. "I suppose I'll have to wear it under the circumstances. I like to sleep in the raw but I can hardly do that here. The gossips would set their tongues on fire if they heard about it."

Footsteps crunched on the path under the window, plainly heard because the rest of the household slept and everything was very quiet. Shona looked from the window and saw a dark figure coming through the gate. "It's one of the Commandos,' she reported. "The one who helped in surgery today."

"Yes, he was good wasn't he? I suppose he feels personally involved. Go down, Shona, before he wakens the house. I can't be bothered with anyone just now."

Shona was back in a few minutes. "He wanted to come up and see Anton but I told him you were getting ready for bed. They're off first thing tomorrow but the military medics will be over in a few days – meanwhile the Home Guard have to keep an eye open." She chuckled. "Can you imagine it? Even Anderson was smirking when he said it. There's some sort of ceilidh going on up at the Manse just now. I think our young surgeon was a little bit merry. He put his arm round my waist and tried to kiss me . . . the cheeky bugger!" With a laugh she turned again to the door. "I'd better away now or Father will be out looking for me. It's daft, I suppose, but he still thinks I'm a wee girl yet."

"At eighteen – you are," said Babbie softly.

Shona's blue eyes widened in surprise. "How *old* you sound, Babbie, and how can I still be a bairn after all the things I told you about myself?"

"Because at eighteen you haven't really grown up. You think you've had all the experiences but there's so much more for you, Shona. You still have a bit of growing up to do."

"You sound as if you've known me all my days." Shona tried to sound light-hearted but the look in Babbie's green eyes made her shiver. In the look she glimpsed the wisdom that lurked in the faraway eyes of the very old. To see it in someone of Babbie's years was disquieting.

"You're a witch," she said lightly. "Niall would call you Caillich Ruadh which means red witch. It's what he calls me to get me angry. Maybe there's a bit of the witch in us all. With Father I often know what he's thinking, he seems to always know what I'm feeling. We're tuned in to each other I suppose. Maybe that's why he likes to keep me in sight though often he hardly says a word when I am. I can just *feel* him caring."

"You're lucky." Babbie sounded wistful. "It must be a good warm feeling to have a father – or a mother – or both. You have one, I have none, yet most people have both and never appreciate the fact."

"Och, c'mon now, Babbie." Shona's voice was gentle. "You must have someone . . . surely everyone has someone."

"No, not everyone. I was lucky, I had an older sister – we were in the orphanage together. She left before me and though she married we always kept in touch. We were always fighting in the orphanage – you know what sisters are – oh, but of course, you don't – so sorry." She paused for a moment then continued slowly. "They say that sisters who fight a lot as kids are really very close even while they're pulling lumps from each other. Well, it's true, the closeness I mean. We had wonderful times when we grew up, even after Jan got married – then – she died, three years ago now – she was twenty-six. I still miss her so."

Shona caught her breath. "Oh, dear God, how sad you must be, to have someone you love die so young. How can you bear not having anyone in the world you can call your own?"

A little smile hovered round Babbie's lips. Her eyes were very green and faraway. "But I'm not alone, Shona. I have friends, I have you here, I have others scattered everywhere and . . ." She laughed suddenly. "Underneath all my heathen ways I'm really very close to my Maker. I'll see Jan again one day, I know that for sure. It's quite exciting when you stop to think about it."

A little groan from the bed made them both jump. Babbie was immediately on the alert, a cool, efficient little nurse again, whose devotion to Anton seemed to divorce her from everything that went on in the world outside the sick room. Shona slipped quietly out of the house and up the lonely moon-washed glen to Laigmhor and the people she loved.

The Commandos left Rhanna early next morning. A bleary-eyed and very subdued Rev. John Gray insisted on squeezing soldiers and prisoners into two traps to drive them over to Portvoynachan. Old Angus, sound asleep under the sofa in the drawing-room, was rudely wakened in order to take charge of Burnbreddie's trap for the journey.

"Ach, but her leddy will be wonderin' where I am lost," he grumbled but the minister would have no excuses and Angus went stiffly to get the horses ready.

Mrs Gray was at the door to see them off. In a neat, grey wool dress, her brown hair in a prim bun, she was Mrs John Gray once more, the minister's wife, instructions ringing in her ears about the church flowers and other such sober affairs. But nothing could keep the twinkle from her eyes. The ceilidh had opened doors in her life that hitherto she had been too wary to enter. Her individuality had been stifled under the cloak of convention but she knew it would never completely envelop her again. Her husband had been full of self-recrimination and dismayed when he divulged to her that certain parts of the ceilidh were a complete blank in his mind.

"We all have our weaknesses, John," she had intoned primly, while her heart surged with delight. "You are only human after all."

"But I only drank tea!" His voice was almost a wail. "*You* know that, Hannah!"

"Of course, dear, of course," she said soothingly but in such a way as to leave doubts in his mind that would never be dispelled.

"Whisky was in that tea, Hannah," he said accusingly.

She patted his arm kindly. "Then knowing that you shouldn't have touched it, John. Take your breakfast now before it gets cold." Early though it was, half the population of Rhanna had contrived to be at Portvoynachan on some pretext or other. Because it was Saturday, the children too were at large, and the normally deserted stretches round Aosdana Bay were reminiscent of a Sunday school outing.

"My, my, would you look at what's coming now?" commented old Joe, looking up from mending a fishing net draped over a large boulder near the edge of the cliffs.

Jim Jim looked up, his netting needle poised in his hand. "Ay, ay, the Jerries must be goin' away," he commented with a bewitching show of innocence.

Canty Tom looked out to sea where, in the soft mist of morning, lurked the grey ghost shape of a naval patrol vessel. "I wouldny like to be goin' out there in one o' they rubber balloon things," he intoned, leering at the pearly turquoise of the early sky. "The Uisga hags have long claws for tearing things up. Yon rubber is no' safe, no' like a real clinker, the Caillichs will just rip the bottom out on them."

"Ach, be quiet, man," spat Jim Jim. "Or it's your bottom will be ripped. Get a hold o' one o' they nettin' needles and make yourself useful for a change."

The traps came nearer and Jim Jim suddenly abandoned his task to move nearer Morag Ruadh. "You were a long time outside wi' these soldiers last night," he said conversationally.

Morag examined her long fingers with great interest. "Ay, you're right there, Father."

"They wereny doin' you a mischief, mo ghaoil?"

"Indeed, hold your tongue, Father! You mind your own business!"

Jim Jim looked crestfallen but pursued the matter grimly. 'Now, now, Morag, as my daughter you *are* my business. I am hoping you are remembering the identity o' the men you were wi' last night – just in case," he finished in a daring rush.

Morag Ruadh tossed her red head haughtily. "Your mind is blacker than the peats you damp all day. I will not be listening to another word!"

She flounced away down the stony track to the bay. Old Joe watched her and gave Jim Jim a conspiratorial wink. "She'll have her man yet, Jim Jim. Look now, there she goes, straight to Dugald Ban. These two were more than a mite friendly last night."

Jim Jim looked at his daughter talking animatedly to Dugald and a smile creased his brown face. "By God, you're right, Joe," he said happily and leaving his nets once more he went down to join the crowds on the white sands below.

The Commandos were retrieving the dinghies from the deep, dry caves that pitted the cliffs. Dunn emerged, a frown creasing his brow. "One of the dinghies appears to be missing," he informed the crowd in general.

"Ach, is that not strange now?" Ranald shook his head sympathetically. "Are you sure you have looked right? It is easy to miss things in these caves."

173

"Hardly something so obvious," said Dunn dryly.

"Maybe it was taken away by a water witch," said Brown with a smothered laugh. But he hadn't reckoned with the islanders who immediately met the suggestion with an eager barrage of superstitious comments.

"All right! All right!" cried Dunn. "We'll make do with what we have. C'mon now, lads, get cracking!"

There was a general bustle to the water's edge and the dinghies were lowered into the speckled green shallows.

Dunn looked at Tam McKinnon whose undoubted popularity singled him out as the unofficial leader of the island's Home Guard. "You will keep an eye open at the doctor's house," instructed Dunn. "I am relying on you, Mr McKinnon. I know McKenzie of the Glen is the Chief Warden but his farming duties take up a lot of his day. In a few days the military medics will be over to see how the German officer is progressing."

Tam's face was red with importance. "We will do a good job, you can be sure o' that, sir. We will make damty sure Mr Bugger will no' run away."

"And I will make sure that Behag is getting her signals right in future," put in Robbie, his round face completely cherubic.

"You will *all* get your signals correct in future!" said Dunn sternly. "No more crossed wires . . . do you hear?" His face relaxed suddenly into a wide grin. "Thanks, lads, for a great time . . . we'll maybe come back one day for a drop more of the water of life."

"You'll no' be tellin' a soul – over there," said Tam anxiously, nodding towards the horizon as if he were referring to another planet.

"Not a soul – scout's honour," said Dunn solemnly.

Jon Jodl was sitting quietly beside Ernst in one of the dinghies. He looked at the green water lapping the edge of the sand. It was a peaceful morning filled with the tang of peat smoke and salt. Even the seabirds were in a placid mood. A curlew poked for small crabs in the shallow pools; a colony of gulls flopped lazily on the gentle swell of the waves. Above the cliffs the sheep cropped the turf with unhurried intent and two Highand cows watched the scene in the bay with silent interest.

Jon looked at it all and swallowed a lump in his throat. For a little while he had found peace on the island. He felt lulled in mind and body. No matter what his future held now he knew he would never cease to bless the reprieve that the landing on Rhanna had given him. The warmth of tears pricked his eyelids and he swallowed again. 'Farewell paradise,' he thought sadly. The memory of Anton strayed into his mind. Dunn and Anderson had escorted him over to Slochmhor at dawn. For a brief moment Anton had opened his eyes as Jon stood over the bed. "You take care, Jon," he had whispered. "I'll see you – sometime."

"Soon – soon, sir," said Jon and left quickly with the Commandos to meet the traps coming down from the Manse. In a way, Jon envied Anton his prolonged stay on the island but he was immediately ashamed of himself for thinking in such a way. Anton was still critically ill, the doctor had said he might lose some of his fingers because of frostbite.

'God forgive me,' thought Jon. 'And let Anton get better so that he can enjoy this place the way I have enjoyed it.'

He got to his feet suddenly, making the dinghy tilt alarmingly. "Slainte!" he cried wildly. "To Anton!" His blurring gaze swept over the homely faces of the people who had been so kind to him. A sob caught in his throat. "Slainte!" he cried again and Ernst was beside him, echoing the words, quietly at first, then in a great surge of sound.

"Heil Hitler," muttered Zeitler but no one heard him because Jon's cry was bouncing out joyfully from the gathering on the shore.

"Slainte, Jon! Slainte, Mr Foch!"

Dunn was politely thanking the minister for his hospitality but the great swelling of the Gaelic 'Health!' bouncing from the pillars of the cliffs and reverberating through the caves, drowned his voice. Dunn turned and stepped into the nearest dinghy and he too took up the cry. The crowd rushed to the water's edge to wave and shout and the Rev. John Gray stood alone.

"Slainte!" He heard Jon's voice above the rest and a hot flush of shame darkened his face. He had been on Rhanna for more than twenty years and never in all that time had he uttered one word of Gaelic. Jon's stay had been less than two days and he was proudly shouting the Gaelic to the skies.

The dinghies were now little dark blobs on the sun-flecked sea, yet still the cry of 'Slainte' tossed back at the crowd surging round Aosdana Bay.

"Slainte," whispered the Rev. John Gray and turned abruptly on his heel to hide the red face of humiliation from the world.

CHAPTER ELEVEN

'Smitted!'

Niall watched Portcull coming nearer. Specks in the bay resolved into the warm-hearted, familiar folk who had filled his thoughts constantly in the past week. He had managed to get word through to his parents that he was alive and well but was staying on in the devastated areas of Clydebank to assist the rescue parties and help with the evacuation of the homeless thousands. What he omitted to say was that he had broken his right arm while rescuing a small boy buried in a heap of rubble, had also sustained multiple bruises, and was suffering from exhaustion having had virtually no sleep for almost three nights after the raids. The picture of the Clydebank holocaust was keen in his mind. He couldn't forget the first night of the raids when his duties as an Air Raid Warden had taken him from horror to horror, and finally into hell on seeing the place that he called 'home' in Glasgow was no more.

The flat in which he had lodged lay fully exposed to the elements. All the furniture in his room was intact but the bed mat had flipped upwards to drape over the wardrobe and a lamp hung from the brass knob on the bed end. Eerie sights, made chillingly macabre by the curious whims of blast. And finally, the greatest hell of all, watching the broken bodies of neighbours and friends being lifted out of the debris; his demented searching for his dear little landlady, Nellie Brodie, finding her quite suddenly, her dead eyes staring up out of the rubble. He had held her close and wondered how he was going to tell Iain Brodie, who was out on fire-fighting duty, that everything he held dear in life had been taken from him. Niall sat very still while emotions raged through him. He looked up into a sky torn apart by the furring vapour trails of the German bombers. All around him the ragged silhouette of the town was thrown into sharp relief by the orange glow of fires. High explosive bombs were falling in the lower part of town, fountains of flame licked the sky, columns of black smoke billowed outwards, moving with the air currents.

His thoughts were bitter. The nerve-shattering experience of Dunkirk came to his mind in vivid flashes. Tears had coursed down his face then, tears of despair, anger, and a hatred for the enemy such as he had never experienced during his time in active service. Then it had been armed combat, soldier to soldier, but this . . . the killing of vulnerable, innocent people . . . he couldn't take that.

He stood on the deck of the boat and with hungry eyes devoured the serenity of the Hebridean island of his birth. After the chaos of Clydebank it was strange to look at a place where people ambled rather than walked and never ran if they could possibly avoid it.

The morning sparkled in a palette of breathtaking colours with the purple of the mountains thrusting stark peaks into a soft blue sky. On the hill slopes a faint fuzz of green thrust through the tawny patches of winter bracken, contrasting with the dark spires of tall pines. The cottages skirting the harbour stood out like dazzling white sugar lumps, each one sending out fluffy banners of smoke.

Niall sniffed the well remembered scent of peat fires. He stared at the translucent blue swell of the Sound of Rhanna. Closing his eyes he let the babble of gulls and the slop of waves wash over his senses till his heart surged with joy.

In the ecstasy of the moment he imagined Shona would be there to meet him as in days gone by but that was all in the past. Because his communication with home had been a one-sided, hurried affair, there was no way of anyone getting the news to him that the girl he imagined to be still in Aberdeen was there, on Rhanna, impatiently waiting for more news of him.

The boat was tying up, pushing and slapping against the pier. A row of pipe-smoking old men sat on the harbour wall, watching the proceedings with languid interest.

"St Michael be blessed!" Old Joe had spotted Niall coming down the gangplank. "It's young Niall, back from the bombs!"

Ranald, who was dividing his time between tarring his boats and reassembling a collection of ancient black bicycles with the intention of hiring them out to unwary summer tourists, threw his tar-clogged brush into a sticky tin, rising quickly from the irksome task to run to the pier. Portcull had rejoiced with Phebie and Lachlan when news came that Niall was safe but no one had expected him home for a while yet.

The men surrounded him eagerly, eyeing his plaster-encased arm with sympathetic interest. "My, my, you've been in the wars right enough, lad," observed old Andrew gently.

A smile lit Niall's weary face. "Ay, but I'm home now for a while. My studies will have to wait for a bit."

"True enough, son, you wouldny get much on paper wi' that arm," nodded Jim Jim wisely. "No' unless you are amphibious. Some folks are – it means you can do things with both hands the same."

Niall laughed and looked round the harbour with hungry eyes. "It's as peaceful as ever. I don't suppose much has been happening on Rhanna."

A clamour of protest followed and everyone vied with each other to regale him with greatly embroidered tales about the crashed German bomber.

"The Commandos took three o' the Huns away last Saturday," said Ranald, so eager to impart the news, he scratched his head with his tar-stained fingers. "But the German officer o' the plane was torn to ribbons on the mountain coming down an' damt near dead when we found him. Your father had to sew his stomach back in but two o' his fingers were rotting away wi' frostbite an' had to be cut off. The lads are guardin' him day an' night for you never know wi' Jerries . . . stayin' at your house he is."

"My house?"

"Ay, he couldny be moved for fear he would die." Ranald nodded eagerly and poked his fingers further into his thick thatch of brown hair.

"The airy-plane came over from blitzed places near Glasgow," Canty Tam beamed, leaning so far sideways it looked as if an invisible weight was pulling him over relentlessly. "Everyone was sayin' they likely killed a lot o' people before endin' up here!"

"Be quiet, you glaikit bugger!" warned Erchy, coming from the boat with a laden sack of mail.

Niall had turned white at the news. The memory of his landlady with the teapot clutched in her hands and her dead eyes staring was extremely vivid. And Iain Brodie, smoke-grimed and red-eyed after endless hours battling with endless fires, his face empty and hopeless on learning the news. Niall felt the bitterness surging through him again, taking away some of the joy he'd felt at coming home. It seemed after all that the scourge of war had touched Rhanna.

The thought of a German under the roof of Slochmhor made him feel sick with anger that his father had calmly taken the enemy into his home. Hot tears of rage pricked his eyes and he turned quickly away, his blurred gaze coming to rest at the Smiddy where a much recovered Todd was sitting outside enjoying the Spring sunshine. Beside him reclined Biddy on a wooden bench padded with cushions. They were both waving at him frantically and he raised an arm to wave back.

"Dear old Biddy," he breathed thankfully. "It will be good to have her moaning and fussing round me."

Erchy shook his sandy head ruefully. "Ach, not yet for a whily. The Cailleach hurt her ankle and is stayin' at the McDonalds' till she is better. Todd had his appendix out and the pair o' them are driving each other daft." A gleam of mischief came into his eyes. "We had a fine young nurse lookin' after us for a whily. A right nice bum and bosoms she has too. We were all thinkin' up ways to see will she come and cure us . . . my ulcer has been bad this past week," he finished, rubbing suddenly at his middle.

"But it's better your belly is now." Jim Jim removed his pipe and spat malevolently on to the cobbled pier. "They are after sendin' over a spare nurse . . . like a gallopin' hairpin she is wi' a face like a forgotten prune! There she is now, goin' up to the Smiddy. Todd has not moved for more than a week though Mollie has been giving him enough liquorice powder to shift a horse. He will be gettin' soapy water through a tube now – I forget what they calls it but I am hearing it does queer things to the bowels – makes them squeal like the bagpipes tunin' up."

Todd watched the lanky figure of the 'spare' nurse coming towards his house and he squirmed with apprehension. Biddy watched also and her lips folded into a thin line of disapproval. Despite her stern words to Babbie, she hadn't meant a word and had been thoroughly enjoying her convalescence. Lachlan had verified Babbie's diagnosis and the young nurse came almost every day to the Smiddy. Like everyone else Biddy had fallen under the girl's infectious charm and they had ceilidhed and cracked over endless 'cuppys'.

Biddy reacted to the spare nurse with characteristic suspicion and the unfortunate nurse, having neither charm nor looks in her favour, was at a disadvantage from the start. Her defence lay in a coldly formidable 'bedside manner' which wasn't designed to endear her in the hearts of the islanders.

"My God!" gulped Todd, his round face crimson. "She is comin' this way!"

"Ach, never mind," consoled Biddy. "If it's an enema she's come to give I'll see she does it right. She has hands like frogs' feets and will not be gentle wi' the tubes like myself."

"Hell no!" Todd couldn't stop the protest. "Not *two* of you! I canny take any more o' this!"

The nurse came through the gate, burying her long nose in the depths of a large hanky. "I have had nothing but sneezes since I came here," she complained. "How are you today, nurse McMillan?"

"Fine – oh yes – much better, thankin' you! It won't be long till I'm up on my feets!"

"Good, then we will all be happy! How are you today, Mr McDonald?"

"Never better, indeed no! I will be back at the Smiddy much sooner than I thought!" gabbled Todd in agitated confusion.

Biddy straightened her specs. "Where is the young nurse? She said she would be over to see how I was keeping."

The nurse sniffed disdainfully. "Too busy with that young German! Said something about taking out some of his stitches. Well, she's welcome. I wouldn't touch him with a ten-foot pole. The child from the big farm was there too, the one with the long hair and innocent eyes." She sniffed again. "Looks like that are so deceiving. She and the nurse are fawning over him like sick kittens. Now . . ." she became suddenly brisk. "Will you come inside, nurse McMillan – I'll do your enema first." She smiled sourly. "Ladies before gentlemen."

"*Me!*" Biddy's yell of indignation sent a clutter of crows into the sky where they flapped angrily.

"Yes indeed, nurse McMillan. I met Mrs McDonald last night and she told me that for a week you haven't been near the – er toilet. She said you had only been passing water into the – hm – chamber pot."

"That Mollie!" roared Biddy while Todd shook with delighted glee. "I'll – I'll never bandage her varicose veins again!"

Niall smiled as Biddy's indignant yells filled the harbour. "Well, *she* hasn't changed anyway! Still the same grumbling Biddy!" He began to move away, calling back, "I'll see you later, lads."

"Ay, we're having a ceilidh tonight at Tam's," grinned Ranald. "You should come down and try some o' his Uisge-Beatha. Like nectar it is."

Niall smiled appreciatively, happy to be among the fun-loving folk of the island again. He walked towards Glen Fallan, lifting his face to breathe the wild, sweet scent of sun-warmed heather. In the high fields above Laighmhor, Fergus and Bob strode among the flocks of sheep. A few tiny early lambs wobbled unsteadily near their mothers. The sheepdogs ran purposefully about their business, answering to the different whistles with an eager obedience that reflected Bob's training. Niall looked with delight at the familiar scene and he raised his arm. The men were engrossed in their work but a moment later they waved in response and Fergus's voice drifted faitnly. "Hello there, Niall! We'll see you later!"

Slochmhor was quiet and deserted. For a moment Niall thought there was no one at home. He knew Fiona would be in school, his father out on calls but, though he wasn't expected, he had anticipated his mother's welcome and he felt unreasonably cheated. The kitchen was warm and homely with two cats sprawled by the fire, one of them using Lachlan's slippers as a pillow. On the window ledge a vase of pussy willows still managed to look graceful though they were parked alongside a jar of frog spawn floating in obnoxious green water. Niall chuckled. Fiona was still pursuing her favourite hobby, a keen interest in all forms of insect and amphibious life. She was a child who kept pet spiders in jars and studied minute creatures with the aid of one of Lachlan's old microscopes. After eight years of struggling to keep her tom-boy daughter's room as feminine as possible. Phebie was gradually giving up the fight and had ceased to be disgusted by the odd assortment of creepy pets she encountered while cleaning.

A light little laugh came from upstairs and Niall stiffened. The laugh was so familiar to him yet the unexpected sound of it made his heart race madly. "Shona, what the hell . . ." he whispered and bounded upstairs. Even while he burst into the little guest room he realised this was where the wounded German lay.

Anton Büttger had made a remarkable recovery thanks to Lachlan's surgical skill and Babbie's devoted nursing. The military medics had been, escorted by a vigilant body of the Home Guard. The medics praised Lachlan, agreed with him that Anton was not fit to be moved, then departed, satisfied that Anton was in good hands and kept well under surveillance by the Home Guard.

The minute the boat whisked them away the Home Guard dispersed about their own business. All of them had clumped up to visit the young German and had come to the united conclusion that 'Mr Büttger is a fine lad, just. Not like a Jerry at all.' Their convictions were further strengthened when the fact became known that he had steered the crippled plane away from habitation before bailing out over the mountains. The islanders applauded such a heroic act and told each other, 'The lad doesny need guns over him all the time. Just a wee visit now and then to see is he still there.' The vigilance of the Home Guard was thus lessened and the McLachlans breathed sighs of relief.

On entering the room Niall got the impression that he had intruded into an intimate little world. Anton, pale but handsome, was laughing up at Shona whose hand was clasped in his, her blue eyes alight in her animated face.

"Shona!" Niall shouted her name in surprise.

"Niall!" She turned from the bed, crossing the room to stare at him in joyous disbelief. "I didn't know or I would have come to meet you! You're hurt, what have you done to your arm?" She put out a hand to touch him but he pulled away.

"I didn't know you were back on Rhanna." His voice held a faint note of suspicion.

"But – I wrote to you when I left Aberdeen! I told you I was coming to see you in Glasgow. I'm just home for a rest – I haven't been too well."

He saw then her pale little face and her incredible eyes, smudged with a delicate blue-black under the lower lashes. He had forgotten how blue her eyes were, how beautifully shaped her small sensitive mouth. Her auburn hair was swept up from her face but gave it no maturity, instead it emphasised her cameo features and pointed chin. She looked like a little girl trying to appear grown up and the nearness of her overwhelmed him for a moment. He longed to crush her to him, to pour words of love into her ears but the picture of her with Anton had roused a stab of jealousy in his breast.

"I didn't get your letter," he said briefly and bitterly. "Mrs Brodie no longer has a letter box – it may still be attached to the door buried beneath the rubble of what was her home! Not that Mrs Brodie will worry about that now . . . she's out of it all . . ." He glanced at Anton accusingly. "Mrs Brodie doesn't need her home now, but Iain Brodie needs it – and thousands more like him who lost everything in the raids last week!" His voice rose menacingly. "Ask your German friend how he would go about helping the people he helped to kill . . . you might not find so much to laugh at then – Fräulein!"

"Niall!" She stared at him shocked. "Stop that! You're raving like a madman!"

"Maybe I am mad – mad enough for a bit of revenge! I keep seeing corpses, they're in my head and I can't get rid of them! I go to bed at night and see my landlady – a tiny wee body who never harmed a soul – lying among the bloody tons of rubble that buried her alive!"

"Niall." Her voice was gentle because she saw the terrible tension in him. "You'll have to try and forget. The raids were horrible, we all know that . . ."

"Do you? Were you there? Pray God you'll be spared anything like it . . ." He nodded towards Anton. "He'll know, he was over the place! He must have seen the hell of it all. After all he must have dropped some of the incendiaries that lit up Clydebank like a Christmas tree. Maybe his was one of the bombers that strafed the streets, spattering bullets about just for the fun of it! Ask him if he knows what it's like to be holed up like a terrified rabbit waiting for a bomb to drop!"

"Ask him yourself." Shona's voice was barely audible. "He can speak English quite well."

"The intellectual type!" answered Niall scathingly.

Anton had struggled up in bed, his keen blue eyes meeting

Niall's angry brown gaze. "Niall." He spoke the name with respect. "Fräulein Shona tells me about you all day. We laugh just now about your times together as children."

To Niall the words were flippant, designed to get him off the subject of the raids. "So, you know my name," he said sarcastically. "And you laugh. I wonder if we'll laugh when we know the names of all the people killed in Glasgow and Clydebank – and all the other cities bombed by the Luftwaffe!"

"Anton's mother, father and sisters were killed by the British in an air raid over Berlin." Shona said the words quietly, her mouth frozen with dismay.

Anton had fallen back on the pillows, his eyes gazing unseeingly at the wall. "I hate the war as much as you do," he said wearily. He reached to the dresser, picking up an iron cross which he dangled idly in his fingers. "This little decoration is meant to signify bravery – all it means is I have killed a lot of people. I am not really proud of it – but I wear it – in the same way the British wear their medals." He laughed without humour. "I am very relieved that I do not have to pin it to my pyjamas – I can forget it for a while."

Niall suddenly felt deflated and uneasy. The sound of Anton's rapid breathing filled the room. A shower of sparks exploded from the coals in the grate and the clear, fluted call of a curlew came sweetly from the Glen.

Shona felt her heart beating swiftly. She could feel the tension spewing from Niall, it showed in his white young face, the clenching of his fist. He looked so forlorn, so unlike the loving, carefree Niall of her memories, that for a moment she was afraid. He'd come through the horrific experiences of Dunkirk, scarred but still buoyant of spirit. The war had wounded him again but she knew it wasn't that which had so crushed him. The first time he had gone to war expecting to meet death and destruction, the second time war had come to him and she realised he hadn't been prepared for it.

"Niall . . ." she began huskily just as footsteps clattered and Babbie arrived breathlessly into the room.

"Oh – sorry." She drew back at the sight of Niall. He turned and her hand flew to her mouth. *"Niall!"* The cry was one of disbelief.

He stared at her. *"Babbie!* What on earth – how did *you* get here?"

They gaped at each other till Babbie finally stuttered. "Shona brought me – at least she asked me to come back with her to Rhanna for a holiday . . . I was leaving the hospital anyway . . . you know me, always jumping around! Pastures new all the time. Your name has been mentioned here constantly but I never dreamt – I never connected . . ." She was unable to go on.

Shona looked from one to the other. "It would be silly to ask if you know one another." She laughed as lightly as she could. "It seems you certainly do!"

Niall pulled himself together with an effort. "Only vaguely," he said briefly. "Isn't that right, Babbie?"

"Oh yes, hardly at all. I didn't even know your second name – till now!"

Despite the careless words Shona sensed unspoken words bouncing between the two. They were trying too hard to be casual. Babbie was fussing with Anton's bedclothes, Niall paying a great deal of attention to a loose thread on his sling. He looked up and his eye's caught Babbie's. She seemed flustered, with a pink tinge staining her pale face and her green eyes unnaturally bright. Shona held her breath but no matter how hard she tried she couldn't stop the suspicions crowding into her mind. Niall and Babbie! There was something between them, something they were trying very hard to hide. Her heart beat swiftly into her throat. She felt weak with emotion but she forced her head high. "I'll have to go now. Father will be in soon from the fields and I promised Kirsteen to help with dinner. "I'll see you – Niall."

"Wait!" Niall stayed her hasty flight. "When will I see you – Ni-Cridhe?"

He said the endearment softly and a sob rose in her throat. 'Ni-Cridhe!' My dear lassie! How long she had waited to hear the caress of his dear, lilting voice but her reply was non-committal. "Whenever you want – though not this afternoon. I'm going over to help Tina – she has a bad ankle."

"I could come with you. I'd like fine to see Tina and the bairns."

"Och, but I'm just going to wash and set her hair. You would feel in the way."

A flush of anger stained his fair skin. "I'm having a taste of that already! Away you go then! A lot of folk are waiting on you it would seem!"

She flew downstairs and hardly saw where she was going for tears. At Laigmhor she flounced about, clattering things on the table. Kirsteen and Fergus exchanged looks. "I see Niall's home," said the latter carefully.

"Ay, that he is! With a broken arm too! Niall always seems to be in the wars." She kept her tone on a conversational level.

"And now you and he are at war with each other," Kirsteen said deliberately.

Shona looked up quickly. "If it's anybody's business, then you are right enough, Kirsteen!" she cried hotly. "Niall would fight in an empty house . . . his temper is even worse than mine now!"

Fergus smiled faintly. "That would take a bit of doing, mo ghaoil."

Shona dumped a pile of plates on to the table with such a clatter that Ginger, a big placid tom, shot out of the door in fright. "And who have I to thank for *my* temper?" she demanded wildly and stamped out of the kitchen in high dudgeon.

She didn't see Niall till well after tea when he came walking down Glen Fallan with Babbie. She was securing the hen-houses and heard their laughter long before they reached the gate in the dyke.

"We're going over to ceilidh with Tam!" called Niall. "Are you coming along, mo ghaoil?"

The sight of them together brought a swift rush of jealousy to her heart. She felt hurt and cheated. When she spoke her voice was high with a mixture of rage and tears. "No, you two get along! I'm – I'm busy and I'm in no mood to go ceilidhing." Niall said nothing. He just stood looking at her for a long moment, then he linked his arm in Babbie's and pulled her swiftly away.

Shona stood looking after them, unable to believe the turn of events. She couldn't believe that Niall and Babbie were nothing more than casual acquaintances. Was it possible that Babbie, whom she loved like the sister she'd never had, could have engineered her stay on Rhanna in the hope that she would be near Niall? Their surprise on seeing each other had seemed genuine enough . . . yet they certainly appeared to know one another quite well, there was no denying that, or the looks they had exchanged in Anton's room.

She felt sick with misery and shivered uneasily. She looked back at the big farmhouse with its soft lights glowing from the windows. It was warm and inviting but in her present mood she felt it wasn't inviting her. Kirsteen's high, light laugh rang out followed by Fergus's deep lilting happy voice. For a moment she wished it was just herself and her father again. She could have talked to him in the intimate way they had adopted through the years. Sometimes just a word from him made her world seem right again, with just a few quiet words of advice he had a knack of making her worries seem trivial. Then she remembered the years of his loneliness and she hated herself for grudging him one moment with Kirsteen. When she went inside Fergus turned from the table. He was enveloped in a large pink apron which was liberally coated with flour. "This daft woman is showing me how to bake bread!" His black eyes snapped with delight. "Me who knows better how to plant wheat! But I'll show her the McKenzies aren't to be easily beaten, eh mo ghaoil?" There was a message in the laughing words and black eyes met blue in a moment of understanding. Smilingly she went into the fray and spent a light-hearted hour in the kitchen before going early to bed.

"Goodnight, Shona," Grant's voice came sleepily. "Will you come and give me a cuddle . . . I know girls like doing that sort of thing," he added quickly. She went in and held him in her arms till his black lashes touched his smooth cheeks. He lay against her contentedly and she felt a rush of love for her little half-brother. Bending low she kissed his warm, plump cheek and his small arms came up to encircle her neck. "I love you, Shona . . . you're not too bad considering you're a girl," he muttered with a sleepy grin. She left the room knowing that her earlier feelings of insecurity had been born of her hurt over Niall.

Nevertheless she couldn't sleep. She was thinking of Niall and Babbie at the ceilidh. It would be a merry affair. Some of the best ceilidhs on the island took place at Tam's house. Niall and Babbie would dance together . . . he would hold her close . . . and then they would go back to Slochmhor together because Babbie was still staying there, though she had moved out of Anton's room. She was in the little box room – which was on the other side of Niall's room !

"Oh God," she whispered, "please help me to be less suspicious – and – and jealous. I can't help it, I love Niall so much yet every time we meet we seem to fight all the time . . ." She snuggled into her pillows and wept. Her arms ached to hold something. Tot, her faithful old spaniel had shared her bed for years, but Tot was dead now and she felt terribly alone.

Mirabelle's rag dolls sat in a floppy row on the shelves. Whenever she looked at them she thought of the plump, homely old housekeeper who had been mother to her during the vulnerable years of her childhood. Every one of the dolls had been lovingly stitched by the old lady for the child she had pledged into her care. They were all somewhat dusty and bedraggled but on the whole had stood the test of time. On top of the dresser was the splendid 'town' doll given to her by Fergus's brother, Alick, on one of his summer visits to the island. The extravagant beauty of the doll had taken her breath away and for a time Mirabelle's rag dolls had been cast aside. But the 'town' doll was cold and hard with none of the cuddly qualities of the others. She had never taken it to bed. Eventually it had become merely ornamental, a pleasant reminder of the uncle whose affection she had always appreciated though she knew he had caused so much trouble in the past. She hadn't seen Alick since last autumn. He had joined the army, surprising a lot of people except those who knew him best. He was still trying to prove himself, making up for the years of self-indulgence of his early manhood.

Shona looked at the 'town' doll with its prettily painted face. "Poor Uncle Alick," she said softly and, getting up, she retrieved it from the dresser, picked out her most favoured rag doll then padding back to bed she cuddled the toys to her like a lost child.

Early next morning Niall met Fergus at the gate of Laigmhor. Fergus looked at Niall's plaster-encased arm and his dark rugged face broke into a smile. "We have one thing in common anyway – for a time at least."

Niall leaned against the dyke and looked towards the sea gleaming in the sun-bathed morning. "There's a lot we have in common, Fergus, though at one time no one would have thought it. For one thing we both love the same girl – with one difference – you know how to get the best out of her. There was a time I thought I could do that too but growing up has brought changes to us both . . ." He shook his fair head in despair, at a loss how to explain further.

Fergus lit his pipe slowly and stood puffing it for a moment. "Take a bit of advice, lad . . . I haven't had a lot of experience with women – God knows I mucked up my own affairs pretty thoroughly. But I've learned that it's no use hanging around waiting for time to sort things out for you, you've got to do it yourself. Time has a knack of changing things. I know my daughter. She's a stubborn wee bitch at times . . ." He smiled. "What else can you expect from a girl with a father like me? You'll have to show her who's boss, be a little domineering! She's in there now mooning around, waiting for you – get in there and be firm with her! She can't go running off in tantrums for the rest of her life!"

It was a big speech for someone usually so thrifty with words. Niall sensed the caring that had prompted them and he gripped Fergus by the shoulder. "Thanks," he said briefly then went through the gate and up the path.

Shona was putting away the breakfast dishes. She had seen him at the gate and she kept her back to him as he came through the door.

"Right now, we'll have no more of your sulks," said Niall firmly. "It's a lovely day, just right for a brisk walk over the hill to Nigg. I want to see old Jock's new piglets and I thought of popping in to see Dodie on the way!"

She turned a crimson face, opened her mouth to speak, but he gave her no chance. "Be quick now, get your peenie off. You'd better wear your wellies for the dew is still heavy on the grass."

She flew upstairs with a singing heart and was back in minutes with a blue cardigan thrown over her shoulders.

"Put your coat on too," he told her sternly. "There's a bite in the wind despite the sun."

"You sound like Mirabelle," she laughed happily as they went out into the sunny morning.

He put his arm round her shoulders and they walked in silence to the hill track that wound over the high moors. The wind blew against the tough sedge grass, rippling it into tawny waves; green fern curls prodded through the tangle of dead bracken and nebulous webs glistened on the rich carpet of moss at the edge of the track.

On the ridge of a hillock a small group of islanders were already skinning fresh peat hags. Laughter and banter went hand in hand with such work because it involved both sexes. Peat skinning meant a lot of hard work yet a casual observer might have been forgiven for thinking the fun-loving islanders were literally having a picnic. Yet, despite the banter, the hags were worked with a skill that could only be carried out by a people imbued by generations of self-sufficiency. While the men cut deeply into the banks with the broad-bladed rutter the women expertly skimmed off the top layer of turf with flaughter spades. At regular intervals the workers fortified themselves from the milk luggie into which they simply plunged a ladle to fill with thick creamy milk.

"It's early for the skimming," commented Niall.

"The weather has been so fine here," said Shona almost apologetically. "There's a good skin on the hags."

"Ay, it has been very warm for the time of year," said Niall absently. "Though I canny say I noticed too much blue skies. Smoke hangs about a long time after the fires have died away."

Dokie Joe's voice came floating down and they looked up to see him waving his spade. "Were you enjoyin' the ceilidh last evening, Niall?"

Niall waved and answered in the affirmative. Shona's head went up. "So, you had a fine time last night, Niall McLachlan!"

"Indeed I did so," he said defensively.

"And Babbie too, no doubt?"

"I don't think so. She went home early."

"And you went with her?"

"No, I did not. Nancy and Archie saw her along. She had to go back to change Anton's dressing!" He stopped and faced her squarely, the wind tossing his fair hair into his eyes and whipping at the old kilt he always wore when he came back to Rhanna. "If you must know, you wee spitfire, I got well and truly drunk last night. To put it rudely, I got pissed! And all because of you!

Good God, you little bitch! I've longed to see you for months – when I do I find you hanging over a German airman as if you never knew Niall McLachlan was born!"

She stared. "You're jealous, Niall McLachlan!"

"All right, I'm jealous, dammit! I have a right to be jealous. If I could look at you without trembling I might not be jealous! But I am, and I do, and if that sounds like a lot of seagull shit you can throw it back in my face if it makes you feel better . . . go on then, start throwing!" he finished passionately.

"Babbie – what about Babbie?" she whispered.

"What about Babbie? She's just a girl I met in Glasgow! I met a lot of girls there – and men too. I have a habit of making friends – casual acquaintances such as you must have had yourself in Aberdeen. It was meeting her here, on Rhanna, that surprised me – us both – so much!"

"It wasn't just Babbie." Her voice was breathless with relief. "It was your attitude to Anton. I know he's a German – the enemy – but he's first and foremost a human being and you spoke to him as if he were a bit cow dung!"

"I know." His voice was subdued with shame. "I apologised to him last night after I got home from Tam's. I was in my room, drunk as a Lord, hating the thought of a German through the wall from me! I spent a good half hour feeling sick and hating Anton. I wanted to go through and spew on him! Then I heard a thud and went in to find the poor bugger had fallen out of bed trying to reach a glass of water. I helped him back to bed and we talked for ages . . . about the war, what it does to people. He's – all right is Anton."

She reached up and pushed a lock of hair from his eyes. "When I saw him, lying so hurt and helpless, it was you I saw on a bloody beach in France. His face was your face. I had to help him in every way I could because, in a way, it was you I was helping. I suppose that sounds silly."

He laughed then, his brown eyes crinkling with joy. "The daftest thing in the world, but I love you for it!" He drew her to him and kissed her harshly, his lips forcing hers apart till the warmth of his tongue touched hers briefly.

"Oh God." He breathed into her silken hair. "I've dreamt of this moment for so long. I want to kiss you for ever! Do you think people are allowed to kiss each other in heaven? If not then I'm never going to die!"

She laughed gaily. "I think people kiss all the time in heaven. How else would they know they were there?"

He reached out to grab her hand and they ran like children to arrive at Dodie's cottage, breathlessly happy.

"In the name of heaven, what the hell's that?" cried Niall, pointing to a ramshackle creation of wood and metal huddled into the bushes near the cottage. The wind soughed through it, rattling metal against metal, eerily whining into cracks in the wood. They didn't need to look too closely to realise that Dodie had built himself a 'wee hoosie' using materials from the wrecked German bomber. The tail piece of the plane served as the roof with the bold symbol of the swastika breathtakingly displayed to the world. The youngsters gaped in astonishment then sped over to examine the monstrosity at close quarters. The door scraped open on ill-fitting hinges. In the middle of the black cavern sat Dodie's large chamber pot, looking like the proverbial pea in a drum. On a small wooden shelf a large assortment of aircraft equipment jostled with a high pile of neat newspaper squares. To the right of the chamber pot the control column was stuck into the ground at a crazy angle; propped in a corner was the broken barrel of a gun, under it, decoratively arranged, a band of ammunition.

Shona pointed at the control column and hissed, "What on earth is *that* for?"

"The mind boggles – but that's not all – look at this! Dodie is certainly going to be well amused when he's using his wee hoosie!"

Affixed to the back of the door was an array of plane's instruments looking decidedly incongruous in such odd surroundings.

"Och, he's the limit!" giggled Shona. "He's made his wee hoosie like the inside of a plane so that he can pretend to be flying when he's in here!"

Niall let out a bellow of mirth which coincided with a terrible bellowing that suddenly erupted from the cow shed. Ealasaid stood in her stall looking greatly distressed and Niall saw immediately that her udder was so distended the veins stood out like knotted rope.

"She hasn't been milked," frowned Niall. "Something's wrong with Dodie. He would never let Ealasaid suffer like this."

They raced to the cottage and tip-toed in. They hadn't visited the place since they were children but it hadn't changed. Threadbare curtains covered the tiny windows, ashes spilled from the grate, treasures reaped from sea and land lay everywhere, lovingly gathered by the old eccentric who saw great beauty in the simple things of life. But one difference was immediately apparent. The old rickety wooden chairs had been replaced by two well-upholstered car seats. They sat, one on either side of the fireplace, comfortably ridiculous looking. Various other car accessories were scattered round the room and Shona held her breath in delight. Madam Balfour had been furious when old Angus refused to recover the car left by the Commandos near Croynachan. By the time she had coaxed Lachlan into fetching it, it had been completely dismantled with only the chassis and the body shell left to rot on the Muir of Rhanna.

Blame was difficult to lay at any one door. Innocence looked out from the faces of the accused who sympathised with each other in pained incredulity that anyone could believe them capable of such corruption. Madam Balfour tried to enlist the services of Dugald Donaldson but he refused to get involved. Eventually Madam Balfour contacted the Stornoway police and she was now awaiting an official visit. Rhanna seldom had a visit by the police. The one who usually came was related to nearly everyone on Rhanna and spent his time ceilidhing at relatives' houses.

But it was rumoured that 'Big Gregor' had been transferred to Mull so when Madam Balfour's plans became known there was a scuffle to cover up any little misdemeanours that might warrant investigation. Tam McKinnon was particularly disturbed by the news and made haste to transfer his 'still' to Annack Gow's secret room inside her blackhouse. A delighted Annack was only too willing to oblige and once again her secret room was fully operational, as it had been in the days of her forebears. Shona knew that no official being would hazard a visit to Dodie's cottage and she hugged herself with glee at the idea of him getting away with his share of the spoils.

"Are you about, Dodie?" cried Niall and was rewarded with a soulful "He breeah" from a door leading out of the kitchen. They went up a short passageway, hung with driftwood cupboards, and came to the bedroom. Dodie's particular odour pervaded every corner, cluttered with old clothes and junk. His old mackintosh hung from a hook on the door over a layer of tattered oilskins. Under the window stood his huge wellingtons and Shona rushed forward to throw open the sash, allowing the fresh, clean air from the moor to swoop in and absorb the smell.

"Ach, dinna open that window!" cried Dodie in alarm. "I'm just about dead wi' cold as it is!"

He was terribly embarrassed, cowering under a threadbare sheet like a frightened animal. He was a pathetic sight with his gaunt, grey face covered in stubbly little patches of hair. On a locker by his bedside a Delft cup held ancient dregs of tea, on a saucer beside it two mouldy crusts adhered to a festering slice of cheese.

Grimy tears coursed down the lines of his face, his mouth was twisted in pain and a band of perspiration glistened beneath the rim of his greasy cap.

"I have a terrible belly ache," he wailed, scrubbing at the tears with one hand and rubbing his middle with the other. "It's been on me for a time now but it has just got worse this whily back. I'm near dyin' wi' the pain . . . and – and Ealasaid, my poor beastie, is ill too. I havny been able to rise out my bed to milk her. She's roarin' in pain and breakin' my heart hearin' her."

"I'll go and milk her now, I saw a bucket in the shed," said Shona, thankfully escaping the room.

"And I'll go and fetch Father before he finishes in the surgery," said Niall. He eyed a heap of gay patchwork quilts lying on an antiquated bride's kist. "Would you like some of these quilts on the bed, Dodie? You're shivering."

Dodie looked terrified. "No, no, I dinna want them! Just shut the window."

Exasperated, Niall banged the window shut and turned out of the cottage. Leaving Shona to keep an eye on things he ran back over the hill track to Slochmhor. Lachlan came at once, having managed with Niall's help to get his neglected car started. They hurtled over the narrow hill track, the sound of the roaring engine making the crowd at the peat hags stop work as one.

"An emergency, just," commented Erchy. The others nodded in sad agreement. "The doctor is having a busy time these days," was the general verdict.

"Who will it be?" wondered Kate.

"Lachlan will see them along," said Jim Jim with conviction.

"If the Lord spares them," sighed Isabel sagely.

There was a move towards the milk luggie where creamy milk was amiably dispensed, together with much speculation about the 'emergency'.

When Lachlan arrived the hens were squawking dismally in the kitchen while Shona boiled a rather sparse 'hen's pot' over a fire made up hastily with cinders and kindling. She knew Dodie would be embarrassed by her presence and Lachlan went alone into the bedroom.

"You dinna have to look at me, Doctor," sobbed the red-faced Dodie. "I know fine what ails me."

"Indeed, and what might that be, Dodie?"

Dodie looked with horror at the pile of patchwork quilts. "It's *these*! I know it's these! I've been *smitted*, Doctor!"

"Smitted with what?" Lachlan saw how distressed the old eccentric was and his voice was gentle.

"With *Shelagh*! You mind, Doctor, she always said it was the winds she had, but I know fine what killed her."

"But, Dodie, that was years ago," protested Lachlan. "I don't see what it has got to do with your condition."

"I have it, Doctor, the cancer! The same as Shelagh. Before she died she told me I was to have these lovely quilts made by her very own hands. After she passed on I took them . . . just to please her because she was always my good friend. My, but they were warm right enough but I havny used them since my bellyache started."

Lachlan sat down on the bed which sagged alarmingly under the extra weight. Patiently he explained. "You don't catch cancer, Dodie. It isn't a germ like 'flu or a cold. Please believe that. I'll examine you and tell you what I think you've got."

Despite vigorous protestations he proceeded with the examination, inwardly shocked when he saw how thin Dodie was. A few minutes later he looked up, his warm smile lighting his face.

"Stop worrying, Dodie, you don't have cancer but you do have an ulcer, probably a duodenal."

Dodie looked terrified. "Ach, Doctor, that sounds worse than the other!"

"It won't be with proper treatment and diet. What on earth have you been eating, man?"

"Nothing, Doctor."

"*Nothing!* But you must be eating something!"

Dodie turned his face to the wall and his big, calloused hands worked nervously on the sheet. Lachlan felt a great surge of remorse and compassion for the old man. His life had been one of misfortune from the start. Against all odds he had battled on, catering for his simple needs by the sheer hard work that had been his lot since he was old enough to hold a spade. Everyone on the island genuinely liked him, but his fierce independence made charitable acts difficult and he was more or less left to his own devices. It never occurred to anyone that the show of independence might be a form of pride born in a man deprived of the basic things in life that everyone else took for granted. His was a big heart, with a great capacity for loving all the creatures, great and small, that God had put on the earth. In his simple world he had created a far happier life for himself than many with all the obvious requisites but it was a lonely existence and no one needed to be that lonely.

"Come on, Dodie," coaxed Lachlan, taking one of his big hands and squeezing it reassuringly. "You can tell me, I'll understand."

"Och, Doctor, I'm starvin' so I am! I used my ration book to help light the fire one morning – I didny know what it meant for I canny read things in the foreign language. When I went to Merry Mary's for my messages, she asked me for it and I didny like to tell her I burnt it. She would think I was daft and it bein' a government thing I thought I would get into trouble so I just stopped goin' to the shop. My tattie crop was a bad one last year and they just ran out on me after the New Year. My poor hens have gone off the laying without the right food – it's terrible to see them starvin' to death."

"You could have boiled one to yourself, Dodie."

"Och, no, never! I wouldny kill the poor beasts!" Dodie was horrified at the suggestion.

"So, you only had Ealasaid's milk?" said Lachlan quietly.

"Ay, but never even that sometimes for she has never been the same since she captured that German cheil." He put out a big hand. "Doctor, it's my baccy I miss most. You wouldny have a wee bit – would you now?"

Lachlan extracted a tin from his pocket. "You keep this, Dodie, but don't chew any till you've had a bite to eat. It's not the best thing for an ulcer but it will do wonders for your peace of mind. Now put your clothes on. I'll take you down in the car to Slochmhor."

"But . . . what about Ealasaid?" came the inevitable wail.

"One of the lads will drive her down." Lachlan's smile lit up his boyish face. "How would you like to go and stay with Mairi for a wee while?"

Dodie's face glowed through the tears. "Mairi," he breathed happily.

"Ay, you know she loves looking after people. With Wullie away she's at a loss . . . you and Mairi get on fine together, and she'll put Ealasaid in with Bluebell."

Lachlan was rewarded by Dodie's radiant eyes. He knew he wasn't taking a liberty, because Mairi had often confided to him her desire to give Dodie "a good bit loving care and plenty food". Lachlan went out to explain matters to the young people who were tidying the kitchen.

"Poor old Dodie," breathed Shona.

"It's up to all of us to see this never happens again," said Lachlan. "He could have died up here and no one the wiser."

Niall swallowed hard. "Surely – Erchy must pop in sometimes with the mail?"

"What mail? I don't think Dodie has ever had a letter in his life. Just now I noticed a picture postcard above his bed. It was tattered almost out of recognition by continual handling . . . probably the only postcard he's ever had."

They went outside and stood silent, each appalled and saddened by their thoughts. Niall looked at Dodie's pitiful attempt to build a 'wee hoosie' in order to be like the majority of islanders, and he said huskily, "Come the summer Dodie will have the finest wee hoosie on Rhanna. I asked Wullie the Carpenter last night if he would give me a job during my summer holidays. I should learn how to knock a few nails into wood. I'll get some of the lads to help me. We can scrounge some bits and pieces from Tam. He has a shed full of junk."

"Good idea," approved Lachlan. Dodie appeared, apologetic because he had taken some time to gather together his most treasured possessions into a large, spotted hanky.

"My hens, what about my hens?" he whispered, holding on to a gatepost for support.

"They'll be looked after too," said Lachlan patiently and bundled Dodie into the car to be driven to Slochmhor in style. There he underwent the rigours of a steaming carbolic bath but the comforts that awaited him more than made up for such indignities. For the first time in his life he was made to feel cherished and important and was the first to admit he owed it all to a 'leddy'.

CHAPTER TWELVE

Children Again

Shona walked quickly over Glen Fallan to Slochmhor. Anton was leaving the island next day and Niall had asked Shona to come over to the house early. They were all sorry that the young German was going. Lachlan had kept the military medics at bay with various plausible excuses but there was no denying that Anton was now ready to leave Rhanna.

The April sun cascaded over the countryside, the heat of it abundant for the time of year. The air was fragrant with the scent of clover, crushed by the frolicking hooves of the lambs scattered in the fields. Shona lifted her bright head and breathed deeply. She loved the spring, with each day breathing the promise of the long, golden summer ahead.

The last few weeks with Niall had been full and happy. In a way, they both seemed to be getting to know each other all over again, with the subject of marriage very far in the background, and she was glad of this because she felt she wasn't yet ready to make any firm decisions. Sometimes the past loomed very near, at others it was so far away it was like a dream, a mad jumble of hurried moments when everything happened too quickly for there to be any lasting impressions.

Her thoughts were far away when she went up the path and round to the kitchen. It was very quiet. Lachlan had taken a day off and had gone with Phebie, Kirsteen, Fergus, and the children to picnic in one of the sheltered coves near Croy. Elspeth had passed Laigmhor earlier on her way to the shops at Portcull, and Slochmhor, nestling against tall green pines, looked rather deserted. But Niall was standing outside the kitchen door and in his arms with her head resting on his shoulder was Babbie. He was stroking her fiery hair tenderly and she was leaning against him crying.

Shona recoiled from the sight and had to push her fists into her mouth to stop from crying out. All her former doubts came flooding back, magnified a thousandfold by the evidence of her own eyes. Niall looked up suddenly and saw her standing there poised ready for flight but Babbie's back was turned and Niall pushed her from him, propelling her into the house without letting her turn round. He came dashing over to Shona and grabbed her arm.

"Let me go, oh, please let me go!" she said in a half-sob.

"Listen – listen to me, Shona!" His voice was harsh and so compelling that she turned to stare at him. "Shona, if you love me, if you love Babbie in the way that you say, then you will do exactly as I ask. There's – something you will have to know – not about us . . . about Babbie! I promised her I wouldn't tell anyone but – you're not anyone and I'm not going to risk losing you over a misunderstanding."

She looked into his honest brown eyes and found herself saying, "All right, Niall, what do you want?"

"Just behave as you normally do, that's all . . . no, listen, Shona. We're all going out for the day . . . you, me, Babbie and Anton. We're going over to Portvoynachan in Father's car. Babbie wants to go to Aosdana Bay, it's one of her favourite places."

"The Bay of the Poet," said Shona slowly. "Yes, one or two people have seen her walking there – alone – always alone." She laughed lightly. "Some of the old folks say she is drawn there by the spirit of the young man who died there."

"Will you do as I ask?" he said urgently.

"Very well, Niall, but who will drive the car? Anton isn't quite up to it with half his fingers gone."

"I will – I learned in the army."

"But – your arm . . ."

"Never mind my arm, I'll manage." He looked at her pleadingly.

"Trust me, darling – and – and – no matter how you feel right now act as if you're having the time of your life! Laugh, sing – anything and I'll tell you why later!"

Phebie had left a bulging picnic hamper on the kitchen table. They went to collect it, then went out to the shed where Lachlan kept the car.

"Does your father know you're taking it?" asked Shona quietly, her mind racing with a million questions.

"No, it only really occurred to me after he left but I'll tell him about it, he'll understand . . . he always does."

They piled into the car, Babbie and Anton in the back, Shona beside Niall at the front.

"I'll steer with my left hand," he told her laughingly. "And you can work the gears . . . don't worry." He stemmed her protests. "Fiona could do it, it's so easy. I'll be working the clutch with my foot. It's a simple matter of coordination, mo ghaoil."

She forced the laughter he had requested but as they got going on the journey she found herself responding to him with a spontaneity that was entirely natural. Niall was in a wild, abandoned mood. His head was thrown back, his brown eyes sparkling as the car hurtled over the rough moor road. The jolting of the car distorted their voices and choked the merriment in their throats. Anton and Babbie clutched each other, the former lapsing into German in his excitement. His pale, handsome face sparkled and he chuckled as Babbie, thrown against him time after time, finally gave up the effort of trying to stay upright. She leaned against him and they both jolted in unison.

Niall began to sing and immediately everyone took up the tune whether they knew the words or not. It was a discordant mêlée but no one cared. They were all mad and young together, the merriment of their voices careered out over the moors, tossed by the fresh spring breezes into a concoction of every note of happiness the human voice was capable of producing. Crofters stopped work to watch the passing of the 'contraption'. Rosy-cheeked children stood by the wayside to wave at it solemnly.

"This day will last forever!" cried Anton, his arms embracing the world.

"Forever and ever!" echoed Babbie, her mysterious green eyes sparkling with a million lights.

Aosdana Bay drowsed in the quiet of morning. The blue sea effervesced invitingly on to the silver-white beaches.

"C'mon, I dare you all to have a paddle!" said Niall, sitting on a rock to pull off his boots and stockings. In minutes a variety of footwear dotted the sands and everyone danced to meet the foaming surf, shrieking in agonised ecstasy as freezing water splashed on to naked skin. They joined hands and ran to meet each wave and though skirts were tucked into knickers and trousers rolled to knees the hems were soon soaked.

For a time the world was theirs to command. Blue sky and sea reeled round as they danced. Aosdana Bay belonged to them. The beauty of youth reflected gloriously in each bright face in those carefree moments. Two fiery-haired girls, two fair young men, pranced together like children and though one of them was a German it mattered to none of them.

"Oh, I'll have to stop," gasped Babbie eventually. "Remember you're just babies compared to me. I can't keep up."

"I am twenty-four, Fräulein, older than you," said Anton quietly.

Babbie smiled carelessly. "Men are slower to grow up. To me you're just a boy."

"The day I joined the Luftwaffe I became a man," he said with dignity but she merely laughed because he looked like a small boy in a huff.

They had left the hamper in one of the cool caves. Niall went with Anton to retrieve it and Shona looked at Babbie. "You'll miss Anton when he's gone, Babbie. You've been closer to him than anyone else these past weeks."

"He had to go sometime," was all Babbie said before turning away to spread a rug over the sand.

After they had feasted on chicken sandwiches and fluffy scones they lay down on the warm beach. Shona turned her head to look at Niall and his hand came out to squeeze hers till it hurt, the strength of his love reaching out to her. A moment later he jumped to his feet and grabbed her hand.

"C'mon, lazy," he said lightly. "You know we said we would pay Alastair Robb a visit."

She began to protest but he pulled her away, saying casually over his shoulder. "We'll see you two about an hour from now. Don't you be running away, Anton. Remember you're in my charge."

When they reached the top of the cliff Shona turned on him. "Niall, if I didn't know you better I'd say you were going a bit daft!"

He turned to face her. "And it seems I don't know you at all,

Shona McKenzie. I credited you with a pretty keen sense of perception yet still you don't know about those two down there!"

Her eyes grew huge with surprise. "Babbie and Anton – you mean..."

"Och, c'mon, mo ghaoil! It's so obvious I thought the whole of Rhanna knew. Mother and Father saw it long ago. They're daft on each other though neither has admitted it to the other. But Babbie told me today. She's mad on him – and her heart is breaking because – of circumstances."

He turned away suddenly and the rays of the searching sun vividly betrayed the deep purple scar beneath the golden fuzz of hair on his neck.

"Oh God, I love you, Niall!" she breathed, drawing him into her arms and laying her warm cheek against his.

"We're lucky, my darling," he said softly. "We've had time to know what love is like – how much better it will be with the passing of each day – they have only a little time left, that's why I wanted them to make the most of it. Can you imagine what it's like? To be in love and never to be alone together."

His voice was strange and Shona drew away to look at him. "There's something else, isn't there?"

"Ay, there is that. C'mon, we'll walk along the cliffs slowly and I'll tell you though I want you to promise that afterwards you'll go on as before – there must be no tears or sadness – promise."

"If it means so much – I promise."

"Did Babbie ever tell you she had a sister?"

"Yes, an older sister, Jan, they grew up together in the orphanage."

"That's right, and Jan died three years ago, she died of a rare blood disease that can run in families and – and – Babbie is going to die too."

"Oh God no!" She couldn't stop the horrified protest. He held her close and stroked her burnished hair. "Be sad now, mo ghaoil, because later, when you're with Babbie, you must be very very strong. She mustn't know that you know. Pity is the thing she fears even more than dying. When she saw me here on Rhanna she was afraid I was going to feel sorry for her. She runs away from that all the time. We knew each other so casually in Glasgow. Each day we went into the same place for a bite – one day we started talking. That's how it happened with us. We never went very far below the surface. She only knew I was training to be a vet and that I came from the Hebrides." He smiled. "My tongue gave that one away. She told me about the orphanage and her sister, things like that. Then out of the blue she told me she was leaving the hospital in Glasgow but she didn't say where she was going. She started to cry, no fuss, nothing, just tears falling silently. After that it all just came out – it's sometimes easier to talk to a stranger. All she wanted was a shoulder. She was afraid a medical check would finish nursing for her so she just moved around a bit. She knew she couldn't get away with it much longer, Aberdeen was the end of the line. Your invitation to Rhanna came in time for her though she's spent a lot of her strength doing the thing she loves best – nursing."

Shona felt drained with sadness. "How long has she got, Niall?"

"Not long, she kept herself going for Anton's sake. When he leaves Rhanna I think she will go soon after."

"Where will she go?"

"To a hospital – as a patient this time." He kicked the ground fiercely. "Life can be a damned cruel thing sometimes! This morning she told me she'd never allowed herself to get too attached to a man since she found out about herself – then she comes to a lonely Hebridean island and falls in love with a German airman. Ironic, isn't it?"

His brown eyes were dark pools of misery. Her tears spilled over and she put out her arms to him. They clung together in the warm, sweet heather and cried for two young people with so little time left to love.

Anton watched Shona and Niall disappearing over the line of the cliffs then he twisted round to take Babbie's cool little hand. "You are shivering, Fräulein, are you cold?" he asked in his attractive broken English.

She shook her head, her oddly mysterious eyes clouding with the sting of tears. "Not cold – happy. It's been a wonderful day . . . thanks to Niall and Shona." She looked down at his hand resting in hers. The two little stumps of his lost fingers had healed beautifully but the sight brought a little sob to her throat. "What will happen to you, Anton?"

He shrugged. "I do not know, a camp, in Scotland or England. It doesn't matter. My home was in Germany with my family. I don't pine for a place where they are no more."

"Poor Anton," she breathed softly.

Anger flashed out of his blue eyes. "I hate pity! Please don't pity me!"

"I don't pity you, Anton, I was thinking how strange everything is. In a way we are both orphans. No family for either of us to go home to."

"Babbie!" His voice was soft again. Very gently he touched her hair where the sun turned it to fire. "Your hair, it is like summer. Whenever I think of you I will think of a summer sun blazing red at the end of the day. These weeks you have nursed me like an angel." He smiled. "You also make jokes like a little devil. I have laughed – and looked – and – loved . . . liebling." The endearment made her heart beat rapidly and she couldn't trust herself to look at him. "Liebling," he said again, his voice barely audible. "I love you and you know it. Niall gave us this time alone together, you know that, don't you?"

"It – it looks that way," she whispered, looking up then at the clear-cut structure of his handsome young face so that she would remember it for the rest of her life.

Slowly he leaned towards her and she shut her eyes to feel his lips caressing her eyelids and when his mouth came down on hers she made no resistance. Instead she put up her hands to trace the curve of his ears, tenderly urging him to kiss her harder. They were timeless moments. The gulls mewed softly, the sun beat down warmly, the creamy foam of the incoming tide rattled the tiny shells of the smooth white sands.

"Liebling." His voice was tense with passion. He touched the softness of her breasts and she cried out, wanting him to love her but afraid that he would hurt himself.

A soft dew of tears shone on his fair lashes. "Please, Babbie, let me – tomorrow I go away – let today last forever."

She was unable to resist his pleas. "All right, Anton, but gently – for your sake."

With trembling legs they walked to the great columns of rock

206

beside the caves. There, in the shadow of the sentinel pillars, he made love to her with such tender devotion she had to press her knuckles between her teeth to stop from crying out in those exalted moments. When it was over he lay quietly, his head pillowed on her breasts. The peace of Aosdana Bay, that had, in years gone by, inspired love, hope and finally tragedy in a love-lorn young poet, washed into the souls of the two lovers with so little time left to love. They listened to the timeless wind and tide that had swept the Bay for aeons past and both of them knew these were the memories they would carry into eternity.

But their time together was coming to an end and Anton finally broke the spell of silence. "Babbie, I want to ask you to be truthful to me. Our acquaintance has been very short yet my feelings for you are so deep it seems you have always been in my heart. I don't know where I am going or how long for. If I am lucky enough to be sent to a Scottish camp then we won't be far apart. Could you – would you – wait for me?"

The welling of her tears drowned out the world for a moment and it was while she couldn't see the love shining in his eyes that she managed to say lightly, "Och, c'mon, now, Anton, be realistic! You'll forget all about me in a little while." Still she couldn't see him but she heard the deep hurt in his reply.

"Forget you, Babbie! How can I forget today – yesterday? You can't forget love! But perhaps . . . I just imagined that you loved me too."

"You will forget, Anton, and someday you'll meet a really nice girl."

"I don't want a nice girl – I want you!" he cried passionately.

She smiled through the mist of tears. "That's not very compli-mentary, Anton."

He was angry now, his blue eyes bewildered. "You know very well what I mean! Good God, Babbie . . ." He spread his hands in appeal. "Don't play games with me now. Tomorrow I must leave this island – I want to know what you feel for me!"

She looked away from him because the pleading in his eyes was taking away all the resolution in her breaking heart. "I – my dear Anton – I feel a great affection for you, but . . ." Her voice broke on a sob. "That's not enough for the thing you ask of me."

He got slowly to his feet and stood looking down at her. "Thank you, Babbie, at least you are truthful," he said huskily. "I will always remember today – even though you may forget." He lifted his head proudly and she stared up at him outlined against the blue sky, tall, slim, fair threads of hair glinting in the sun, already a million miles away from her.

Niall and Shona appeared on the skyline and Anton cried brightly, "Hey, there, you two, you are just in time! I was beginning to miss my escort. You have grown on me like a bad habit!"

The island gave Anton a good send-off. Cries of good wishes for his future well-being filled the harbour at Portcull. He stood for a few moments, observing it all, the spring green on the mountains, the smoke that drifted as dreamily as the people of Rhanna, the bronzed slopes of Sgurr nan Ruadh that reminded him of a girl with hair the colour of a fiery sunset. In his pocket was a package which Elspeth had pushed brusquely at him when he left Slochmhor for the last time. "Some tablet to put strength in your feets," she told him sourly. "With the sugar on rationing it wasny easy but we must all share what we have – after all – we are all alike in the eyes o' God though sometimes I think He must be needin' specs."

He had surprised her by taking her hand and saying quietly, "Mein Frau – thank you – and it is not God who is needing the spectacles – it is ourselves. He will bless you for your thoughtfulness – Elspeth."

His pronunciation of her name was beautiful and, with crimson staining her cheeks, she hurried quickly into the house to dab at her eyes with the corner of her apron.

Fiona also had given him a present, a glass jar containing a large hairy spider. "For luck," she said briefly for it had cost her a lot to part with her most prized specimen. "His name is Geallachas, which is the Gaelic for faithful, so mind you take care of him. Keep the jar open so's he can catch flies and get a parcel of midgies together. Mind give him a drop of water too for spiders get gey thirsty."

Anton laughed and stooped to look into the child's bright eyes. "Thank you – jungfräulich – that is the German for maiden. I know Geallachas will bring me luck – perhaps enough for me to come back to this island and marry a beautiful princess called Fiona McLachan!"

"Ach, you'd be too old!" she told him but her smile was coy and she threw her arms round his neck to kiss his forehead.

The military escort were impatient to be on their way but Anton's blue eyes were scanning the harbour hoping to catch a last glimpse of Babbie. She hadn't said goodbye to him, she had barely spoken a word to him since yesterday. There was no sign of her at the harbour and his heart lay like a pebble in his breast.

He extended his hand to Niall who had come down with him. "Thank you, my friend, for yesterday. It is a day I will remember. Will you tell Fräulein Babbie I give to her my love. Thank her also – for healing my body – just say that, Niall."

Niall gripped Anton's hand so hard he winced. "I'll tell her, Anton," said Niall. Desperately he tried to think of something comforting to say but there was nothing. "She couldn't come down to see you off," he said as the young German turned away. "She said you would understand."

A pink stain touched Anton's pale cheeks. "Perfectly," he said shortly and walked quickly to the waiting boat.

Two days later Totie Little was walking back home over the cliffs from Portvoynachan. Breasting a rise she paused for breath and stood looking down at Aosdana Bay. Something green was swaying gently at the edge of the tide race. It looked like a piece of material and Totie frowned, trying to remember where she had seen such a garment before. But of course! It was right here at Aosdana Bay, the cloak worn by that young nurse, Babbie Cameron on her lonely walks on the white sands below. Totie drew in her breath uneasily then began to run down the track to the beach.

Babbie lay face upwards in the water, her green eyes staring up at the infinite blue sky, the bright strands of her hair swirling to and fro in the surging sea.

"Poor lassie," whispered Totie gently. "Poor, poor lassie. Who will weep for you but the spirits o' the sea?"

Rhanna was appalled at the news. The old folk shook their heads sadly and told each other, "It was the spirit o' the poet that lured her. Now they will both be haunting the Bay together."

"It was maybe she was a Green Uisga Caillich," smirked Canty Tam. "You can never be too sure of a body who dresses themselves in green all the time."

Biddy cried openly at the news, her heart turning over as she remembered Babbie's last smiling words. "You'll soon be up on your feets, you old cailleach, and I won't have to listen to you telling me how to give enemas again."

Shona felt numb with sadness. "Do – do you think – it was deliberate?" she asked Niall but he shook his head.

"No, not Babbie. She would never have taken that way out. She was far too considerate to inflict that kind of tragedy on the island. She was having a lot of dizzy spells, she probably took a bad one at the top of the cliffs and fell over."

He paused, remembering eyes that were like pools of amber-flecked sea, seeing in them the terrible loneliness of a young woman who knew that she must soon say goodbye to all the dreams that are the right of the young. "It's maybe better this way," he continued slowly. "At least she won't have the agony of waiting to die."

The people of Rhanna saw to it that the young nurse was laid to rest in style. During her short stay on the island she had visited nearly every croft and cottage, 'cracking' and ceilidhing like a true native. Everyone had a soft spot for her and gave generously towards the funeral of the girl with no kin to call her own. The children of the island began to build a cairn on the cliffs above Aosdana Bay. In days to come whenever anybody passed the spot another stone was added till eventually a tall monument stood in Babbie's memory. It was soon given the name of Carn Camshronach, which meant the Cairn of Cameron, and if Babbie was observing all this from the heaven she had so firmly believed in then she would have smiled her mysterious smile, knowing that her earthly spirit really belonged somewhere at last.

Rhanna droned lazily in the heat of high summer and Shona ran swiftly over the green fields of Laigmhor. Out on the Sound of Rhanna the ferry sounded its deep mournful horn and she stopped to watch it gliding into the harbour before she walked into the cool, silent woods that skirted the road. Pine needles rustled beneath her feet, the sunlight dappled on the rich brown earth. She sat down on a mossy tree stump to hug her knees while she waited for Niall the way she had waited countless times before. She was wearing a dress of palest green which was a perfect foil for the deep gold of her tanned limbs and the luxuriant auburn hair which she had swept upwards and pinned carefully in place.

She had taken long to get ready that morning, exasperating both Kirsteen and Fergus by running downstairs during breakfast, deciding to change from her white dress into a yellow one before the meal was over, deciding she liked neither and changing to the green. She had wondered whether to wear her long hair up or down and when Fergus said, "I like it flowing down your back the way it was when you were a wee girl," she had answered.

"I am *eighteen*, Father!" and had gone immediately upstairs to pin up the thick waving curls.

"You're too grown up for me to *talk* to now," Grant told her disgustedly.

"And you're too much of a baby for me to care!" she had snapped at him. She was tense and irritable as so often happens when a keenly anticipated event is nearly a reality.

Sitting among the cool trees she was ashamed of her outburst. The atmosphere at Laigmhor was usually one of happy contentment and it was wonderful to live in a house where laughter prevailed above all else. There was going to be another child in December. Kirsteen had confided the news to her a fortnight ago and they had celebrated by holding a gay ceilidh.

Grant's feelings were mixed on the matter. He dreaded the idea of a 'silly wee sister' and half-heartedly decided a brother might come in useful 'once it grows from a smelly baby into a real human'.

"Are you pleased, Father?" Shona asked.

His black eyes had regarded her for a long moment. "Ay, delighted," he said eventually. "But, no matter how many bairns may come along there will never be one to match you."

"That could mean a lot of things," she had answered with a smile.

"You know what I mean, mo ghaoil," he said with an intensity that made her put her arms round his neck and nuzzle his thick dark curls.

"I know, my dearest father," she said gently. "It's easier for me, I only have one father to adore . . . you have more than one child – and you must never show you have a favourite."

Shona clasped her knees and thought about her father. The years they had spent together at Laigmhor had been stormy but beautiful years in her life and she knew she would always treasure the memory of them. But always there had been Niall. All through her tempestuous childhood he had been the other prop in her life and undeniably an even stronger one than her father whose pride had been the cause of unhappiness for a lot of people.

She watched a baby mole ambling blindly among the moss. A squirrel washed its whiskers on a branch above her head and she held her breath, loving the peace of the pine-scented wood, treasuring it even more because it was a part of Rhanna, the island she loved with every fibre of her being. Yet soon she must leave it if she wanted to remain with the man she loved. Niall had given her an ultimatum. "When I come back to Rhanna in the summer I want your answer, Shona." These had been his parting words when he left to go back to his studies at the vet. college.

A jaunty whistle came faintly on the breeze. Niall! At last, Niall! The thought of him so near quickened her heart. That whistle! It suddenly came to her that she hadn't heard it for many months. It had always been a part of Niall yet on his last visit to Rhanna she hadn't heard it once. The gay sound of it came closer and she got to her feet. Niall was back! The Niall of the carefree years before the war! The dear, sweet Niall of her early memories. She saw him through the trees, tall, sturdy, his hair gleaming like a field of summer corn. His hands were deep in his pockets, his stride firm and sure as he walked on past the woods and into Glen Fallan.

"Niall!" She burst from the trees in a breathless flurry and he turned, holding out his arms to embrace her. He held her away and looked at the graceful beauty of her golden limbs and slender body. The upswept hair enhanced the curves of her delicate neckline and showed to perfection the symmetry of her pointed little face.

"Hey!" he laughed joyously. "You're all grown up! My God, you're beautiful. I won't tell you that too often though in case you get big-headed. And that tan – you make me feel like a ghost!"

Tenderly he tucked away a small tendril of fine hair. "You've got your hair up again I see."

"Yes, do you like it? I did it especially for you."

"It makes you look – sophisticated – the way some of the town girls look. I always thought of my Shona as a tom-boy, hair flying all over the place."

"You don't like it!"

"I never said that – Caillich Ruadh!"

"Don't call me a red witch again, Niall McLachlan! You know I hate it!"

"Temper! Temper!" he scolded, his eyes dancing. "Now, if you were Fiona I'd take down your knickers and skelp your wee arse!"

"You're a barbarian, that's what you are – and a glaikit one at that! I don't know why I bother with you!" she cried, her cheeks red with rage.

"Because I'm irresistible, that's why." He grinned delightedly.

An ancient van trundled towards them on the dusty Glen road. Behind the windscreen two heads bobbed in unison, one a flaming red, the other a startling white. Morag Ruadh beamed at them, her ruddy face radiant, Dugald Ban peered out and nodded acknowledgement.

"That was Morag Ruadh!" gasped Niall. "What is Dugald Ban doing riding about with that Caillich Ruadh?"

"It *was* Morag Ruadh," said Shona politely. "Now Mrs Dugald Donaldson, mistress of Dunbeag, Portvoynachan."

"Never – never Morag Ruadh! How did she do it?"

Shona couldn't help laughing. "In the same way as her cousin Mairi, only Morag Ruadh, the one-time saint of Portcull, was far more blatant than poor Mairi. Old Behag says she's never seen such sinful flaunting in anybody – but of course she says that about everyone who strays from the narrow path . . . I got it all too . . . and from Morag too, the besom."

"But how did poor old Doug get caught? I thought he and Totie were pretty thick!"

"They were – up until that time the Commandos came and there was a ceilidh at the Manse. It seems Morag and Doug were very friendly that night. When Morag knew she was pregnant she blamed him, and Isabel and old Jim Jim gave him no peace till he took Morag to the altar. The baby's due in December. The cailleachs are saying that the Manse ceilidh was no more than an excuse for drunken lechery."

"One up for Morag," grinned Niall. "Though I'll never know how poor old Dugald Ban got himself into that one."

"Neither can anyone else. The gossips' tongues are red hot for some say that Doug wasn't the only one with a hand in the affair. When Jim Jim first asked Morag who was the father of the bairn she said calmly, 'Will you take your pick, Father? I have been a loose woman.' When Jim Jim heard that he nearly went up in a puff of peat smoke and said he hoped the father wasn't a Jerry. After that Morag pinpointed Doug. Morag was such a confirmed saint Doug just took her word for it so he must have been *one* of them." She giggled. "All these years, Morag without a man then suddenly we are to believe they are queuing up!"

"Totie must be furious! She kept Dugald dangling long enough."

"She doesn't seem to mind at all. Morag is kept so busy typing all Doug's notes and looking after the house she doesn't have time for the Kirk organ so she signed it over to Totie. Doug got himself that old van and takes Totie's goods all over the island. She's delighted but Behag and Merry Mary are furious because it has taken away business from them."

They arrived at the gate of Laigmhor in a merry state, but Niall's face became serious when he said, "Will you come out with me after dinner?"

"Och Niall," she scolded happily, "I haven't waited this long just to wave to you from the gate. Where will we go?"

"To the moors – to visit the cave at Dunuaigh."

She recoiled from him. "No, no, Niall! Don't ask that of me!"

"Please, Shona," he begged earnestly, "I have my reasons."

"Very well," she faltered unhappily. "But there are nicer places on a beautiful day like this."

In days gone by they had sped to the cave on swift, carefree feet, but when he met her at the dyke outside Laigmhor she looked pale and apprehensive. He put his arm round her firmly and led her towards the long heat-hazed stretches of the Muir of Rhanna. The sun beat down warmly. Furze, needle-whin, and broom nestled among tawny tussocks of sedge, banks of butterwort popped shy violet faces through the leaves of the more boisterous marsh trefoil whose dazzling white flower spikes carpeted the moor bogs. A Hebridean rock-pippit winged overhead, muttering deep in its throat. Bees, already laden with little sacks of pollen, prodded frenziedly into the heather; delicate moths fluttered uncertainly over the wild flowers, restlessly roaming from one clump to the next.

Niall was very quiet. Shona looked at his boyish profile and wondered why he was taking her to a place that had no meaning for her now. They were skirting the edge of Burnbreddie Estate. Very soon they topped a rise and stood looking down at Dunuaigh with the Abbey ruins nestling in a hollow. It was very peaceful. The shaggy sheep of the hill cropped the long, sweet grasses; contented cud-chewing cows sat in the cool shadows of rock out-crops. In the distance the deep blue of the Atlantic sparkled to the boundless horizon.

Shona drank in the scene avidly. "It's so beautiful here," she said wonderingly. "I'd almost forgotten the enchantment of it."

"Come on," he said softly and they ran then to the sun-drenched hollow where the silence of forgotten places descended on them in a thistle-down blanket of peace.

"Oh!" Shona was staring at the little birch tree that Niall had planted to mark the entrance to the cave. It was more than a year since her last tortured flight to this place of memories. How eagerly she had looked then for the little birch tree and how near to panic when her desperate gaze had nearly missed the twisted little sapling that had weathered the terrible winter winds that bowled over the moors. She couldn't miss the tree now. Though warped cruelly by the weather it had grown big and sturdy, its silver bark shining in the sun, banners of green foliage throwing shadows among the gorse.

Niall glanced at her. "It's weathered the storms all right. Can we say the same, mo ghaoil?"

But she didn't answer. She was running to the cave, pulling back bramble and bracken, snagging her dress, pricking her fingers, pulling and tearing while the tears choked up into her throat. "Hey, steady on!" Niall rushed up to her but she wasn't aware of him. She sat on her heels gazing into the cool, dry cave, going over every little detail that was etched in her memory. Mirabelle's dolls flopped on the shelves, jostling with cups. The cruisie, containing the remains of the candle that had given her light during the agonising hours of her labour, still hung from its chain; the wickerwork chairs, carried over the moors on a far-off morning of childhood, still sat, one on either side of the rough stone fireplace. And in the corner, the roughly hewn bed of stone, piled with cushions and a sheepskin rug now grey with dirt. Everything was covered in cobwebs. It was neglected and forgotten, but she looked and remembered; the happy echo of childish laughter; the whispered hopes and dreams; the discovery of carefree young love. She tried to push her mind on further but couldn't. The agony of her lonely childbirth was a blank in her mind; the lifeless body of her tiny son a dim blur almost beyond recall.

Niall slid his arm round her waist. "Well, my darling little girl, what now are your strongest memories of this place? Sadness or happiness?"

"Happiness . . . oh, so much happiness I can hear the laughter now!" She buried her face into his neck. "I can look down the years and it's all so real – you and me and dear old Tot . . ." She pulled away to look at him and continued slowly. "The only thing that isn't real to me is – the – the last time! Oh God! I feel so guilty! It's my last experience of this place yet it's the dimmest. In my mind I can see Tot with her golden ears covering her white muzzle – yet – I can't see the face of our little baby! Why, oh why can't I?"

"There now," he soothed. "Have a good greet if you like. I had an idea this place would get things into perspective, that's why I brought you. You can see the old spaniel because she lived before she died . . . our little boy didn't," he finished gently.

They were quiet for a long moment then he asked, "Well, am I going to be a bitter bachelor all my days or an old married man?"

She reached out and touched the scar on his neck. "An old married man, so long as you're married to me. You didn't have to bring me here to make up my mind. I keep thinking of Anton and Babbie, how such love was so dreadfully wasted. We're not going to waste any more of ours. I've done a lot of practical thinking this summer. Rhanna has given me back my health . . . I'm ready to go back to nursing – I want to take my full training and what better place than Glasgow? Being married means terrible things like bills. We'll need money for all that so – don't tell me I can't do it."

He smiled wryly. "Who ever tried to stop a McKenzie? But I won't have a wife of mine being the sole breadwinner. Glaikit wee Niall has found himself a weekend job . . ."

"And we have Mirabelle's legacy to tide us over at the beginning." She caught her breath. "I wish she could be here now, I owe so much to her. Oh God! It's so wonderful not to feel guilty about the baby anymore!"

"He'll come back to us." He took her hands and looked at her with quiet joy. "We'll have other sons – and daughters – lots of them – we'll fill the world with our children!"

Their shout of laughter echoed through the cave. He embraced her and they sank to the heather as one, their mouths meeting over and over. His tongue touched hers and she responded wildly till they drew apart to look at each other longingly. "Enough," he said shakily. "Two minutes of you and I'm shaking like a leaf."

A sprite of mischief danced in her eyes. "It's a good job you've got your kilt on, Niall McLachlan! Being the bull you are you wouldn't have room in your trousers."

His brown eyes glinted. "Remember old Burnbreddie? In the hayshed rutting at some old yowe? He wore nothing under his kilt then. How do you know I'm decently covered? Would you like a quick peep?"

She got to her feet in an outrage. "*Niall McLachlan!* You dirty bugger!"

She ran and he chased her, in and out of the crumbling pillars of the Abbey. He caught her and she tilted her head for his kiss, delighting in the firm strength of his young body. Her face was cupped in his hands and she could feel a small pulse beating in his thumb, the rhythm of his life throbbing steadily. She heard a sob catching in his throat and saw that his eyes were clouded with tears.

"My dearest, dearest love," he murmured unsteadily. "I feel so lucky to have you back again." He studied her intently for a few moments. "Something's missing! That beautiful hair, sliding through my fingers like silk! Let me unpin it so that it flies loose and wild like it used to. We'll be children again for a while! We'll

dance and sing like idiots and we won't grow up till we're ready!
We have the whole lovely summer ahead of us!"

For a brief moment their hands entwined. A playful breeze
lifted the loose strands of her hair, blowing it over her face, throwing it into a ruffled bronze mane behind her back.

"Race you!" he shouted. Their feet took wings and they were
running, children again, their breath catching with laughter in
the mad flight over the perfumed shaggy moors.

They were married when the soft, golden days of the Hebridean
summer were growing shorter. The island waited with a subdued
excitement for the event while Laigmhor and Slochmhor bustled
with unhurried preparations.

The Rev. John Gray spent many hours rehearsing the wedding
ceremony in Gaelic while his long-suffering wife sat with her
knitting and made automatic sounds of approval. In her opinion
his loud, booming voice was entirely unsuited for the soft pronunciation of the Gaelic language. Once she said mildly, "You need
some lilt, John. If you listen to the islanders you will hear the lilt."

"I *am* lilting, Hannah!" he roared indignantly. "Your trouble
is you don't listen properly. Put those knitting needles away and
you will *hear* my lilt!"

It seemed as if the whole of Rhanna was crowded into the Kirk
on the Hillock to watch the ceremony. Shona was radiant in a
simple blue dress with white marguerites braided into hair that
tumbled down her back in rich thick waves. At the altar stood
Niall, tall and straight in a lovat tweed jacket and McLachlan kilt,
his fair skin flushed with a mixture of pride and nerves. Strong,
rugged Fergus wore the McKenzie kilt with pride but he felt a
moment of panic at the idea of walking into Kirk and all eyes
staring as he gave his daughter away. Then Shona was beside him
and he braced himself.

"Well, Father," she whispered. "Another man will have to put
up with my tempers now."

He nodded slowly. "Ay, you're right there, lass. Not only your
tempers but those awful dumplings you make and your cheek at
the breakfast table . . ." His black eyes were very bright. "And
your singing when you're doing your chores and your wee voice
bidding me goodnight . . . these are all the things I'm giving away

to another man, together with a million other things I love about my lass." He gave a wry smile. "You didn't know your old man could make speeches like that, eh?"

"Not my old man," she said with a little sob. "My handsome big boy, remember? I haven't called you that in years but I still think it."

Behind them Fiona and Grant fidgeted impatiently. "I'll *never* marry," hissed the former, pulling disgustedly at the frills on her dress.

"Nobody would want to marry *you*," returned Grant. "You're more like a boy than a girl."

"I'm glad of that even though boys are horrible they're better than silly girls. I'm going to be an explorer when I grow up and live in a tent in the jungle."

"I'm going to be a fisherman like old Joe and sail all over the world. I'll never get married either cos it's stupid. Mother and Father fight one minute then make goggle eyes at each other the next – and they have babies all the time," he finished in aggrieved tones.

The wedding march struck up, the door opened and the wedding began. The Rev. John Gray had listened to his wife after all. His subdued tones lacked the 'lilt' but his Gaelic was perfect. The old Gaels looked at each other with a mixture of surprise and delight.

"Ach, he's speaking the Gaelic in English," muttered Jim Jim. Isabel poked him in the ribs. "The man is doing his best. He means well right enough. Just you leave him be, Jim McDonald."

Despite the lack of the lilt, the ceremony was beautiful. The Gaelic words echoed round the old Kirk and the ancient walls seemed to soak them in for a moment as if joyfully savouring a familiar tongue, then they were released again to go bouncing from wall to wall, one upon the other.

"Oh God," gasped Phebie, dashing away a tear. "I promised myself I wouldn't cry."

Lachlan moved closer to her. "Lend me your hanky," he said with a watery sniff. "Men aren't *supposed* to cry at weddings." He gripped her hand. "If they have a marriage like ours – then they couldn't ask God for more . . . my bonny plump rose."

"Ay, you're right, Lachy – my darling," she said huskily and blew her nose as quietly as she could.

It was over and they were all moving outside. Erchy and Todd stood one on either side of the door, the bagpipes wheezed into life, the gay tunes filled the air. Laughing, the islanders linked arms and began to dance. The ceilidhing was already starting.

Biddy fanned herself with her hat. She was fully recovered now. The 'galloping hairpin' had long ago departed the island, glad to escape Biddy's criticism and the eccentricities of the older inhabitants.

Shona and Niall were accosted from all sides but Biddy, her ancient box-camera at the ready, was the most persistent. "Look you now, will you be standin' away from these gravestones," she commanded. "Todd, get out of the way! I'm no' wantin' your hairy legs in my picture."

Dodie galloped up, knocking her elbow just as the shutter clicked. Turning, she clouted him on the ear as if he was a small boy. "You are just like a herd o' elephants!" she scolded. "Now I have nothing but a fine picture o' the clouds!"

"Ach, I'm sorry, Biddy!" he wailed. Mairi had restored him to such a degree of good health that his cheeks popped out from his face like wizened brown apples and his bony frame had filled out considerably. But he was a creature who needed the freedom of wide places. After weeks of cosseting he was glad to escape to his lonely little cottage in the hills though he showered Mairi with such a continual flow of simple little gifts it had been suggested to her by the opportunist Ranald that she should open up a craft shop for the summer tourists.

Dodie turned hastily from Biddy, knocking her hat off in the process and amid a stream of abuse he shouted to the newly-weds, "Will you be waiting a minute. I have a wee wedding gift for you." It was a dewy spray of harebells, bog myrtle and white heather, lovingly wrapped in a square of toilet tissue such as was used at Burnbreddie.

"It's a lovely present, Dodie," said Niall gratefully.

"Ach well, it will be mindin' you of the moors when you are being gassed by the smelly smoke in the city. The heather will bring you a lot o' luck. I had a job findin' it but I wanted to give you something after the fine job you made o' my wee hoosie."

"Is it all right then, Dodie?"

"Ay, lovely just." His grizzled face shone with pride then he looked ashamed. "I am after putting back my own roof wi' the nice pattern."

"But, Dodie," laughed Niall. "That's the sign of the swastika – the Nazi sign!"

Dodie's face showed no comprehension. "Ay, ay, a lovely sign it is! I like it fine," he enthused.

"Daft, daft he is," smirked Canty Tam. "The British planes will be shootin' his wee hoosie down in flames else the Peat Hags will haunt him for takin' the pattern away from them."

Shona had stolen away from the crowd to the part of the grave-yard that held the remains of so many who had been her dear friends in life. Pausing at each grave she laid a single white rose on the grassy earth, each one plucked from her wedding bouquet. The only person she had never known was the one who had given her life and for a long moment she stood looking at her mother's head-stone, then she stooped to lay her garland of marguerites on the mossy brown earth. "Thank you for my life, Mother," she said simply and turned to walk down to where her father was waiting quietly a few yards away.

That evening Tam's Uisge-Beatha rocked the foundations of Laigmhor with its happy effects. At ten o'clock Niall and Shona stole away and sped hand in hand over the dark fields to the harbour. There Ranald was waiting to take them out to a fishing boat which was sailing with the tide to Stornoway where they were to spend their honeymoon.

Ranald's face beamed at them in the darkness. "I kept a special boat for you," he confided. "I've been waitin' for a chance to use it and it bein' your weddin' night you must have everything done proper." He led them to the dark blob of a rubber dinghy floating in the shallows. "In you go now, mo ghaoil," he said, courteously helping Shona aboard. "If you feel like you've been walkin' all day on air then now you're goin' to be floatin' on it."

"But, Ranald, this dinghy belongs to . . ." She stopped short and chuckled. "Ranald McTavish," she finished and the wily Ranald said a polite and utterly innocent "Right enough, now," and began to row away from the shore.

The dim lights of the fishing boat loomed nearer and they could hear the laughter of Torquil Andrew and Fingal who were having their own ceilidh on board.

Shona looked at Rhanna slipping away. The rugged peaks of Ben Machrie and Sgurr nan Ruadh were outlined in the remnants of a deep golden sunset that still hovered in the north-western sky. Sounds of merriment came faintly on the breeze; on the sands skirting Port Rum Point a family of gulls squabbled quietly; the dark shape of a lone heron glided on silent wings, uttering a sharp 'cra-ack' as it passed over the dinghy.

Shona's heart rose into her throat but Niall's arm came round her and his warm lips touched hers. "Slainte – Mrs Niall McLachlan," he murmured softly. "You belong to me now."

"We belong to each other," she said firmly, dashing away the tears that had sprung to her eyes. "Always you seemed to leave me behind on Rhanna . . . you can't do that anymore – and I'm happy to be coming with you – my darling husband . . ." She pointed upwards to where the sliver of a young moon peeped out shyly from a fluffy cloudbank. "Look, Niall, the new moon! Mirabelle always made a wish whenever it appeared. We must each spit on a piece of silver, hold it in our hand and wish."

Solemnly they carried out the ancient ritual. "I've made mine," said Niall seriously. "I hope it comes true."

She nodded with assurance. "It will – so long as you never tell anyone what it was. Some of my best wishes came true on the new moon."

High in the fields above Laigmhor a tall figure looked out to the Sound of Rhanna, watching the dark little dot of the dinghy moving over a velvet sea faintly flecked with gold. It was a lovely autumn evening, filled with the sharp tang of peat smoke and fresh salt wind, the kind of weather Shona had always loved. Fergus breathed the scent of it deeply into his lungs, looking at the picture before him till it became a blur.

"Goodbye – Ni Cridhe," he said, so quietly it might have been the sigh of the wind.

Kirsteen came up behind him and slid her arms round his waist. "I knew you'd be up here," she murmured, "saying goodbye to her. Don't be sad, Fergus. She'll be back."

"Only to visit us," he said huskily.

"Perhaps, she has her own life to lead now but I think one day they'll both come back – to stay." She linked her arm through his. "Come down now, darling. That little devil Fiona gave Grant a glass of sherry and I swear he's drunk. He's doing a Highland fling with Biddy and her teeth and specs are rattling like mad!"

Turning his back on the sea he put his arm round her waist and they walked over the dew-wet fields to Laigmhor and the happy sound of laughter that drifted to them on the playful breezes that eternally caressed the lonely high places of Rhanna.